ROBERT E. WATERS

DEVIL DANCERS

And Other Tales

Pennsville, NJ

PUBLISHED BY
eSpec Books LLC
Danielle McPhail, Publisher
PO Box 242,
Pennsville, New Jersey 08070
www.especbooks.com

ISBN: 978-1-942990-98-7
ISBN (ebook): 978-1-942990-97-0

Interior Design: Danielle McPhail
Cover Art and Design: © Mike McPhail, McP Digital Graphics
Cover Background Art: #46591424, Enrico G. Agostoni, fotolia.com
Copyeditors: Greg Schauer and Danielle McPhail

DEDICATION

*To the real Apache warrior and chief,
Victorio, aka Bidu-ya, "he who checks his horse."
Born 1825; Died 1880.*

You will be remembered... today and in the future.

CONTENTS

AHAGAHE!

I STUDIED CULTURAL ANTHROPOLOGY IN COLLEGE, AND NATIVE American cultures have always fascinated me. All of them do. But tribes of the American Southwest, to this wargamer's heart anyway, held particular interest.

The Apaches were tough. They lived on a tough land and they fought hard to preserve it. Great chiefs like Geronimo, Cochise, Juh, Nana, Naiche, Coloradas, and Victorio fought against the Spanish, the Mexicans, and the Americans. In the end, we know what happened to them, to their culture, but that does not mean that we should forget them.

In the mid-1990s, I took up fiction writing. I had this idea to introduce an Apache warrior in a science fiction setting as a... what? I did not know. I studied Apache history, in particular their warrior traditions, and packed away—in the back of my mind— several ideas, but none of them evolved until I met the McPhails. Danielle and Mike invited me to submit a story to their, then, newish military science fiction series, *Defending the Future*. From all the ideas knocking around in my head, Victorio "Tomorrow's Wind" Nantan and the Devil Dancers were born.

I do not know if I'm the right person to write these stories. I'm born from hearty European stock. Many of the Apache chiefs of the Indian Wars would probably refer to me as "White Eyes." But I hope I've done their culture and traditions justice; in a futuristic setting against an alien race known as the Gulo, true, but I've tried to portray their culture as honestly as I can no matter the setting. As Victorio might say, *"I am the lightning flashing and streaking! This headdress lives; the noise of its pendants sounds and is heard!"*

Now hear The Devil Dancers as they dance and wage war against an alien foe among the stars. Wish them well, and enjoy!

Robert E Waters
July 2, 2019

DEVIL DANCERS

Victorio Nantan, Captain Victory, Squadron Leader of the Devil Dancers, looked over the smoke-filled room. Somewhere within its cavernous swill of booze, laughter, music, and celebration, were his men. They were the Devil Dancers. Aces every one; the finest fighter squadron in the fleet. They deserved their seventy-two hours of R&R. Their record kills at the Battle of Pallid Musings had earned them their playtime. But the war continued, and Captain "Victory" had just received secret intelligence about enemy fleet movements near Castor V. It was out of his squadron's designated deployment zone, but an opportunity that could not be ignored. The finest pilots in the Federated Union had to keep pushing themselves, and at such a critical moment in the war, time was imperative. The enemy was on the verge of collapse.

That enemy was the Gulo, a wolverine-like race that had nearly cut the Union in two. Feral, savage fighters, their technology was on par with that of the humans. They were a formidable foe. Deep in his heart, Victorio could not help but admire their prowess in battle. But the war had waged for over thirty standard years, and even personal admiration grows pale over time. He and his men were working hard to defeat the Gulo. A turning point was at hand. Victorio could feel it. He had seen it in his dreams. One more push, one more decisive rout, and the scales could be tipped.

The Devil Dancers were not going to be left out.

He crossed the room, pushing through the partiers, responding in kind to the salutes of junior officers from the 3rd Sol Fighter Wing. He even recognized some crew members of the *Star Chariot*, an old carrier that had been refitted to accommodate a full battalion of troopers and their drop pods. Among these men, he and the Devil Dancers were legend, and whenever they were present, they received much respect. Victorio passed through them politely but kept his eyes set on one of his pilots who sat on a plush red sofa near the bar, surrounded by adoring women and sycophants.

Naiche looked up from his drink and recognized his brother. "Ah, Captain Victory!" He stumbled to his feet, the beautiful ladies surrounding him shifting their bare legs to let him pass. "You've decided to crawl out of your wickiup and join us."

Victorio grabbed his brother before the younger man embarrassed himself by hitting the floor. Naiche's face was flushed red, his breath rancid with drink, his eyes dilated and distant. "You're drunk."

"You're goddamned right I'm drunk!" Naiche said, receiving cheers and laughter from his friends. "And I intend on staying that way for another forty-eight hours."

"We need to talk, brother," Victorio said, pushing Naiche away. "Now."

"Nonsense," Naiche said. "We need to drink. Pull up a chair and join us." Before Victorio had a chance to respond, Naiche said, "Ladies, let me introduce you to our *na-tio-tish*, our war leader, Captain Victorio "Tomorrow's Wind" Nantan, the *second* finest pilot in the galaxy." He tapped his brother's chest with a blunt, lazy finger. "This man single-handedly wiped out an entire Gulo squadron at the Battle of Two Dwarves. He's received six commendations for bravery, and a score of Silver Wings. And ladies," he put his hand to his mouth and lowered his voice, "he's got the cutest little tattoo on his—"

"Enough!" Victorio grabbed Naiche's shoulders and shook. The drink in his brother's hand toppled to the floor, spreading red liquid across the plush white carpet. The internal lattice-mesh of the floor began sucking the fibers dry. "We will talk, now." He turned and looked at the women, whose expressions had become quite still. "Will you excuse us, please?"

Naiche wrestled himself free and stumbled to the sofa, apologizing profusely to his fans. He gave each lady a small kiss and promised to call on them. They shuffled past Victorio without a word and disappeared into the throng of dancers.

"You waste yourself away with all this," Victorio said, finding a seat near his brother. "Father would not be pleased."

Naiche rubbed his forehead and chuckled. "Father is just as boring as you, big brother. You are the worst kill-joy I've ever met. If you had played your cards right, one of those ladies would have given you a—"

"Everything comes so easy for you, Naiche. Not so for me. I've had to bust my ass for everything. While you were off carousing with your friends at Boot, I had to double down, pull second shifts, commit overtime. And you'd waltz right in the next morning and ace your—"

"And yet here you are," Naiche interrupted, "*Captain* of the Devil Dancers."

Victorio had gotten the promotion in the field during an engagement in the Kuiper Belt eight standard years ago. His calm, serious demeanor had impressed Star Marshall Kinski Shu, who said, 'You're not like others of your kind, are you, boy?' Images of his father's hostilities toward the White Eyes came to mind, but Victorio kept his mouth shut like a good soldier. He always kept his mouth shut. 'No, I guess not, sir." And so it was that he took command, and the rest was in the common record.

"There are reports of heavy Gulo activity near Castor V."

Naiche perked an ear. "And?"

"And I've asked Star Marshall Shu to give us a temporary transfer to Peregrine Task Force."

Naiche sat straight in his seat, the effects of the alcohol washed from his face. "Are you nuts? That racist is going to get us killed!"

Victorio shot glances around the room. Luckily, the music was too loud and the patrons too drunk to notice his brother's insubordination. "Keep your opinions to yourself, pilot."

Naiche lowered his voice and leaned in. "The men need rest, sir. We won at Pallid Musings, but it was a near-run thing, and you know it. Blue Bird just had her foot reattached. Shines Like the Sun has a new heart, and—"

"They can rest and recover *en route*. The *Exodus* does not depart until eighteen hundred hours."

Naiche's expression grew still, his eyes silent. "We're leaving that soon?"

"Yes."

"Shouldn't I have been consulted on this, sir? I am second-in-command."

"Second being the operative word."

Naiche shot out of his seat. They stood there, faces close. Victorio was taller and so he towered over his brother like a bitter tree. Naiche was shorter, indeed, but very fit and muscular, and if he wanted to, he could bring Victorio down and make short order of him. Around them, patrons began to take notice, pretending to party, but with a curious eye turned toward the disruption. Word of two Devil Dancers fighting would spread throughout the fleet; questions would be asked, demands would be made. It was an untenable situation. Hitting a superior officer, even if he was your brother, would be tantamount to suicide. Naiche blinked and stepped back. "And so that's how it's going to be, huh? Captain Victory has made his decision, and all shall bow to him."

"Don't be dramatic, brother. You have a taste for Gulo blood as strong as any pilot."

"Yes, but why now? And why this particular action? Enemy fleet movements have been reported all over the Caustic Drift. What interests you so much about this particular report? You hate Captain Shriver of PTF. Why would you—"

"Gingu-sha has been spotted with that fleet."

Naiche's mouth dropped open.

The greatest Gulo fighter pilot was Gingu-sha. His kills alone matched those of the entire Devil Dancer squadron. His name drew fear even from the crews of capital ships. One story told of how Gingu-sha single-handedly dispatched a Union destroyer, crashing into its hull with a burrowing torpedo and then fighting his way to the bridge, where he massacred the crew and drove the ship into Starbase Calvin, only to escape unscathed on a shuttle. A destroyer did indeed strike the starbase, but whether or not Gingu-sha was responsible was unclear. Since everyone on the ship died on impact, there were no eye-witnesses to confirm the event, only hearsay from nearby ships. But that hardly mattered. The stories were out there, and his reputation and skills were undeniable.

Over the years, the Devil Dancers had had opportunities to take the Gulo ace down. The Battle of Two Dwarves, Cassini Station, the Emerald Rim, Ambush at Three Moons. Battle after battle, and yet the *na-de-gah-ah* had always slipped the net. On one particular occasion, Gingu-sha had turned his fighter upside down and aligned his cockpit with Victorio's, after he had shot a hole through Victorio's engine and left him for dead. They drifted there for a long while, and the beast could have, at any time, looped around and fired his guns. But he didn't. They just drifted, both of them looking at each other through the cockpit glass, an arrogant smile spread across the creature's black lips. Perfect black teeth with a darting pale tongue. His pure-white fur was as beautiful as the first snow of winter, his eyes blazing red hot like fire. And then he gunned his engines and was gone in a flash of blue energy.

From that moment on, Victorio vowed to find and kill Gingu-sha and put his pelt on the wall of the Devil Dancers' headquarters on the light carrier *Justice*.

"Gingu-sha is your albatross, brother," Naiche said, "not mine."

Victorio ignored his brother's insult. "And I've decided that you will be the Clown."

Naiche's expression turned from anger to surprise. "Me? But what about Music-Maker?"

"He's down with fever. He'll not be ready when we depart."

"But you have never allowed me to play the Clown. Why now?"

"The opportunity is here, Naiche. Do you accept this honor or no?"

Naiche stood there rubbing his face. Victorio could see the passion behind his brother's dark eyes.

Naiche nodded. "Yes, I will accept the honor. I will be the Clown."

Victorio breathed a sigh of relief. "Good. Now gather the men. We leave immediately."

Naiche stiffened and saluted. He was back to his old self. "Don't worry your fat, arrogant head, brother. I'm the best goddamned pilot you have. I won't let the Devil Dancers down."

Yes, you are the best, brother, Victorio said to himself as he watched Naiche leave the room. *But let's see just how good you really are.*

Victorio moved his head and eased his fighter up and down the spread of jagged rocks along the crest of the mountain. He could have easily steered the craft above the bright, white spires and let it whisk unimpeded through the low clouds. But no. He would not do that. He would not shame himself by taking the easy path. He would neither shame himself nor his brother who lay wrapped in a blanket behind him on the cockpit floor.

He blinked thrice to disengage his head from steerage and peered out the cockpit window. His eyes widened. The blur of rock, sand, and arrowweed below jogged memories. Memories of boys with brown, ratty hair, sun-browned skin, and dirty buckskin leggings. Memories of breathless runs up mountain paths with mouthfuls of water. Memories of wrestling matches and bareback races. Good memories. Bad memories. Memories even the dark, cold vacuum of space could not erase. But as he eased over the last crest and focused the landing reticule on a black concrete pad in the distance, his heart raced.

He was home.

His craft, a single-seat, fixed-wing Radiant-class fighter was an older model with inherent up-draft problems. It was made for space battles and did not fly well planetside. But he—and thus his squadron—refused to change. And they did what their captain told them to do…even if it killed them.

He set the fighter down carefully on the landing pad, its anti-grav chutes turned downward, engaging automatically as it wavered in place, then inched down until its three deployed legs touched the hard surface, cushioned, then solidified. A perfect landing. Victorio allowed himself a tiny smile. It had been a while since he had had to do that. It was good to know that the old skills were still there and could be called upon quickly. But his smile turned sour when he looked out the cockpit window at the small man standing twenty meters portside. "Yusn Life-Giver," he whispered to himself and took a deep breath, "give me strength."

Victorio removed his helmet, shook his long brown hair free, wiggled his nose, then sneezed. Damn allergies! He'd been on Earth for only a few minutes and already they plagued him. He wasn't used to the fresh, warm air of a planet. He suppressed the urge to sneeze again and tapped his fingers along the pulsating red line of the engines panel. The engines wound down and the red line turned orange, then green, then yellow, until a slight hum replaced a whirling chaos. He did not want to turn them off completely. He was not staying long.

He tapped the cockpit hood and it opened like the mouth of a snake. Despite his allergies, Victorio breathed deeply. He unbuckled and stood up. He was weak and tired, the weight of gravity causing him to pause and gather himself. The artificial gravity of the *Radiant* was supposed to slowly adapt to all outside environments so that the pilot's body had time to adjust before disembarking. But this never quite worked in practice. There were always slight differences in pressure, and a less hearty pilot could become ill or break bones if he moved too quickly. Victorio stood there and let the warmth of the morning sun bake his brown skin.

Then he turned and lifted his brother off the floor from behind the pilot's seat. His body was heavy in death, but still flexible. In his belly had been placed a small silver tablet that released an enzyme that kept the body warm and the blood liquefied. It also softened the joints. In time, the tablet would dissolve and the body would stiffen, just as all humans do in death. Victorio pinched his eyes shut momentarily, then stepped out onto the wing.

As he reached the tip, the fighter dipped slightly to create a ramp that Victorio stepped down slowly, careful not to stumble or slip and lose his hold. He stepped off the wing and the fighter stiffened gently. He walked across the black pad, his heart in his throat, his eyes fixed on the man who waited.

He stopped in front of the man who stood several inches shorter, clothed from head to toe in light tan buckskin leggings and vest. His long hair was braided with turquoise beads and false rubies. Two hawk feathers were stabbed into the hair and waved in the warm breeze. His eyes darted back and forth between Victorio and the wrapped body. There were tears rimming the bottom of those dark eyes, and his cheek muscles worked nervously as if grinding bone.

"Father," Victorio said, holding himself steady, showing no signs of fatigue though his arms shook with the weight of his brother. "I bring you your son, Naiche "Blackclaw" Nan—"

The man put up his hand quickly. "Do not say his name. It will never be spoken again."

Victorio bit back his frustration. "He has a strong name, Father, and it is well-respected in the Federated Union. He is a warrior, the Champion of Europa and the Ward of the Crimson Sun. He received the Golden Spear for his actions at Alpha Centauri and clusters for bravery. He is a Devil Dancer. His name deserves to be spoken."

Father ignored his son's outburst and pointed to the ground. "Set him down, please."

Victorio did so. Father fell to his knees and put his hands on the blanket. "Father," Victorio said, "I don't think it's a good idea for you to look—"

"Do you think I'm afraid of death?" Father said, looking up at his son, his eyes now glaring in anger.

Victorio shut his mouth and the old man opened the blanket. Reconstructive surgery had reset Naiche's jaw and had re-grafted the skin that had been peeled away with fire. The ribs on his right side, where the energy bolt had landed after piercing the cockpit, had been re-formed as best as possible. The rest of his body, severely burned, had been left alone. There was little reason to do much more on a corpse.

Father ran his fingers across his dead son's jaw and down his chest. He lingered there for a moment, his weary eyes moving up and down the shattered body. "How did he die?"

Victorio told him.

Father nodded, folded the blanket back over the chest and face, and stood. "He was not a Devil Dancer," Father said, so low that Victorio almost did not hear. "He was *Ga'an*, a mountain spirit, sent by Yusn Life-Giver and so are you. 'Devil dancer' is a White Eyes term."

"There are no White Eyes anymore, Father," Victorio said, lifting his brother back into his arms. "There are only human beings...and *others*. We are all in this together."

Father huffed. He turned and walked toward the rancheria, which sat far in the distance. From here, Victorio could barely make out the domed roofs of the three dozen or more wickiups that dotted the harsh landscape. But he followed in silence and thought about the Life-Giver and *Ga'an* mountain spirits.

Father was right in that the term "devil dancers" was a name given to the *Ga'an* impersonators by a white man who had mistaken their dancing as erratic, out of control, evil. But that was hundreds of years ago, long, long before Father was born. And in the bitter vacuum of space, perception was just as important as rockets, torpedoes, lasers, ion cannons, and energy bolts. A "devil" garnered respect, from colleagues and enemies alike. That much, at least, Victorio had learned about war in his time among the stars.

Victorio shook his head. "Why do you persist in this harsh land, Father? I send you money all the time. You can afford to live a better life, in a better place."

"And where is that?" Father asked.

"Many other tribes have already left Earth. They are living good, peaceful lives on other planets."

Father snickered. "Peaceful... until the Gulo arrive."

All my fault. "We are winning the war, Father," Victorio said as they reached the bottom of the hill. The rancheria lay a quarter mile away. "The Gulo will not prevail. I promise."

"Yes, White Eyes promises much, but delivers little."

His anger welled again. "There aren't any White Eyes, Father. How many times do I—"

Father turned on his son and raised his hand again. "Spare me your lectures, son. You may live among the stars, but you have a lot to learn. I have seen the end in my dreams. The Gulo *will* sweep the Union away, and at the end of time when they come to punish Earth, when they come to this desert, this inhospitable place of rock and brush as you call it, we will make our stand, and Yusn will decide our fate."

Father turned and walked away. "Now, come," he said, "and bring He-Who-is-Gone. We have a lot do to. The ceremony is at dusk."

Victorio stood and watched his father walk away. He could not contain his anger any longer. "His name is Naiche "Blackclaw" Nantan," he shouted. "And I am Captain Victorio "Tomorrow's Wind" Nantan. These are the names that you have given us. They are proud names, respected names. They deserve to be spoken."

But Father did not speak them.

The command squadron arrived near midnight, dropping out of the sky like metal birds and churning the desert floor into sand sprites and dust clouds. The heat off their engines warmed Victorio's skin as he waited for their landing, the scent of *tula-pa* heavy on his breath. He had drunk too much, his mind hazy and unclear, but what did it matter? By morning, none of it would matter. He wiped away a tear and waved them down.

There were three squadrons that comprised the entire Devil Dancers unit. One command squadron (Alpha) and two auxiliary squadrons, Beta and Gamma. The auxiliaries contained junior officers and pilots recently added to the roster. In time, some of them might be so honored to be bumped up to Alpha, if they possessed the right mental and physical capabilities…and if a spot became available. As Victorio watched the pilots of Alpha approach him through the swirling dust, it was strange not to see his brother among them. He could not remember a time when Naiche was not there. Now Naiche's place was occupied by Warren "Red Moon" Benito, a capable but very young Apache lieutenant brought up from Beta just three short days ago. Would he survive? Victorio wondered. Time would tell.

The air cleared and Blue Bird and Shines Like the Sun stepped forward. Victorio relaxed. It was good to see old, familiar faces again, pilots that he had flown with for years. Blue Bird still limped from her foot reattachment and Shines Like the Sun, his face in a perpetual smile, breathed deeply, still growing used to his new heart. But they had fought bravely at Castor V and had survived.

Victorio kissed Blue Bird on the forehead and hugged her deeply. "It is good to see you, Captain," she said. Her voice was soft, tinged with grief, but strong.

Victorio pulled away. "It is good to see all of *you*. I'm glad that you came. Naiche would be proud."

"What are your orders, Captain?" Shines Like the Sun asked.

Victorio looked to the ground. There lay a grave of freshly dug earth, rocks and soft soil piled on top. He bent down and placed his hand on a stone and rubbed it gently as if it were the head of a baby. The funeral had gone well, and Naiche's spirit was now on a horse and making its way, like a true warrior, into the hereafter. "We dance," he said. "We dance for Blackclaw."

And they danced, adorned brightly in their Ga'an costumes. Buckskin kilts with large, richly-colored headdresses of green, red, and white. Feathers were attached here and there to wave in the desert wind like fingers. Fixed to the top of the headdresses were u-shaped arms with lines of sharp human teeth that jutted into the night sky to connect the flesh to the great cosmos. They danced, like Yusn Life-Giver had instructed when he sent the mountain spirits down to the Apache to teach them how to live a good, honorable life. Be good to others, good to yourself. Aid the poor, heal the sick. These were the things that they danced for. They danced for these things in honor of their fallen brother. And they sang too, though it was forbidden to sing over the grave of a fallen warrior. They sang the old songs. They sang to Yusn.

In the middle of the Holy Mountain,
In the middle of its body, stands a hut,
Brush-built, for the Black Mountain Spirit,
White lightning flashes in these moccasins;
White lightning streaks in angular path;
I am the lightning flashing and streaking!
This headdress lives; the noise of its pendants
Sounds and is heard!
My song shall encircle these dancers!

They built a bonfire. They stoked it until the flames reached into the dark sky. The four main Ga'an impersonators approached the flame, their bodies moving to music that only they could hear. They approached, they fell back. They approached, fell back. Again and again, like tradition demanded, to reflect the mountain spirits moving rhythmically into the world of the living. Victorio watched and waited. This time...he was the Clown. He had put on his brother's uniform and headdress, lined his face and bare chest in red, black, and white clay. He waited until the movements of Blue Bird were so erratic, so violent, that she fell to the ground.

Then he sprang, running straight to the fire, howling madly, shaking his arms, twisting his chest. Around him, he imagined scores of people, young children laughing and pointing. The Clown was a thing of mirth and joy. The Clown made funny faces and made people laugh, to lighten the mood for such a serious event. That was the traditional role of the Clown. But among the stars, against the Gulo, a Devil Dancer Clown was a thing to fear, a warrior not afraid to put himself out there, alone, to draw fire and allow the other dancers to swoop in and take victory. That is how Captain Victory had twisted and distorted the tradition for his own selfish gains. How many bright young men and women had he sent to their deaths? How many "Clowns" had been blown out of the vacuum to cover his walls with white, black, and tan pelts?

Tears streaked down his face. The shimmering people around him pointed and laughed. *Murderer*, their lips said silently. *Murderer.*

"I'm sorry, brother," he said, twisting and turning his body as if possessed by a Ga'an itself. "I have failed you, and I will not allow my weaknesses to kill anyone else."

He stared into the fire. A doorway opened, a large funnel of sand swirling down into the underworld. He smiled. Out of the orange-white flame came hands. Yusn's voice, calling him home. *Come, come,* a whisper tickled his ear. *Come to me.*

Victorio stopped dancing, raised his arms like wings, and leapt.

He fell into the middle of the flame. The fire roiled across his flesh. His body tensed against the searing heat, but he did not burn. He opened his eyes. He looked at his hands. They were soft, fresh skin ruddy with red clay. They were cool.

He blinked and suddenly he stood outside the bonfire, alone in his pilot's uniform. He felt a hand on his shoulder. He turned and stared into his father's face.

"What are you doing here?" he asked the image.

"*Saving you from making a terrible mistake,*" Father said, his face weary, old, wind-swept.

"But I am guilty."

"*Of what, my son?*"

"I killed my brother. I killed Naiche."

Father's face grew stern, serious. "*Did you kill him, or did the Gulo?*"

"I sent him to his death."

"*You did your duty. I could ask no more. Now don't be foolish and kill yourself. Do you think I want to bury two sons in one day?*"

"But I have failed you, Father. I'm an embarrassment. Naiche was the one you loved, not me."

"*That is not true. I love both my sons equally.*"

"Why have you never said so?"

"*I—*" But that was all Father managed to say. Victorio blinked and the image disappeared.

A large black bear appeared in front of him, claws bloody, teeth bared in a loud roar. It stood on hind legs. "*Attack me!*" it said, the words coming out of its foul muzzle in puffs of steam. "*What are you afraid of?*"

"Everything," Victorio said. An Apache feared the bear, for the spirit of an ancestor often came back to earth as a bear. To kill one, then, risked killing an ancestor.

"*But your brother killed a bear, and nothing bad happened to him.*"

Maybe, maybe not. That was the story perpetuated by Naiche himself and oftentimes Father to show the fearlessness of his son. Victorio knew the story well but had discounted it as ridiculous.

When he was a year old, Naiche had wandered away from the rancheria. He was missing for many hours, and night came and went. When they found him, he was covered head to toe in dried blood and dirt, hypothermic with the evening's dew. But in his hand he held a single black bear claw. *Where did you get it*, they asked him. He was too small to say, but the speculation grew. Naiche Nantan, now "Blackclaw" Nantan, was a little bear killer, the bravest of the Nantan boys.

"I cannot kill a bear."

"*You must, or you will die.*" The bear said, and rose up high on its legs. Then it leapt.

Victorio ducked and rolled, scrambled left to keep from being mauled by the beast's massive paw. The bear leapt again, snapping with its powerful jaws, catching him in the chest and throwing him across the fire.

Victorio screamed, rolled, and stood. The bear was on him again, grabbing his arm in its teeth and slinging him about like a doll. "*Kill me, or you will die.*"

"I want to die."

"*Then you are a coward like they say.*"

"Who says?"

"*The Gulo. They speak about you. They laugh at you. Gingu-sha laughs at you.*"

Gingu-sha's pristine white face came to his mind. The black teeth, the pale tongue, looking at him through a cockpit window...laughing.

Rage filled Victorio's mind. He pried himself away from the bear's grip and hurled himself onto its thick, broad back. The bear twisted and turned, snapped at his moccasins to pull him off. Victorio held tightly, and with all his strength, with all his anger, he plunged his hand into the bear's back, drove it through its spine, through its lungs and liver. He pushed his fingers into the warm flesh, found its heart, and yanked it out.

The bear dropped dead and Victorio hit the ground, rolled and skidded into the dirt. When the dust settled, he picked himself up, brushed off his pants, and walked over to the bear.

But it was no longer a bear. What lay there, in a heap of blood and fur, was something even more deadly. Something white, something...

Victorio opened his eyes. He lay beside the bonfire. Fuzzy images hovered nearby. He blinked several times, clearing his eyes of dust, tears, and sweat. Blue Bird's face was there, her expression quiet, comforting. She smiled. She raised her hand and rubbed a soft, wet cloth across his forehead. He let her do this a couple more times, then he sat up and looked around.

No blood, no bear, no Gulo. Just the steady crackle of the fire and the hard, dry ground against his legs. He stood, letting Shines Like the Sun steady his shoulders.

"Are you okay, Captain?" someone asked.

Victorio gained his balance and looked around. Was he okay? That was a difficult question to answer, but he nodded and said, "Yes, I think so. What happened?"

"You passed out," Blue Bird said.

"For how long?"

"Fifteen minutes?"

Victorio rubbed his face. It was a dream. All a silly, useless dream brought on by too much beer, too much excitement, too much emotion. He chuckled and shook his head. He raised his hand to rub his face again, but there was something in it this time. Victorio opened his palm.

A long, sharp black bear claw lay there. His heart sank. *Naiche's claw.* Where had it come from? It had been lost in the fire, it had not been found—

Then he remembered his dream, his Father, the bear, the Gulo. His mind raced. His heart soared. He gripped the claw and looked into the night sky.

"Would you like to sit back down, Captain?" Shines Like the Sun said. "Do you need rest?"

Victorio looked at his lieutenant, at his crew. He shook his head. "No. No rest for me, my friend. Suit up and strike the engines. We're going to war."

Behind him, the Devil Dancers fanned out in Eagle Pattern, the portside of their carrier Justice shielding them from the radiation of the nearby star. It was a bright, white-hot sphere of the Pollux Cluster, a perfect backdrop to the frontal attack called for by Admiral Cho. The enemy fleet sat a mere thousand kilometers away, cruisers and carriers mostly, and they had already seeded the field with anti-matter mines, energy sears, and radiation dampeners. But Captain Victory did not care. He had mapped out the best approach, and in Eagle Pattern, they would fly through the prepared defenses like broad wings in the sky, and the powerful light from the star behind them would give them the advantage.

"When we clear this field," he spoke over the comm to Alpha Squadron, "shift to Raven Pattern."

"So soon, Captain?" Blue Bird asked. "We don't even know the enemy fighter positions yet."

"Yes we do," he said. "I've already seen it."

And he had, twenty days ago as he danced around the bonfire and his brother's grave. He had seen everything clearly, concisely.

Shines Like the Sun screeched as his fighter nicked a mine. It ignited and tossed the fighter out of the pattern. "Watch your periphery, Lieutenant!" Victorio said.

Shines Like the Sun pulled the fighter out of its spin, rejoined the pattern, and said, "Yes, Captain. My apologies."

"Stay sharp, people," Victorio said, tilting his head and shifting the squadron to port. "We do this for Naiche."

They cleared the minefield. Before them lay the cruisers *Na-Ta-She* and *Vichu-Pa*. The Devil Dancers had fought against these mighty ships before. In fact, they were never seen separately, nor were they ever more than a few hundred kilometers apart in a Gulo capital ship formation. Gulo chatter captured on broadband always grew more steady and rhythmic when these ships appeared on view. There was something sacred, something profound about these vessels that went beyond their military purpose. The Gulo treated these ships with a reverence that, to this day, was not fully understood by Union Intelligence. The fact that they were here, and on the front line, meant that the Gulo were serious. They had staked out their position and had no intention of giving ground. Victorio sensed his pilots' apprehension at the sight of the enemy cruisers. "We've no worries about *them*, my Devils. Let them have their gods. Our target is much smaller."

Scores of red dots appeared on radar. "Enemy fighters, sir!" Red Moon said. "Straight ahead."

Gulo fighters did not fly in any defined pattern. Chaos was their pattern. As best as they could tell, there were no squadron leaders or captains in any fighter group. Every Gulo pilot was an individual weapon, whose mission was simply to find a ship that didn't look like one of theirs and blow it away. They were extremely skilled at that, Victorio had to admit. But it was also easy to exploit their lack of order, divide them and pick them off piecemeal.

"Raven!"

Victorio pushed a button on his cockpit panel and the exterior of his *Radiant* turned pitch black. The others followed suit, and against the bright light behind them, they seemed invisible to the untrained eye, and in the chaotic mass of enemy ships that swirled into view, they would fly in and wreak havoc.

The formation tightened, closing the wings. "Rockets!" Victorio said and pressed a button on his weapon's pad with a quick jab of his thumb.

Six rockets burst from each fighter, screaming through the deadly space between them and the Gulo. Such a large rush of munitions seemed to shock the enemy. They divided, some ramming into their own ships. The rockets spread out and captured the emission trails from Gulo fighters, locked on, hit, and exploded.

Victorio's cockpit windows grayed momentarily to protect him from the blast. The problem with Raven Pattern, unfortunately, was that your position was almost always exposed on the first launch of rockets. That's what Blue Bird was concerned about, but now was not the time for caution. The rockets exploded and their sudden flash of light alerted the enemy fighters to the Devil Dancers' position.

Gulo energy beams sprang to life.

"Scatter!" Victorio said, gunning his engines and rolling right, barreling down swiftly. Such a move was difficult to control, even for a pilot as skilled as himself. He lifted his head sharply to activate the stabilizing rockets so that the ship did not float against the vector too quickly, lose control, and drift aimlessly into enemy fire. Many Devil Dancers had been killed that way over the years.

Victorio righted his ship and flew into a mass of Gulo fighters. Blue energy zipped around him, scorching his wings, but failing to find impact. He looped twice, flew upside down, tapped his weapons pad, and sent red laser light into an oncoming fighter. But before the beams impacted, Red Moon swooped down and blew the enemy away with a spray of anti-matter bolts.

Victorio tensed as he burst through the shattered wing of the Gulo fighter.

"Woohoo!!" Red Moon's voice filled Victorio's helmet. He winced at the young man's screech.

"That was my kill, Red Moon!" Victorio said.

Red Moon silenced. "I'm sorry, Captain. I thought you were in danger. I was trying to, I was—"

"Forget it! Next time, stay out of my frontage."

"Yes, Captain." He paused for a moment, then said, "May I claim its pelt, sir?"

All activity on the enemy fighter had ceased, and it was falling away. Inside its cockpit, Victorio could make out the brown and yellow pattern of the Gulo's thick fur, riddled with holes, but still relatively intact. What a lovely display it would make on his wall. Victorio sighed. "Very well, you may claim it. It was a good kill."

Red Moon yelped. A tiny missile shot from his fighter and connected with the dead ship, splayed open, flashed red, and began emitting a signal. After the battle, they would salvage the wreck and Red Moon would skin the Gulo on the floor of the carrier bay, cut out its heart, and dance around the carcass. Victorio smiled. It was a good day for the young lieutenant.

Where are you, Gingu-sha? He was out there somewhere, Victorio knew. Waiting, perhaps, behind the cruisers, letting less capable pilots weaken the Union force before showing himself. "Where are you, you white son of a bitch! Show yourself, or are you too afraid to fight?"

The comm link was on and the others could hear him, but they dared not speak. Their captain was calling out an enemy, challenging him to fight. They would not give their voices to the challenge, but they would give their support, in any way that he asked.

"Ga'an Pattern!" he said. "I'm the Clown."

He could sense Blue Bird's apprehension, her fear for what was coming. Not because she was afraid of the fight. She was one of the bravest pilots he had ever known. But fear for what her visions, her own dreams, had shown her. She pulled her fighter up beside him. They looked at each other through the dim gray. She mouthed words so that they would not be heard across the comm, kissed her fingers and pressed them to the glass. Victorio smiled and kissed her back.

Victorio gunned his engines, and into the swirling mass of enemy fighters, he flew alone.

I am the lightning flashing and streaking! Over and over, Victorio mouthed the song, drawing strength from its cadence, its rhythm. *My song shall encircle these dancers!* In his mind, he danced around a fire, his face lined in red and white stripes. Mountain spirits whirled around him, filling his lungs, his heart, his arms, and legs, holding him up, keeping him steady as the enemy's weapons boomed in his wake. A Union fighter alone among the Gulo was a thing of respect, and a Devil Dancer Clown always got the respect it deserved. Naiche had gotten it, Victorio remembered. They had parted before him, letting him fly into their midst as if he were one of them. And then Gingu-sha appeared, and the respect and the dance were over.

Victorio tapped a panel to his right. Radio waves burst from the sides of his fighter in short staccato blasts. The Gulo had extremely sensitive hearing, especially in the high-decibel range. Their radios would pick up these blasts and emit the noise through all the fighters until they changed their frequency. It was a short-term solution, but it gave Victorio a moment to work without hindrance. He rolled and tapped his weapons panel. Anti-matter bolts shattered the hull of a Gulo fighter. It ignited the missiles inside and breached the hull. The collateral damage took out another two fighters. Victorio skidded left to avoid the chunks of armor tumbling in his path.

"Come out, Gingu-sha. *Come out, come out!*"

And then he was there, on the radar, a bright blue dot closing fast.

The Union had customized its radar so that they could tell by color what kind of enemy fighters were closing. Gingu-sha now flew a new model, one that they had experienced only a few times over the past several engagements. Union designated it *Saw*-class for its circular hull with extractable alloy teeth. Victorio gulped. If those teeth connected with a *Radiant* hull...

The enemy ace did not give him time to think. He flew across Victorio's vision cone slow and steady as if he were taking a mild stroll through a meadow. Victorio followed the ship with bursts of laser fire. Nothing connected. He turned the nose of the *Radiant* up and spun like a screw. Stabilizer rockets slowed the rotation and he dropped, tapped his weapon's pad, and released the last of his rockets. They swirled off-radar, twisting and turning like one massive torpedo, zeroing in on the Gulo's emission trail. The *Saw* listed to the left and turned upside down. Scores of tiny needles shot out of the hull and shimmered madly like a swarm of hornets. Victorio watched in awe as each of his rockets, one after the other, fell into the swarm and exploded harmlessly. The Gulo righted his fighter and was gone.

"Dammit!" Victorio said, gunned his engines in pursuit.

He's playing with me, Victorio thought. This was the Gulo way, a kind of counting-coup: How many times could Gingu-sha avert death before ending the chase? How many times had he averted death against Naiche? Victorio could not remember. The moments of that fight were fuzzy now, a blur in the mind. *You won't play with me, Gingu-sha. Not for long.*

He followed closely, matching the enemy pilot's every turn, every twist. Victorio kept his finger on his lasers, short bursts, then long, short, long, keeping the Gulo guessing, uncertain about whether to run or to stop and return fire.

Blue energy beams slashed out of the *Saw's* aft weapon's pod, singeing the *Radiant's* wings and taking out an anti-matter bolt tube. The strike knocked Victorio away. He rotated his ship to compensate for the blast and tried to renew the chase. But that part of the dance was over.

He slowed and watched as Gingu-sha looped back on the pattern, the brilliant, smooth silver hull of his round ship bristling with lights and activation queues. "Great mountain spirits," Victorio said as he waited. He tapped his helmet to activate his comm. "Come and give me strength."

Scores of missiles launched toward him like shards of glass. Victorio activated his point defense and nudged his fighter forward, letting the missiles set their deadly path. A cloud of metal balls infused with passive sonar drifted out in front of his ship and created a glistening mesh. He waited, watching the tiny dots on his radar come closer, closer, closer, until he could wait no longer. He activated the mesh, then gunned his ship and turned hard to the right, tumbling over and over as each Gulo missile found a patch of balls and exploded. The shock wave of the strike pushed Victorio further than he wanted. He arched his back and pulled up. The radar screen still beeped with enemy munitions. *Damn!* The wall hadn't gotten them all. A half-dozen still moved toward their target.

He flew, pushing his *Radiant* as fast as it could go. He twisted left, right, until the missiles were lined up correctly to hit his wings. He ignited his fore stabilizers and brought his ship to a halt. He waited, tensed against the impending strike, and closed his eyes.

The missiles pounded his wings, one after the other like a line of meteors striking a moon. Victorio held the arms of his chair tightly. His security belt dug deep into his shoulders. With each strike, he was tossed around the cockpit, banged left and right, as the *Radiant* lost power and tumbled away like a leaf in a strong wind.

Then all was silent. The light of the Pollux star lit up his cockpit windows. He could not see, could not hear. The face of his father came to him, his brother, a loud, smoky room where he heard Naiche's laugh for the last time. A bear. A Clown. Earth. Mountain spirits.

A shadow fell over his cockpit. Victorio looked up. Gingusha's bright, white face was there, arrogant and proud, staring at him again through the cracked glass. His pale tongue flicked, his black teeth popped together. He was happy, Victorio could tell. Joy was a universal feeling. The Gulo was elated by the fact that he had his prey where he wanted him. His red eyes glowed hot and his beautiful, thick fur glistened in the starlight.

Victorio smiled back. "I know how you feel, brave warrior. I've been there before." He straightened in his seat and mouthed the words though he knew the Gulo could neither hear nor understand them. "But you forget who you are facing. I am Victorio "Tomorrow's Wind" Nantan, Captain Victory, leader of the Devil Dancers, and proud brother to Naiche "Blackclaw" Nantan. We are the lightning flashing and streaking. We are the

Ga'an. We are the mountain spirits. We are Apache. And we *never* fight alone."

Laser light and anti-matter bolts slammed into the Gulo ship, a relentless array of firepower that blew Victorio back into his chair and knocked his fighter clear.

Blue Bird and Shines Like the Sun came into view, their fighters swirling, their weapons hot. The enemy ship looked like a pinball as Gingu-sha worked his panels desperately to get away, to fire weapons, to do anything, but it was too late. Rockets launched and slammed into its hull. Fire swept the cockpit. White fur burst into flames. Gingu-sha mouthed a silent scream. The *Saw* exploded.

Victorio rested in the dark, cold cockpit of his fighter. He thought about something Father had said, something he had seen in his dreams. *'The Gulo will sweep the Union away.'* He nodded. Perhaps one day, yes. The war was far from over, and the Gulo were still very strong. But not today. "Today, Father," Victorio said, reaching into his breast pocket and pulling out Naiche's black bear claw, "today, your son...your *sons*, prevailed."

Blue Bird pulled up beside him and launched a drag cable around one of his mangled wings. She pulled him close and they looked at each other through the glass. "Cutting it a little close, weren't you?" Victorio said through his headgear.

Blue Bird smiled. "Sorry, Captain. We were giving you a chance to win."

He smiled, nodded, and looked out toward the battle. The capital ships were closing. Torpedoes were being fired, ion cannons were belching. The war raged on.

"What are your orders, Captain?" Shines Like the Sun asked.

Captain Victory breathed deeply, tucked the claw away, and said, "Let's go home, my Devils. Let's go home."

CHILD OF THE WATER

Two boys sat in the flow of frigid water, neither willing to move, to give the other the satisfaction of knowing he had been bested. They were young. They were warriors. Well, not yet, but someday they would be, and neither harsh mountain rock nor freezing water would keep them from their destiny. Captain Victorio "Tomorrow's Wind" Nantan, Squadron Commander of the Devil Dancers, 3rd Sol fighter Wing, was proud of them.

"I saw you move," Deer-Caller said, his skinny body shivering as the river water flowed around him. Around his neck, a small piece of deer antler bounced just above the waterline on a strand of leather cord. The day was hot, but the water seemed incapable of accepting the sun's gift. "Captain, sir, I saw him move."

"Liar," Little Boy said. He had indeed moved a finger, Victorio had noticed, but the boy would never admit it. "*You* moved, Deer-Caller. You wiggled your nose."

"Gentlemen," Captain Victorio said from the bank, "Devil Dancers work together to solve problems. When the Gulo strike, do you think they will care about who moved a finger, or who wiggled a nose? The Gulo will kill you where you sit, and care neither for your fingers or your noses. Focus your minds, and deal with the pain of the freezing water. That's what matters."

The boys tried to focus. Little Boy was younger than Deer-Caller by a year. He had already tried this challenge once before when he thought no one was looking. But Victorio had noticed, and had tracked the boy in silence to this very river three days ago, and had watched him sit obediently in the stream, shaking at the incessant rush of cold water around him. It was against the rules of training, indeed, but Victorio let it go. It never hurt to do a little pre-planning, he reasoned. Little Boy seemed good at that, good at anticipating situations and putting himself in a position to prevail. *Let others call it cheating*, Victorio had thought as he had watched his novitiate endure the freezing cold. *I call it smart.*

They sat for several minutes more, neither taking his eyes off the other. Little Boy made faces of evil spirits, *Godeh* trolls, and the *Ga'an* Clown. He spoke silly gibberish and made Deer-Caller snicker. "Captain," Deer-Caller said, no longer containing his mirth. He pointed at his younger rival. "He's making faces at me."

"Enough," Victorio said. "Time's up. Out!"

They crawled to the bank and rolled out, letting the sun warm their frozen skin. Little Boy shivered and rubbed his arms. "Ha, I knew it," Deer-Caller said, pointing with a shaking hand. "I knew you were cold. Admit it."

"Come," Victorio said. "Let us continue."

They stood and huddled around their captain. From a pouch tied to his waist, Victorio pulled two small tubes of water and handed them over. "Uncork these and pour the water into your mouths. Hold it there, but do not drink."

They did as directed, then handed the tubes back. Victorio tucked them away and said, "Now. . . ," he pointed to the east, ". . .you will run to the top of that hill, taking the path I have shown you. It will be a long and difficult run, but a warrior would not drink the water, no matter how thirsty he is. A warrior knows how to control his body and his urges." He pulled the boys close and squeezed their hands. "This is not a competition to see who will get there first. You must both get there with the water intact. Do you understand?"

He waited until both boys nodded agreement, then said, "Now go."

Little Boy moved first, getting the jump on Deer-Caller. The older boy's eyes glared in protest, but the younger was gone.

Victorio followed closely behind, keeping pace as best he could. This would be an interesting run, he knew. As stated, the goal was not to be the winner, but he couldn't help but wonder who would actually reach the summit first. Deer-Caller was the fastest by far, but Little Boy was the smartest. No doubt about that.

The way grew steeper as the flatter terrain of the river valley gave way to harsh rock, twisted brush, and sharp cactus. Little Boy pushed hard, his body washed in sweat. The water, now clearly warm in his mouth, was making it hard to breathe. He must be terribly thirsty, his throat so dry. *Perhaps he'll take a sip*, Victorio thought as he jogged beside them and observed. *Who would miss one little drop?*

Then Deer-Caller was beside Little Boy, pumping his strong legs and taking the lead. The older boy's face was brilliant with joy. His thin lips were pulled back in a big grin, but not a drop of water escaped them. Little Boy shook his head, clearly trying to figure out how he had let such a lead evaporate. He doubled his efforts, pushing into Deer-Caller and jumping over dead wood. Deer-Caller stumbled and fell back again, trying to keep his footing. He yelled something indiscernible, not wanting to open his mouth and lose the water. Little Boy ignored the words, smiled triumphantly, and kept moving.

The summit was near.

With thirty paces left, Deer-Caller took the lead again and kept it. Victorio could see the anger and disappointment on Little Boy's face; he had lost another race to Deer-Caller.

Victorio watched Deer-Caller stumble forward, gasping for air. He clapped Little Boy on the back. "Well, Little Boy, looks like you've lost again. Don't be too upset. You can't win them all." He chuckled. "You can't win any of them, looks like."

In the midst of Deer-Caller's cackle, Little Boy stood straight, smiled, winked, then bent over and spit his water onto the bleached rock so his captain could see. "Wanna bet?"

Deer-Caller's face flushed with panic. He fished around in this mouth with his tongue. His head dropped, his shoulders slumped. The water was gone.

He had sipped too much.

Little Boy edged his *Radiant* fighter into Raven pattern. His left wing was four degrees out of synch.

"Caje Muchacho!"

Captain Victorio's voice boomed over the comm, commanding. A chill spread down Little Boy's spine at the sound of his full name. It reminded him of his mother. "Sir?"

"Keep formation! This is not a drill!"

"Yes, sir!"

He was the third in a five-fighter formation, moving rapidly toward a line of cometary knots in the Helix Nebula known as The Necklace. Deer-Caller flew at point, and Little Boy fumed. *What's four degrees*, he wondered, as he slowly shifted his fighter into the correct position. *Deer-Caller was twenty degrees too far forward just a moment ago, and the captain didn't chew him out.* But Captain Victorio never seemed obliged to explain his often-times erratic and inconsistent command style. Erratic in Little Boy's mind, anyway. Then again, what did he know about command? He wasn't a Devil Dancer. Not yet, anyway.

The brilliant, white cusp of the cometary knot came into view, and Little Boy instinctively flicked on his fighter's radiation shield as a precaution to the harsh environment. The Gulo had thought it clever to run their heavy cargo hulls along The Necklace as a way to screen out Union attacks. And it had worked for a while, but a crease in the line had been breached, and the fleet was determined to exploit the opportunity. It was a perfect way to get in real, practical flight-and-fight training at low physical risk.

And Little Boy was flying third. *I should be in front,* he thought, as he shifted left on cue with everyone else. *I should be the Clown!*

"Keep tight!" The captain said, coordinating the effort from position two. "We get in and out quickly. Spray the platform and fly. No funny business. No delay. *Ahagahe!*"

The war cry repeated through the squadron. Little Boy checked his sensors and flipped on laser and missile arrays.

I'm ready.

His scanner pulsed with enemy blips. Fighter craft were converging on their location. "Sir, three *Wasps* are. . ."

"I see them," Victorio said. "Let them come to you. It's a screening force. Nothing to worry about. Maintain formation, lock targets, and wait."

Little Boy did as directed. "Hey, Deer-Caller," he said over secure comm, ". . . watch this."

He waited, waited until the *Wasps* were in optimal range. On his dashboard, their weapons flashed active, and Little Boy threw his weight to the right as he leaned into the stick. He touched his dash, maintaining formation, but barrel-rolling such that his laser array was at a proper firing angle. He fired, and the *Wasp* closest to him swerved and roiled off course, striking the one next to it and breaking the entire formation. The Wasps reacted by laying on their flechette guns, but Lieutenant Red Moon, a veteran holding position five, ended the flurry with a carefully placed rocket into the lead *Wasp*. It burst into a thousand tiny bits, causing collateral damage to the one next to it, forcing the third and final to break off.

Deer-Caller snickered through comm. "Shut up!" Little Boy said. "I broke up their formation at least."

"Stay focused!" Victorio said, interrupting. "Here we go."

They burst into The Necklace. The light from the Helix star lit the dust in brilliant white, red, and green. Little Boy had never seen anything so beautiful and if time were convenient, he'd like to just drift, alone, in quiet, soaking it all in. There was a peacefulness in space that one could not acquire planetside. That was one of the reasons why he wanted to be a Devil Dancer. He wanted to be one with the cosmos, to be a *Ga'an* dancer, to dance around a bonfire until exhaustion and dehydration gave him the visions he needed to succeed, not only as a human being and as an Apache, but as a pilot as well. That's how the senior members of the squadron gained their courage, and he was working toward that goal. All he had to do was show himself on this mission, show his talent, his. . . genius, and he would be accepted.

There was nothing he wanted more.

They cleared the knot and before them, in a small dustless corridor within The Necklace, lay the Gulo carrier platform. Open-faced and about five kilometers long, stretching further than Little Boy's eyes could see, but not too far for his sensors.

It was also about a half kilometer wide. Wide and long enough for several cargo ships to set down, unload, and launch once more.

He reengaged his weapons and shifted left with the formation.

Now the surface of the platform was visible, every detail, every scratchy Gulo symbol and diagram. There was also a blue shimmering dome above it.

"Sir," he said, "will our weapons penetrate that shield?"

"Yes," Victorio said. "It's for radiation only. But we'll need to fly through it to get a good strafe. It's going to get a little bumpy. Be ready."

Little Boy noticed something else on the platform. He was about to mention it when Deer-Caller chimed in. "Sir, aren't those green hatch markings missile designations?"

Victorio grunted. "ISR has fucked up once again, gents. This is going to get bumpier than I thought. Okay, increase speed by twenty percent, and let's reform to Sparrow."

Damn you, Deer-Caller. I saw it too! It was my turn to impress.

Sparrow was a tight formation, with a potential Clown flying point. Deer-Caller maintained that position, and Little Boy obeyed the order and pulled his Radiant in, until they were flying nearly wing to wing. It didn't make sense to him at first, and then he saw the logic in it. A smaller, tighter formation made for an even smaller moving target, and one that could fly past each battery faster and thereby confuse Gulo tracking.

The captain was right. Flying through the shield made his dashboard flicker, and for a moment, Little Boy thought his entire cockpit would go dead. Then it revved up again, and he lay hard on the stick to keep in line, then settled in once the entire formation had pierced the blue haze.

"Fire!"

Little Boy lay on his stick, digging his fingernails into the trigger as if doing so would make them fire harder, faster.

First, laser fire. Five lines of green cutting light tore into the Gulo platform, ripping huge chasms in its floor. Then they emptied their missile tubes. Each high-explosive round struck the platform, some penetrating deep into their mark, igniting fuel and ammunition reserves. Damaged pieces floated everywhere.

Gulo batteries tried responding, and a few shells went forth to find targets. But the *Radiants* were too fast, too small a target, and by the time the Gulo batteries locked on heat signatures, the entire formation was well past the danger zone.

But Little Boy saw it. And this time, *he* was the only one who did. While the others were cheering and glorifying in a successful strafe, including the captain, Little Boy saw a long, powerful prow cannon arching up at the end of the platform, faster than any barrel its size should move. The gun wasn't a small-craft weapon. No. It was designed for larger hulls, destroyers, cruisers, capital ships. But if it hit the squadron. . .

He didn't waste time thinking. He gunned reverse thrusters and drove his fighter into Lieutenant Red Moon's. Red Moon fell left at the impact, hitting the Captain's and forcing him into Shines Like the Sun's position four. This chain reaction caused all four ships to fall port. Only the lead fighter, Deer-Caller's, kept moving forward, unaware of what was happening behind him.

The prow cannon disregarded the fighters falling away, locked itself on Deer-Caller, and fired.

Brilliant white light flashed before Little Boy's eyes, and Deer-Caller was gone.

Victorio didn't give Little Boy time to clear his cockpit. He bounded up the fighter's lowered wing, grabbed the boy by the scruff, and hoisted him out of the cockpit. He pulled the boy down the wing, tore off his helmet, and let the boy's bare-brown novitiate war cap fall to the tarmac.

"Why did you break formation?" Victorio screamed into Little Boy's face. "Why?"

Little Boy did not speak, his eyes wild, fearful, glued to Victorio's face. "I—I—"

"Deer-Caller is dead! Incinerated! His soul will never greet Yusn Life-Giver, to follow the *Ga'an* into the mountain. He will never dance!"

"I know that!" Little Boy shouted, and then lowered his eyes again, realizing that his voice was too harsh, too confrontational. "I did it to save you. To save Lieutenant Red Moon and Lieutenant Shines."

Little Boy described the cannon and its uncharacteristic speed. Victorio stood there, listening to every word, letting his angry breathing subside, his heart slow. He released Little Boy and stepped back. "Caje, do you know why the back four in a Raven or Sparrow formation must maintain tight control over their position?"

Little Boy nodded. "Yes, sir. So that, when and if the captain of the formation orders the fifth and lead fighter, the Clown, to assume his or her role, the back four can maintain a tight and orderly force against any attempt to destroy the Clown upon its leaving the formation. Without that tight control, weapons targeting can be hampered, slowed, so that the Clown is vulnerable."

"And what is the key word or phrase of that rule?"

Little Boy considered. "To maintain the formation to protect the Clown on his or her departure."

"No!" Victorio snapped. "The key word is 'captain'! It's the captain that will make the decision. The captain did not order a break in the formation, did he? Because the novitiate did not radio his captain and warn him of the threat."

"With respect, sir, I made the judgment that there was no time to radio such concern. The cannon was tracking too fast, sir, for such communication."

"And you are qualified to make that decision on your own?"

"I—" Little Boy paused, gnashed his teeth. Victorio could see him trying to find the right words to say, the right response to end this confrontation. "Yes, sir, I am. I was the only one who could."

Victorio sighed, rubbed his aching eyes. A headache was coming on. "Go," he said, motioning behind him to the exit leading to crew quarters. "Clean up, get ready for mess. There will be a debriefing at 0800."

Little Boy straightened, saluted, but Victorio could see the boy's hand shake as he held it to his forehead. Victorio saluted then stepped aside to allow the boy to leave.

Victorio leaned over the *Radiant* wing and watched Little Boy disappear through the exit. At his feet lay the brown novitiate war cap. He picked it up and looked at it. Bare, nondescript, bereft of metals, service ribbons. But of course, it would be.

Little Boy had not done anything yet to warrant metals or ribbons.

Or had he?

"Goddammit!" Victorio hissed the word and threw the war cap down as he saw Deer-Killer's terrified face in his mind. "Goddamn it all!"

"He reminds me so much of Blackclaw, it's scary."

Victorio stood in his office, looking up at the rows of Gulo pelts on his wall, each one an ace. Dozens of tan and grey coats, some a mixture of white and black, or white with brown spots and stripes. Only one was pure black, and Victorio smiled as he remembered that dogfight ten standard years ago. None were pure white. There was an empty frame at the very end of the display where a pure white coat should be, but it had been incinerated in a cockpit fire. *Praise Yusn Life-Giver for small miracles!*

His brother's nameplate now rested in the middle of that frame, and beneath it, scores upon scores of medals, ribbons, and clusters. Naiche "Blackclaw" Nantan had been one of the Federated Union's most decorated pilots. Now, he was dead.

Lieutenant Blue Bird came up behind him and wrapped her arms around his chest. He breathed deeply. She smelled good. She always did. She felt good too, more relaxed than he had seen her in a long time. R&R had agreed with her.

"Your brother was an ace ten times over," she said, resting her head on his back. "He was born a wolf, a fighter. He killed a bear when he was only three."

Victorio chuckled. "That was Davey Crockett."

Blue Bird laughed. "Well, he did *something* to that bear to earn his name."

He leaned into her but kept his eyes on his brother's achievements. "I shouldn't have grabbed him. That was uncalled for. But I'm so goddamned tired of losing young men."

"Then you're in the wrong business, dear heart. Fighters are all expendable, you know that. Though we've beaten the odds."

She was right. The Devil Dancers had the best survival rate of any squadron in the Federated Union fleet; the most kills and the most aces. But that record wouldn't last long if they kept losing novitiates.

Blue Bird pulled away and stepped up to the wall, ran her fingers along the bottom of the frames. "So what have you determined?"

"The boy was right." Victorio turned from the wall and fell into a chair. He tapped a display on his desk, and Red Moon's vid-data appeared. "I've looked at it for hours, at every angle. The prow gun is some kind of new type. It has a trajectory near three times the speed of their typical cannons. The Gulo are innovative little bastards, aren't they? Always throwing a surprise our way." He shook his head and turned off the display. "The boy was right. There was no time to communicate the threat. He fell back into Red Moon to create a domino effect to throw us all out of formation, thus forcing the targeting system on the cannon to choose one of us; it chose Deer-Caller. Caje Muchacho disobeyed orders to save the majority of his squad. He made. . . a command decision."

"So, no disciplinary action? No Court Martial?"

Victorio shook his head. "No."

"Then perhaps you should recognize his valor in an official capacity and apologize to him."

Victorio sprung up from his chair and walked back to the trophy wall. "There is no precedent for giving trainees citations. It just isn't done. Besides, he still disobeyed orders. He broke formation without authorization from his squadron leader. What do you want me to do? Kiss his ass? Praise him before the entire squadron? And then what? His willful, arrogant spark grows to such an extent that somewhere down the line, he believes in his own invincibility as Blackclaw did, and makes a decision that *isn't* the right one, and he gets himself and everyone else killed in his squadron. I can't do that, Blue. He's not ready."

"He's a Devil Dancer, love. He's a warrior."

"Not yet he isn't. He's still a child."

She moved to him and placed her hand on his. She looked deeply into his eyes and Victorio couldn't help but look back, back into those clear blue irises that accentuated her name. He knew what she was going to say before she said it.

"Are you sure?"

Little Boy shivered uncontrollably. He sat cross-legged below the shower head in the crew quarters' shower bay, letting the frigid water trickle down his body and congeal into icy slush at the drain. *Don't move,* he told himself, as he tried controlling his erratic motions. *You have been ordered to keep formation. Do not break it!*

He imagined himself in the cockpit of his *Radiant,* flying Raven Pattern, off the port side of his captain. *Don't break it! Don't break it!*

"Aaahhhh!" He howled under the cold flow. "I can't stand this any longer! I must break formation!"

No! The voice screamed in his mind. *Maintain your course.*

"I must break course, or I will die. We will all die!"

Deer-Caller died following orders.

"It should have been me! I could have sped up. I could have knocked Deer-Caller off course. Then I would have died instead of him."

But you didn't speed up. You fell back. Why? Why did you allow him to fly into his death?

"I wanted to save the rest."

Save them? Or impress them?

"Save them!"

You hated Deer-Caller.

"Yes. . . no! I didn't hate him. I was. . . jealous of him. There, I said it. I was jealous. But I did not hate him. He was a good human being. He was a good Apache. He was—"

"What are you doing?"

Captain Victorio's voice cut through the water. Little Boy scrambled to his feet, reached behind him and turned off the spigot. He pushed his wet hair out of his eyes and swirled around to face his captain, naked and shivering.

"I was showering, sir."

Captain Victorio nodded, paused a moment, then said, "Dry off, then come out here."

"Yes, sir."

He dried quickly, then threw on green utilities hanging on a peg just outside the shower. He rubbed loose water out of his hair, rubbed his face, straightened up, and walked out into the crew quarters.

Captain Victorio stood in brilliant, colorful *Ga'an* attire, waiting. Little Boy went to him and saluted. "Yes, Captain."

The captain cleared his throat. "Tell me. . . why did Yusn Life-Giver send the *Ga'an* to Earth?"

"To teach the people how to be good human beings, sir. To teach them how to serve as moral creatures. To heal the sick, clothe and feed the poor and hungry. To glorify in life and to give thanks to the spirits."

"And how do they teach the Apache these things?"

"They dance, sir."

Captain Victorio reached into a small pouch at his side. From it, he pulled several feathers. From his belt, he pulled a brown war cap.

"You left this on the tarmac," Captain Victorio said, unfolding it and placing it on Little Boy's head. "Wear it at all times, Muchacho, for it will give you strength like the *di-yin*."

He then drew a feather from his hand and fixed it to the cap. "Take this oriole feather, for it will keep your mind clear in times of stress and danger. Take this eagle feather, for it will protect you from harm. Take this pinfeather from the left wing of a hummingbird, for it will give you speed. And take this quail feather, for it will aid you in surprising your enemy. Wear these feathers at all times, as they will help guide you in life and in the tough decisions that you will have to make as you walk your path."

Little Boy waited until the last feather was placed, then he reached up and felt each in turn. Tears welled in his eyes, but he forced his emotions deep. A warrior, a Devil Dancer, does not cry in the presence of his captain.

"Now, come with me," Captain Victorio said. "You're ready."

"Ready for what, sir?"

Victorio placed a hand on his shoulder and smiled. "You're ready to dance."

In the launch bay, around a simulated fire, they danced. They were dressed in fur-lined buckskin kilts of tan and black, with white streaks of clay running length-wise along seams and pleats. They wore headdresses with multiple feather patterns that fanned out like hands reaching toward Yusn Life-Giver and the great cosmos. Affixed to some of their headdresses were u-shaped arms of sharp teeth, and these gave the entire ensemble a dark, fearful visage that Little Boy found both disturbing and awe-inspiring. The four *Ga'an* impersonators from Alpha Squadron approached the flames in a rhythmic pattern to reflect the mountain spirits flowing ghost-like into the world of the living.

Little Boy watched and waited outside the ring of dancers. He had been given the honorable role of Clown. He wore a uniform and headdress that had been made specifically for him, had lined his face and bare chest in red, black, and white clay. He waited until the movements of Blue Bird, who had replaced Deer-Killer in the squadron, brought her close to the flame so that her brightly-colored mask shown in the light like a devil.

Then he joined her. He shook his arms and howled madly. He ran straight to the fire, twisting his chest, his hips, and halted just before falling into the embers. In his mind, he was surrounded by people, many of them children, laughing and pointing at him. How could they not laugh? He was the Clown, and the Clown brought joy to a somber ceremony such as this one. But there was little joy in the vacuum of space, and a Devil Dancer Clown was the most feared pilot, a warrior not afraid to put himself out there, alone, to draw fire and allow the other dancers to swoop in and take victory. As he danced, Little Boy wondered if he was that kind of warrior, stalwart, fearless, ready to give his life for others if the need arose. He was not sure, but he danced, as he had been taught through the squadron's liturgy. He danced and imagined he was that kind of warrior.

Across his bare chest lay an *izze-kloth*, a cord of powerful medicine affixed with war charms. Clipped to his belt were a tiny bag of pollen and a war club. All of these things a warrior took into battle, to protect himself from evil spirits if such a bloody end was near. All of the dancers had them, and they wore them proudly as their rhythmic movements and singing filled the launch bay.

Little Boy pulled his war club and waved it violently in the air, letting the heat from the fake flames wash his face as he leaned into the fire. He pinched his eyes shut and imagined himself back home on Earth, just a mere three years ago. A child then, longing for space, for war, looking up into the night sky and wondering what it was like to be among those stars. And now here he was, dancing around a 'fire' in a launch bay on a carrier, light years from home, defending the Federated Union from an insatiable enemy, a powerful wolverine-like foe that seemed intent on wiping out every last human being. Dancing around this fire, Little Boy was becoming a man. No, not yet. Not until he had killed the monsters.

He opened his eyes and saw the first monster lurch out of the flames, a four-armed Gulo of pitch-black fur, all teeth and bleeding gums. Like the stories told in his youth, Little Boy imagined himself the Child of Water, the supernatural being whom all novitiates imagined themselves during their training. At his neck, he touched the line of turquoise beads that were placed there for protection and drew a bow and arrow from his side.

The monster leapt at him, howling madly, scraping the air with its powerful claws. Little Boy notched his arrow and drew it back, aimed carefully, and let it fly through the beast's eye. The monster fell dead at his feet, shimmered like a vid image, then disappeared.

Another monster flew out of the fire, this one wrapped in brilliant red burning wings. Little Boy nearly dropped his bow in fear. A Gulo with wings. *Holy Yusn, give me strength.*

The monster rose into the stale air of the launch bay, flapped its long muscled wings, bared its black teeth, and swooped in for the kill.

Little Boy shook in terror, felt broiling heat flap off the monster's wings. He could smell its foul breath on his face. He closed his eyes again against the sheer terror of the image. *I can't do this*, he said to himself as he pulled the arrow back. *I can't. . .*

The arrow loosed and a mighty roar escaped the monster's cavernous maw. Little Boy crouched, huddled like a turtle, and waited for the image to dissipate against his back.

He sighed with relief, but it was short-lived as another, even more terrifying, monster rose out of the flames.

Standing easily ten feet tall, the pure white Gulo stepped forward, cords of muscle rippling beneath its beautiful coat. Little Boy dared to look further, dared to admit to himself how lovely it was how glorious in its power, standing upon haunches bulging with strength, its claws two inches long and dripping with human blood. It did not roar, it did not flex or crouch to attack. It stood there, stiff and watching, glaring at Little Boy with its impenetrable black eyes.

And then he knew what it was. An aspect of the Gulo fighter ace that had killed Captain Victorio's brother. Less than one standard year ago. The one the squadron honored by placing an empty pelt frame on their trophy wall. There he stood, but surely this wasn't a real image of the beast. No Gulo was this tall, this monstrous. Most of them were no larger than humans, and perhaps a little shorter in some cases. No, this was a fake. Wasn't it?

Little Boy found the courage to rise, to notch another arrow on his bow. He pulled the arrow back, but something in the monster's face stayed his hand. Something in its expression. A longing, perhaps, a sorrow. It stepped forward, and Little Boy lowered his bow, smiled at it. The creature did not smile back, though its long muzzle was capable of that kind of expression. It licked its teeth instead. It moved its pink tongue across its fangs as if it were savoring a meal. Little Boy fell back, losing his smile. He notched his arrow again. He pulled it back. He stumbled over his own feet. He lay there as the Gulo monster drew closer. He closed his eyes once more, prayed to Yusn to give him strength, courage. *I am a Child of the Water*, he told himself. *I am not afraid of monsters. . .*

Captain Victorio and Blue Bird and the other Devil Dancers attacked, having come up behind the creature in silence. They stabbed it with ceremonial blades, jumped on its back, slit its throat, and pounded its legs with war clubs and hatchets. The slaughter went on and on, and Little Boy marveled in the brutality of the attack, the sheer violence of it. The beast tried to fight them off, but it was outnumbered, outmatched. It fell under the weight of its assailants, shimmered in rage, and then popped out of existence at his feet.

Little Boy did not realize that he was still holding a notched arrow, until a hand grabbed the bow and gently set it aside.

"Rise, Caje Muchacho."

He did as Captain Victorio ordered. He opened his eyes and saw his captain standing before him, headdress removed.

"I could not fire at it," he said, lowering his head in shame. "It was so terrifying in its calmness. I did not have the courage to—"

"Nonsense," Captain Victorio said. "You did what a Clown is supposed to do. You lulled the enemy into a complacent position, and then you let the rest of the squadron attack. You fought like an Apache today. We are Apaches, Little Boy, we are Devil Dancers. We fight together, always. Do you understand?"

Little Boy nodded. And he *did* understand. For the first time since his training began, he understood what it meant to be a Devil Dancer, to be a part of this elite force.

"Now," Captain Victorio said, "go and clean up. And this time, with warm water and soap, for tomorrow, you go to war. Not as a child this time, but as a man."

He was lead fighter in the formation, the place that Deer-Caller had held in death. He was honored, if not a little nervous. Captain Victorio had given him a further honor as well: he, Little Boy, would call the formations as required during flight. Such a responsibility had not been given to Deer-Caller, and for a moment, he was not sure that he could do it. But the decision had been made, and there was no way out of it. . . except to fail. And today, Little Boy would not fail.

"Raven Pattern!" he said over comm, holding his position but waiting until the rest of the squadron made the change in mid-flight. No objections came from anyone, so he calmed and checked his exact position in the formation. Just slightly out of synch, but not enough to matter. The rest moved swiftly into position. He did not need to remind them to activate their guns; that was a standing order in any combat approach.

They were assaulting the cometary knots again, but this time, at their furthest point, in the transition between The Necklace and a cloud of thick dust forcing itself through, threatening to annihilate the entire string of comets. ISR had declared that the Gulo held a small task force there, and that that task force must be neutralized and scattered before it received reinforcements to threaten the entire Union operation. The *Star Chariot* had been brought in closer to support an entire wing of fighters set loose on the Gulo fleet. It was the biggest formation Little Boy had ever seen, and he could not contain his pride and excitement, or his fear. The Devil Dancers had their mission, and it did not require much coordination with other squadrons, but being a part of such a large and dangerous endeavor. . .

"Careful, now, Ensign," Captain Victorio said, as if he could feel Little Boy's anxiety. "It'll be all right. Just stick to the mission, and make your calls as best you can. We're in support."

"Yes, sir."

Gulo *Wasps* flashed deadly on the radar, a ten-fighter formation, though the Gulo didn't really fly in formation. More like a chaotic mass, with seemingly no unit commander. That made them erratic, prone to mistakes, but also unpredictable and deadly. Little Boy relayed his data to the rest of the squadron but did not order a formation change. Raven was perfect for what was to come.

He dipped his fighter forward and down. The rest followed suit, and Little Boy saw their rocket packages heat up on the dash. He swung wings left and right, dodging a few scattered lasers from the front *Wasp* swarm. He tapped his rocket display and activated them all. Once each rocket was fully green, he said, "Fire!"

All five *Radiants* lit up on his display as their rockets tore into the void.

One after another, *Wasps* exploded in brilliant flashes of green and red as rockets found targets. The chaotic mass of enemy fighters became a jangled mess, as single survivors fell away, seeking advantage in their speed. A *Wasp* was much faster than a *Radiant,* but could not take many direct rocket strikes before falling apart. The back end of the *Wasp* formation, however, maintained its course and speed, and when close enough to respond, answered the *Radiant* rocket launch with a launch of its own, sending needle-infused shard packages into Little Boy's flight path.

He could not respond fast enough. He slammed into the needle cloud. The Radiant's shield took care of most of them, but some were slender enough to penetrate the strong energy curtain and strike his hull. Little Boy fought against his stick to maintain speed and formation. "Abort the mission, sir?" He asked over comm.

"No," Captain Victorio said. "Maintain course and speed. That was nothing; a few minor stings."

But Little Boy could tell on his array that it had been more than just a nuisance. The left wing of Red Moon's fighter had been severely damaged. And Blue Bird's fuselage casing integrity was at forty percent. Another "sting" like that and the entire squadron would have to pull out.

He checked his mines again. Thank Yusn. None of them had been compromised, nor had their protective casings been damaged in any appreciable manner. Good. The mission would continue.

They blew through the last of the Wasp formation. Little Boy allowed his AI tracking system to designate targets. He thumbed his firing pinion and took another two, three out with a flash of laser fire. He rolled left, fell dangerously close to Shine's fighter, got a stern cussing from the lieutenant over comm, then managed to pull out of the roll just in time to clear the remaining *Wasps* and see the object of their mission become visible through thick stardust.

The *Vichu-Pa*. One of the Gulo's most prized and revered cruisers. A companion vessel to the even more venerable *Na-Ta-She*, for some inexplicable reason, it was flying independent in The Necklace. Both capital ships usually flew together and gave each other near impenetrable support, so what luck to find one alone and ripe for the picking. Its haughty, over-extended prow looked like a hook-nose, but the coil gun running its length was nothing to laugh about. Against Union capital ships, it could rip holes through hulls like butter, and its point defense was worthy of respect. How they were supposed to get close enough to set mines, Little Boy did not know. He had not been given that detail of the mission yet.

"Sir," he said as they reformed into a tighter Raven attack pattern, "we are moving into the designated strafing line. I recommend that we change to Eagle Pattern to—"

"No, sir," Captain Victorio said. "I am now taking command of the operation. I thank you, Ensign, for getting us this far. You have shown your value, your heart, and you are no longer a Child of Water. You are a Devil Dancer, like all of us, and you have a more important mission to fly. Are you ready?"

Little Boy's stomach turned, but he said, "Yes, sir. What do you wish from me?"

There was a pause as if Captain Victorio was reconsidering his statement. Then he said, "You will now become the Clown."

The captain detailed Little Boy's new responsibilities, and Little Boy listened intently. When he was finished, Captain Victorio said, "Do you understand your orders as I have told them to you?"

Little Boy swallowed his fear. "Yes, sir. I am ready."

"Very well. . . now go!"

Little Boy killed his engine and drifted down and away from the squadron, though he still moved at speed toward the *Vichu-Pa's* coil gun. From his passive array, he saw the squadron re-form into Sparrow Pattern, pulling in tightly to ensure their mines were set as the captain had designated. He closed his eyes momentarily and allowed himself to drift unhindered, knowing that as soon as he flicked on his pulse beacon, his quiet, pleasant solitude would disappear. He breathed deeply, and recited a prayer in his mind—

Oh, Yusn Life-Giver,
Whose voice I hear in the wind,
Whose breath gives life to all the world,
Hear me; I need your strength and wisdom.

—then flicked on his beacon.

He gunned his engines and leaned into his stick, pushing the *Radiant* beyond regulation. But none of that mattered now. What mattered was that Captain Victorio and the others fly unhindered toward the Gulo cruiser. What mattered was the pulse that he sent out to bring all Wasps his way. What mattered was the mission.

"Come on, you sons of bitches!" he screamed into his comm. "Come chase the Clown!"

They did, scores of them, picking up the beacon and interpreting it as a suicide pulse, like the ones that they had registered in the past. *What fools!* Little Boy thought as he turned his *Radiant* swiftly to the left and headed straight toward the barrel of the coil gun.

Oh, if only he could fly out of the sun like ancient pilots did back on Earth, and with the enemy blind, pepper Fokker wings with a 7.62mm Colt-Browning. That was real dogfighting, and Little Boy had never flown a craft in a gravity well, but what fun it must be.

He opened lasers and shot through a picket of *Wasps* that had lain a minefield before his craft. He wavered back and forth, setting off the mines with his wings as practiced at flight school. With each explosion, the powerful munitions rocked him back and forth, but the true focus of their blasts erupted away from him, and he escaped their trap with minimal damage.

He was less lucky against a swarm chasing from behind, trying desperately to stop him before he reached the barrel. They scorched his hull with laser fire, and one even managed to detonate a rocket that sent him reeling. Little Boy fought against Gimbal lock, working his stick madly to pull out. They struck him again with more laser fire, and his shield display bleated its dissatisfaction. Down to 63 percent efficiency. A few more strikes like that and there wouldn't be a Clown to worry about.

But he was strong, stronger now that he had beaten the beasts in the fire, had proven himself to his captain and to the Devil Dancers. He could beat this problem.

And he did. He rolled until he was close enough to the *Vichu-Pa* to use its own gravity. With that support, he regained control and slowed his craft until he was upright and flying straight, straight down alongside the thick barrel of the coil gun.

Now point defense opened up, throwing radiated chaff into his flight pattern like flak from AA. He didn't have much time.

He tapped his panel, and the mines in the belly of his *Radiant* activated. He smiled as he lined up for a strafing run.

Then his dash bleated another problem, one that he could do nothing about.

Lieutenants Red Moon and Shines had lost control of their fighters. One lucky round from the *Vichu-Pa* had found a seam and had blown them both off course, and too far out for them to recover in time to make the run. Captain Victorio and Lieutenant Blue Bird had maintained their course, had lain their mines, but it was not enough. Explosions from their mines rocked the cruiser and threw a few armored plates off the coil gun's casing, but it did little damage.

Captain Victorio's voice was loud and commanding. "Abort mission! Abort!"

I can't do that. . . Little Boy thought he said it to himself, but the captain yelled, "You can and you will, Ensign. I'm giving you a direct order. Abort the mission!"

"No, sir," he said, as he keyed in a detonation time for each mine.

"You are a Devil Dancer, and you will—"

"No, sir. I'm not a Devil Dancer. You know this. I'm more like your brother than I am you. You knew that this would be the result when you ordered me to Clown. You've known all along. I'm not a Devil Dancer. I'm your brother. I'm the Child of Water. . . and I'm not afraid of monsters anymore."

He killed the comm. There was nothing more to say, and anyway, Captain Victorio was too far from his position to react in time. There was nothing anyone could do. He turned the nose of his fighter into the pulsing light of the coil gun.

The mines grew red with heat. His panel screamed danger. Little Boy smiled. "This is for you, Deer-Killer. We serve to die!"

He struck the center of the coil gun. The mines ignited.

Victorio laid Little Boy's Union Cross, Distinguished Service Medal, and Commendation Medal in the center of the frame. The Clusters for bravery he pushed into the fabric of the service medal's ribbons. He then placed the glass panel over the display, sealed it tightly, held it up in the light of his office, then placed it carefully next to his brother's medals. He looked at them both, side by side. His heart was heavy. He shook his head.

"What a waste."

Blue Bird placed her hand on his shoulder. "Some pilots are lone wolves, Vic. They are born to be Clowns."

He shrugged. "Perhaps I should retire the position. Do we really need them?"

"Yes, we do. Without them, we could not do what we do best. They serve to die."

Victorio turned to look at her. He touched her face, kissed her gently on the lips, and said, "Someday, I may have to order you to be the Clown."

Blue Bird kissed him back, smiled. "No, sir. You will never order me to be the Clown. When that day comes, I will volunteer."

Victorio nodded, fought back tears, and stared again at Little Boy's medals. He placed his hand on the glass frame, and Blue Bird did the same.

And together they prayed for the Child of the Water's soul.

THE SORROW SEA

Captain Victorio "Tomorrow's Wind" Nantan knelt beside the body of the young woman. Not a spot of skin remained on her frail bones, and only the tattered scraps of a blue uniform lying nearby indicated that she had once been an ensign. Young, inexperienced, and perhaps thinking a billet on a Union freighter would provide a few years of calm and uneventful service before joining a real warship. *So much for that,* Victorio thought, as he placed his hand on her cold forehead, closed his eyes, and spoke a silent prayer to help aid her soul into the hereafter.

He moved to the next body, a young man, a bosun perhaps, his flesh equally desecrated. His lips had been cut away, revealing swollen gums and a ghoulish Clown grin of messy teeth. Victorio had to turn away lest he become sick at the sight of it. All around him, the crew of the *Genoese* lay equally still and dead. Not a man or woman alive. The massacre had been swift and brutal.

"The Gulo?"

The sharp voice behind Victorio startled him. He had quite forgotten that Shines Like the Sun was video-logging everything for Admiral Cho.

The captain stood. "Perhaps, but I doubt it. The Gulo would have breached the hull. They would have crippled the ship, swarmed it, taken what they wanted, then scuttled what remained. Whoever did this docked and gained access through deceit. The Gulo would not have wasted so much time."

"But the bodies, sir. They've been skinned."

Victorio nodded. The savagery of the attack was, indeed, Gulo in its nature. He shuddered. Even after thirty standard years, the name of that wolverine-like race gave him chills. The Federated Union had been at war with the Gulo forever, it seemed. They were feral, savage fighters, their technology on par with that of the humans. They were a formidable foe.

But this was different; this attack, this massacre, was something else, perpetrated by... who? By what? He did not know for sure, but he had his suspicions. The skinnings were precise and carefully administered with deft hands, with patience. The Gulo would have simply ripped them to shreds.

"Captain!" Blue Bird called from across the bridge. "Come look at this."

He stepped over bodies and went to her side. His second-in-command knelt beside a young boy. His skin was intact but his hair had been removed, a clean and efficient scalping, a *bitsa-ha-digihz*, that Victorio had seen many times as a young Apache boy on Earth during the Rebellion of 2235. Blue Bird's face grew pale and her hand quivered as she held up the knife that had obviously done the deed.

Victorio grabbed the blade quickly. His heart fluttered. He turned it over in his hand. It was a crude weapon. The handle was cured buckskin wrapped tightly over deer bone and smeared with red clay. The blade was a piece of grey chert chipped to razor perfection. This was not a Union-issued knife.

"It's him, isn't it?"

Blue Bird's question cut like the hewed stone in his hand. As much as he wanted to say no, he could not deny the truth that lay in bloody heaps around him.

Captain Victory gritted his teeth, then tucked the blade into his belt. "Yes," he said, "it's him."

Mangus Coloradas flipped the knife effortlessly from hand to hand, then jabbed it into the stale air before him. A sharp, clean thrust. A killing thrust. It was a skill he had perfected in prison with a small blade fashioned from shop scraps. He'd gotten a good beating when the guards had found it beneath his bedroll, but it was worth it now so many light-years away from that dank cell. The weapon in his hand had had a handsome partner. But he had foolishly left it near the dead White Eyes boy who had tried to open his belly with a Muck Carbine. Or had it been so foolish? In his dreams, the great lord of the People, Yusn Life-Giver, had shown him the face of the one who would come for him. A pilot. A captain. A Devil Dancer. The one who had conspired to steal his command so many years ago.

And they call me a pirate!

He flipped the knife over again, caught the tip between thumb and index, then hurled it into the neck of the target ten meters away. The feeble wood and foam of the mannequin burst into a cloud of dust and splinters as the stone blade bit deep. "That's what I'm going to do to you, *Captain* Victory!"

The comm signal on his armband flashed green. "Red Sleeves," said a scruffy voice, "we are approaching the *Loch Ness*."

He always smiled at his true name, his Apache name. He was, indeed, the resurrection of that great warrior that had brought pride and dignity to The People. But to his enemies, he was Coloradas, a pirate, a butcher. He was proud of both the name and the status.

"Keep us steady and a thousand kilometers down on her port-side," he said, wiping sweat from his face as he exited the training cube. "And keep those asteroids between us. We can't be seen until we're close."

"Aye, sir!"

The Union did not consider him and his Red Paint People a threat to a full destroyer, especially the *Loch Ness*, which had fought honorably against the Gulo so many times. That's why they had sent it into the Sorrow Sea to root him out, to get him back on the "reservation" as it were. But this vast field of asteroids and dust in the Carina Nebula held incalculable places to hide and to wait out anything White Eyes might send in. The supply lines that ran along the edge of the Keyhole Nebula, a smaller and much darker expanse within the Carina, was a font of goods and material that could sustain an entire fleet forever...

as long as the freighters moved. The Union could not afford to shut down this supply line; the human colonies beyond the keyhole were under Gulo pressure (or so White Eyes claimed). So send in the *Loch Ness* and whip those pirates!

But White Eyes will get an education, he thought to himself as he stopped in front of a door panel, *and that right soon.*

He tapped the security panel, and the blast door on the main cargo bay opened to wild activity. His crew was scrambling to tiny fighters strapped into this honeycomb of a ship. His ship. The *Ahagahe.* It was the size of a small freighter, but in truth, it was an old abandoned drill platform modified to serve as a small carrier. The length of its hull was a cylinder that had originally housed an ion beam used to carve through hundreds of meters of solid iron ore. The cannon was gone, replaced by rows of lockers that, when opened, scattered fighters like broken glass. The Union did not know that he had such a ship, and he was going to make damn sure they never did.

"Strap in, you wild coyotes!" he screamed over the hum of the chaos. Someone handed him an oxygen mask. He took it and placed it over his face, strapped it around his head, and breathed deeply.

"You should activate your boots as well, sir," said a small man to his right. "The launch bay will depressurize in thirty."

Coloradas sighed. Little Dog was always yapping at his heels, always telling him his business. The runt had a gift for stating the obvious. "Look to your own deportment, Little Dog. I know my ship better than you."

"Yes, sir. But this is the Loch Ness we're up against. A warship. We've never taken one on before, and I'm just making sure everything goes—"

"I know my enemy, boy." Indeed he did. Rocket and torpedo tubes fore and aft; broadside point-defense; retractable cupolas along its spine. Everything it needed to render a pirate fleet inoperable. *Everything,* Coloradas thought, *but the Sorrow Sea.* The *Loch Ness* had sailed into his battleground. Its crew did not understand where it was, did not understand the lay of the land. The Sorrow Sea would provide, he knew, as Yusn Life-Giver had shown him in his dreams. The Sorrow Sea provides.

Little Dog offered the captain an *izze-kloth,* a tiny bag of pollen, and a war club. He tied them all to his belt to ensure his protection from evil spirits if such a bloody end was near. But he was not afraid; neither the Union nor an aged destroyer could move him to fear. If the end would come today, so be it. Mangus Coloradas would happily die a warrior.

He dipped his fingers into a palette of red paint, then ran them across his skull. With these lines, he would meet the enemy, and they would know who he was. "Is my fighter ready?" he asked as he punched a button on his belt and felt his boots tighten against the hard floor.

Little Dog nodded. "Aye, captain. Refitted and ready."

The bay walls opened and Coloradas felt the rush of decompression. He stopped for a moment, however, to enjoy the view. The Sorrow Sea opened to him, like the petals of the desert flowers he remembered as a child. An unending ocean of rocks floating effortlessly in the void, grabbing bits of light from the nebula around her, and casting them back ten-fold. He smiled. She was brilliant, beautiful. Beautiful and deadly.

He stepped up to his fighter, climbed in and lowered the cockpit hood. He could feel the hum of her small engine as it warmed his legs. He strapped in tightly and activated his dashboard, which lit up white, red, and green. Somewhere beyond the myriad green dots lay the *Loch Ness.*

"All steady now, you Mimbres, you Red Paint People!" Coloradas said into the comm connecting him to every fighter. He gunned the engine and tapped a touch-pad four times. "Roll the cylinder!"

Not all his crew of one hundred and fifty-nine were Mimbres Apaches, but many were. And many were from other tribes that had fled earth to find a better life among the stars. But White Eyes always had a way of making their lives miserable even light years from earth. The war with the Gulo was such an aggravation. An unnecessary, useless war that went on and on, far longer than it needed to, ending the lives of (at least) a billion Union citizens, many of them of Native American descent. He had tried to warn them, had tried to bring a peaceful end to the war years ago. And what had it gotten him? Pain. Sorrow. Exile. But he would show them, and make White Eyes and their native traitors pay.

They will pay.

The cylinder began to roll, and its impetus moved the mining platform forward. Cries filled the comm as his men whipped themselves into a frenzy. This was the first time the entire fleet was mobilized, but such a target required a war party and not just a simple raid of a few dozen ships.

Through the Sorrow Sea, they sailed, their tiny fighters turning over and over like a Ferris wheel, spinning around the mighty cylinder as it gained speed and crashed through the fine stardust and pebbles that lay quiet and unfettered in their path. In a way, Coloradas was sorry to disrupt such a beautiful field of rock. But the sea would fix itself anew in time, providing, again and again, the protection he and his men needed. And a field of larger asteroids lay ahead, and they did indeed need those mighty rocks.

"Disembark!" he yelled, and one by one, locker doors opened and out streamed corkscrews of fighters. Like finely-tipped arrows from bows, they streamed outward as the platform fell away and took its hiding place among the stellar winds.

"Okay, boys!" Coloradas said. "Set sights on those rocks. Fifty up, fifty down. Claw Pattern. Land and set grapples!"

They did as commanded, half the fleet breaking away and pulling themselves up and behind a line of asteroids many times larger than themselves. Coloradas picked his rock and moved to it, bringing his fighter down gently on its backside, then locking it down tightly. He waited until the white dots on his monitor clamped themselves fully to other asteroids, then said, "Now is the time, my friends, where we put White Eyes in his place. He has come to make his war upon us, and we will show him the error of his ways. We will drown him in the Sorrow Sea." He heard more joyous cries across the comm His men were ready. Coloradas breathed deeply, then said, "Strike the engines!"

And so a hundred fighters strong-gunned their engines, and the asteroids they were on began to roll, and roll, and roll, like cannonballs on a tilting deck. Beyond the wall of rock, already the *Loch Ness* was trying to keel left to meet this unexpected threat. In his mind, Coloradas could hear the mighty ship answer with point defense, but it would do no good. He was *di-yin*, and he had seen the end in his dreams. "Release!"

The fighters unclamped themselves from their rocks and burst upward and out of harm's way. *Let the Sorrow Sea do its worst,* he said to himself as he burst from behind the line of whirling asteroids and refreshed his targeting reticule. *And then, like brave Mimbres all, we will finish the job.*

"*Ahagahe!*" Coloradas roared, turned his fighter toward the destroyer, and opened fire.

Victorio watched the video display as the asteroids smashed into the *Loch Ness*, breaking its spine and crushing its bridge. Its point-defense and shields had thwarted some of the attack, but not enough, as he could see its gunnery teams frantically tap monitors to launch hopeless volleys of rockets and torpedoes. And then a horrible cry, like mothers wailing their sorrow over fallen sons, as the pirates swarmed the battered hull like mosquitoes, pricking here and there, ripping the ship apart. Over the crackling audio of the crippled destroyer, he could hear the word "Ahagahe" shouted again and again.

Admiral Cho turned off the screen and fell into his chair. He rubbed his eyes and said, "What does the word mean, captain?"

Victorio cleared his throat. "It's a battle cry, sir. A challenge."

"Who is he challenging?"

Me. "The captain of the *Loch Ness*, sir. The Union in general I suppose."

"You know this man?"

Victorio nodded. "Aye, sir."

"Tell me about him."

Admiral Cho was a relatively new admiral, having come up to Barracuda Task Force after the Gulo had massacred Admiral Estrela Frome, her crew, and most of her subordinate fleet. It had been the worst Union defeat in the entire war, and the young Cho had been brought in to replace her and to cobble together the remains of the TF. Victorio was surprised that the admiral did not know of Mangus Coloradas. But then, perhaps he did, and he simply wanted to measure Victorio's answer. He might be young, but Admiral Cho was as cagey as Coyote.

"Mangus Coloradas used to be my captain, sir, and dare I say, a good friend. He was older than me, but our families shared the same village on Earth until shortly after the Rebellion. They left, and I did not see him again until I joined The Devil Dancers. He had served as their captain for five years before my brother and I came along. Two years later, he made me his second-in-command, where I remained until his court-martial."

"Ah, yes, the Paladin Conspiracy." Admiral Cho's dark face wrinkled in disbelief. "I find it hard to believe that this *butcher* was involved in that treason."

"Coloradas was not always a violent man, Admiral. There was a time when he was quite passive, despite his skills as a fighter pilot. In many ways, he made the Devil Dancers what we are today. He believes that he is the reincarnation of Mangus Coloradas, the great Apache chief. He has the stature and bearing, for sure, and the temperament at least before his incarceration. But, like his namesake, he's been betrayed again and again. It is clear that he has not forgotten what White Eyes—as he would call the Union—did to his family and to his career."

"And what do you think, Captain? Did the Union betray him?"

Victorio measured his answer. The memory of the court-martial was strong in his mind still, as if it had happened just a week ago. "I did what I had to do, sir, to protect the integrity of the Devil Dancers and for the fleet as a whole."

The Devil Dancers were the finest fighter squadron in the fleet. Its kill ratio and its number of aces rivaled that of whole flights. Comprised mostly of Apache warriors, it was named after the *Ga'an* Mountain Spirits that Yusn Life-Giver had sent to earth to teach the People how to live a good and virtuous life. The term "devil dancer" was one given to them by a White Eyes who had mistaken their ceremonial dancing as erratic, out of control, evil. Though he did not particularly like the name, it was an effective one in the Union's struggle against the Gulo. A devil garnered respect, even from its enemies.

"There is one other thing you should know about Coloradas, Admiral," he said, clearing his mind of painful memories. "He is *di-yin*."

"*Di-yin?*"

"He's a shaman. One of great stature. And he has ghost power. He believes that he can touch the dead and subsume their spirit. That is why he is being so brutal in his attacks on our ships. He is collecting the spirits of those he kills violently because he believes that their unsettled spirits give him strength."

Admiral Cho rose to his feet. "How do you know this, Captain?"

I've seen it in my dreams. "I… just know, sir. I know."

"And you believe this foolishness?"

Yes. "No, sir. But he does, and that makes him unpredictable, dangerous."

"I don't need a lecture on ancient Apache mythology, Captain, to know that." Admiral Cho stepped from behind his desk and faced Victorio. He was short, but Victorio did not bow his head to show any disrespect. Yet he could see the lines of stress and anger on the little man's brow. "Let me bring the matter back to reality for you, Victorio. Mangus Coloradas and his Red Paint People, as you call them, have captured and/or destroyed twenty Union cargo ships. He has stolen a million tons of weaponry and supplies along the Keyhole transit line. He has massacred at least a dozen crews." He pointed to the blank video screen. "And he has just scuttled a destroyer. The *Loch Ness!* All attempts to end his terror have failed. He's holed up somewhere in the Sorrow Sea, and we can't get him out. The matter is desperate. Do you understand?"

Victorio nodded. He knew all too well. He waited to see if the admiral would say anything further, but he did not. He just stood there, staring up with those strong, green eyes that could intimidate even the most stalwart naval officer. *We're all in this together…*

"Yes, sir. What can I do to help?"

The admiral let a smile cross his thin lips. He returned to his chair. He scooped up a small tablet and punched out a noisy code. "Effective immediately, you, your squadron, and the *Justice* are hereby assigned to Barracuda Task Force for special duty." He finished tapping out the transfer order, then laid the tablet on the desk. He looked up. "Captain Victory? You are hereby ordered to take your Devil Dancers into the Sorrow Sea... and kill that sick son of a bitch."

Victorio's heart leapt into his throat.

In his dream, he danced like a devil. Like he used to in better days, when he was a young captain full of hope and honor, fighting against the common enemy. He moved in the rhythmic patterns as ordained by the mountain spirits of his people. On his body, he wore the buckskin kilt and headdress of the Ga'an, and attached to his hood, the various spiritual accoutrements that would bring him closer to Yusn Life-Giver and the great cosmos. He danced for the well-being of the People; he danced for victory; he danced for himself.

Out of the dried bushes leapt the Clown, its bare chest and stomach smeared with white and red clay. It hopped around wildly, its face a twist of silly expressions that made the young children watching nearby giggle. As the crowd laughed and pelted the Clown with tiny pebbles, he moved forward. *It will not steal the show*, he said to himself as he doubled his efforts to win back their attention.

So they danced and danced, he and the Clown, each pushing the other, desperate to win the crowd's cheers. The Clown tripped him, and he grew angry. He stood up to protest and felt a warm, sick feeling in his stomach. The dance stopped and he faced the Clown, whose contortions now smoothed to reveal its true face.

You! He whispered. He looked down and saw a blade of stone sticking out of his belly and warm blood trickling down his breechcloth.

The Clown laughed and said, *I see you... Can you see me?*

The comm signal on his armband buzzed and blinked to life. Coloradas sat upright on his bunk and wiped sweat from his brow. He clicked the comm. "What is it?"

Bright Star's voice was anxious. "Freighter sighting, sir. Three cargo ships. In good shape."

He sniffed and cleared his throat. "Any escorts?"

"A few small squads. Nothing of concern."

He was surprised by that. After destroying the *Loch Ness*, he would have expected a better showing. *Are they stupid*, he wondered, *or do they not fear me*? He could not decide which was the worst offense. Either way, it was humiliating. He gnashed his teeth. "Rouse the crew. All of them."

"Are you sure, sir?"

"What do you mean, Star?"

She hesitated, then said, "It's just that, we suffered a lot of casualties against the *Loch Ness*. And many are exhausted. I think it best to just let this one—"

"If the Union sees fit to continually try me, Star, by sending in near-defenseless cargo vessels, then so be it. We will keep the pressure on until they fear and respect us. We will attack, in force, and leave none alive. Is that understood?"

A pause. Then, "Yes, sir."

Coloradas shut off the comm and stood. A sudden rush of heat and dizziness washed over him. He sat back down and placed his hand on his stomach. He gasped as he pulled his hand away and looked at it.

It was covered in blood.

Victorio sat cross-legged on his meditation quilt while Blue Bird ran thick lines of red-and-white clay across his face, neck, and chest. He opened his eyes and saw the worry in hers. "What do you fear, kind heart?" he asked.

Blue Bird was a warrior, as true as any Devil Dancer. She was fearless and uncompromising in the seat of her *Radiant*-class fighter. She had performed her duties marvelously after the death of Victorio's brother, Naiche "Blackclaw" Nantan, at the hands of Gulo fighter ace, Gingu-sha. He had promoted her to second-in-command. He loved her. It was forbidden, of course, for captains and their officers to express such feelings, but he could not help it. She was beautiful, powerful, and he wanted nothing more than to steal away with her to some quiet planet and make "a thousand babies," as she would say. But not today. The war with the Gulo still raged, and now this matter with

Coloradas. He would do his duty as ordered. He would do it... even if it killed him.

"I fear the agitation of troubled dreams," she said, "that cannot be tempered by waking." Her eyes watered as she bit back the growing trepidation in her voice. "I fear the Sorrow Sea. I fear Coloradas. I fear the *di-yin*."

He took her hand and stood. He put out his arms and she helped him into his blue shirt and buckskin vest. He buckled his belt and took his *izze-kloth* and war club, his holstered pistol, and bag of pollen. He accepted his helmet but did not put it on. Instead, he rested it on his hip, took Blue Bird's arm in his, and whispered, "These things I fear too, sweet. But they cannot burden our minds now. We must keep these feelings hidden away, until such a time as we can think upon them clearly. Out there, he waits. We have danced to Yusn for strength, for honor, for courage. He will keep us safe. We are Devil Dancers. We are mountain spirits. And if today is the day I die..."

Blue Bird put her finger to his mouth. "Shh! Do not speak anymore." A tear fell down her face, but she took his helmet and placed it on his head, leaned into it, and kissed him firmly on his face-plate. "I want to keep your smiling face in my memory. Just go... and be safe."

She let him go. Victorio turned and walked to his fighter. It waited patiently, its engine humming as it pulled on the chains that held it to the floor of the cargo bay. He turned once more to her, saluted, then climbed in.

Blue Bird pulled a lever on the floor and the chains fell away. His fighter was free, and he guided it slowly to the bay door. It opened, and the light of the Sorrow Sea flooded in. He leaned his head back and the fighter fell back as well until it was through the door. He waved goodbye, but already Blue Bird and the rest of the Devil Dancers were mere specks in his vision. The bay door closed and he was alone.

He tapped a dashboard panel, his engine went dead, and he floated away silently into the brilliant cold and dust of the Sorrow Sea. He closed his eyes.

Let the dance begin.

Coloradas and his pirates corkscrewed off the *Ahagahe* in long, roping lines. They spun out in wave after wave of fighter craft, armed and determined. Around them lay such a quiet and serene stretch of space; it seemed almost blasphemous to disrupt the beautiful tranquility of the Sorrow Sea. Yet despite Star's and Little Dog's constant yapping to sit this one out, he gave the order. He wrapped his wound tightly and did not let them know of it. They might have mutinied right then and there had they discovered the blood on his stomach. Nothing, not even a little scratch, would stop him. But it wasn't such a little scratch, was it? It was something more, something... What? The images from his dream flooded back into his mind. He tried blocking them out, but he could not wipe away the face below the Clown mask. But where was he? Where was Victorio? Ahead of them, three cargo ships awaited, flanked by a tiny and insignificant escort that would quickly fall at the first volley of rockets.

Where are you, Victorio? I can't see you.

"Sir, there is a line of asteroids ahead three hundred kilometers. Shall we make for them?"

"No," Coloradas answered Little Dog's question sharply. "Not this time. Today, we go straight in."

"But, sir—"

"Enough talk! We go in, and that's an order. Triple lines and rotating packages. Leave no ordnance unfired. We will make them bleed today!"

"Yes, sir."

He cut the comm link. There would be no more communication, no more talk. Today, he would sweep the Sorrow Sea of any trace of White Eyes. Today would be his greatest victory yet.

He closed his eyes, gunned his fighter forward, and tried to discern the face in the fog of his mind.

Victorio floated quietly through a vast field of rock and dust, the automatic thrust of his passive alignment coils the only thing keeping his fighter from being destroyed by the tumbling debris. He was cold, frigid in fact, but he would not bring his engines on-line until the right moment.

And when will that moment come? he wondered. The Red Paint People had already begun their attack against the Union freighters; three empty and old freighters. Empty, save for three squadrons of the Union's finest... plus the Devil Dancers. One of the freighters had already been destroyed and their hidden squadron decimated; another listed badly to its port side. Victorio listened to the chaotic radio chatter over his comm link; listened but did not respond for he would not give away his position. He wanted badly to be among them, with Blue Bird and Shines Like the Sun and all the others. But he would grit his teeth and wait, wait for the one that had not shown himself yet.

"Where are you?" Victorio whispered in the dark of his cockpit. "Where are you?"

I'm right here...

The words flowed through Victorio's mind like water, and before he could gun his engines, something nicked his fuselage and he went spiraling round and round. The thick dust of the Sorrow Sea collided across his wings and threw him dangerously close to an asteroid. He blinked furiously, cocked his head, and lit his engine. The *Radiant* sprang to life and flew upward, catching the wind of the nearby sun and disappearing in a flash of heat and energy.

But his pursuer was relentless. Rockets raced along his side, and Victorio had to twist between two massive rocks to keep from being incinerated. Another rocket sprang off his side, the *Radiant's* point shield turning it away. The rocket hit an asteroid, exploded, and knocked him starboard. Victorio worked his dash frantically.

He cursed himself. Blue Bird had warned him. *I fear the di-yin*, she had said. He had listened to her warning, but he had been too confident in his abilities to reject the shaman's mind-spirits. His old captain was stronger than he had imagined. *I'm such a fool. I should have been more cautious. I should not have let him in my mind.*

"And there I will stay, old friend," Coloradas spoke over the comm. "It's good to see you again."

Victorio grunted. "You should have stayed in the brig, Coloradas. That old *Zoot* won't last long in this rock field."

Coloradas laughed. "We shall see."

In truth, the *Zoot* was fast and agile, the perfect fighter in an asteroid field and a good pirate craft. Yet it lacked power and stamina. It worked best in packs. It had to strike first, expel its munitions, and then dog its opponent with laser fire. But laser fire did not work well in the Sorrow Sea. So why such an antiquated ship?

Victorio banked left and spun through another line of asteroids. He purposely knocked apart smaller rock clusters with his wings. He would suffer damage, but the swirl of dust left in his wake was enough to blind even the most sophisticated sensors. He turned and turned, leaving Coloradas and his tiny *Zoot* choking.

It worked. Whatever rockets the *Zoot* had left tried to penetrate the swirling stardust, but the radiated heat ignited them all. Victorio smiled, turned his fighter right, and barrel-rolled through a maze of boulders the size of tiny homes. He rolled his finger up a line of pads on his dash, then tapped the last one.

Thirty rockets burst from his wings.

He watched as the tiny specks on his radar closed in on their target. They closed and closed as Coloradas zigged and zagged through the heavy dust, spinning and spinning his *Zoot* with a fury that Victorio found quite impressive. His old captain had not lost a bit of his flying skills. Still the best pilot in the Union. *What a waste to see it blown to cinders*, he thought as he watched and waited for the end.

But it did not come. As they closed, each rocket in turn suddenly changed course and impacted against a meteor cluster. Ten, then twenty, then thirty. Every one. All of them. *How in the hell did—* Of course: the *Zoot* had an old, outmoded homing signature, and *Radiant* rockets were tuned to different, more modern frequencies.

Coloradas laughed over the comm. "An old, yet effective, trick."

"Goddamn you, Coloradas," Victorio said, "stop playing games. Face me and fight like a man. Fight like a true Mimbres."

Coloradas laughed again. "When a pirate, act like a pirate. My world is different than yours, Victorio. I live by the rules of the Sorrow Sea, and she loves a good chase." Coloradas pulled up beside him; Victorio could almost see him through the bright haze. "But you're right," he said. "I grow tired of this dance. Follow me, and let's go fight like old times."

Victorio followed his old captain out of the sea and into a small patch of hollow space. Was this a trap? Perhaps. He would find out soon enough.

As they burst out of the sea, a large, long cylinder emerged in his vision. A mighty ship, almost as long as a Union frigate, but it lacked any sizable amount of point-defense. It was beautiful in a way. It caught the light of the sea and shone it back bright and vibrant. Almost blinding. Yet, peering into the glow, Victorio felt at peace. This was clearly the vessel he had seen in his dreams. This was...

"Yes, the *Ahagahe*," Coloradas said over the comm. "My ship. Isn't she wonderful?"

Victorio nodded, then stopped himself quickly. He was being manipulated again. The *di-yin* was getting into his mind, affecting his perspective. He blinked quickly and edged his fighter down to keep pace with the *Zoot*. "She is. But stop the tour, Coloradas. If you've led me into an ambush, then spring the trap. I grow tired of your babbling."

"No one is here, Victorio," he said. "My people are fighting and dying against yours. We are alone. This is our fight."

"Then let's have it."

They flew around the Ahagahe twice, then panels on the starboard side opened and out rolled a circular and domed platform. It slid into space and detached itself from the ship and floated gently in place. On either side, thrusters equalized its mass and kept it from tipping. Coloradas dropped his *Zoot* until it hovered just above the top of the dome. Then the dome irised open. He centered his craft over the opening, then slipped through the gap and disappeared inside.

"Come," he said calmly. "I welcome you."

Victorio reluctantly followed, bringing his *Radiant* down and squeezing through the opening. His wings barely fit through, but he dropped in and watched as the dome shut behind him.

Below was a paradise.

Not paradise exactly, but nearly so. A jungle, with carefully planted trees and vines of lush, green palm-sized leaves. Through the cockpit window, he could see a waterfall and a small stream circling the splendor. He almost didn't want to touch down, for fear of disrupting the delicate balance of flora that blanketed the floor. But he followed Coloradas down until they set their fighters beside each other. Victorio killed his engines. He let them come to a complete stop, then depressurized the cockpit. He waited for a moment, then opened the canopy. He removed his helmet, unlocked his belt, and stood up. Clear, fresh air filled his lungs. He breathed deeply. It had been a long time.

He climbed out onto a wing. He stopped to enjoy the scent of lilac and rosewood, but then held his breath when he saw Coloradas standing on the ground, tall, still, and commanding, holding a stone knife in one hand, a war club in the other. Victorio dropped his helmet, reached into his boot and drew out the stone knife that he had found at the *Genoese* massacre. Then he unclipped his war club from his belt and dropped to the ground. He ripped his shirt open to show the long red-and-white streaks running down his chest. Coloradas did the same.

Victorio moved cautiously toward his old captain. He stopped and raised his weapons.

"*I am the lightning flashing and streaking,*" Coloradas said as he bowed to his opponent.

Victorio knew the phrase well and replied with a phrase from the same song that Yusn Life-Giver had given the *Ga'an* mountain spirits long, long ago. He bowed and said, "*And my song shall encircle these dancers.*"

And they danced.

"I trusted you. You betrayed me."

"You betrayed yourself," Victorio said, watching carefully Coloradas move as they jockeyed for position inside the battle platform, daggers and clubs held tightly. "And more importantly, you betrayed the Devil Dancers. You and your conspirators willfully disobeyed orders or implemented such orders so slowly as to affect the same result. Millions died because of your inaction."

Coloradas nodded. "And billions would be alive today had you listened. This war with the Gulo is destroying the Union. They are no longer a threat."

"That is a lie! They attack us at every turn."

"Only to defend what little space they have left. The war has been over for a long time, Victorio, and you know this. You have had the same dreams as I, old friend. The Gulo have been removed from every segment of Union space. Now it's just genocide." He jabbed with his blade. "They fight simply to stay alive, to keep White Eyes from taking more. In your own life, you have *seen* what White Eyes is capable of. You've seen it in your own family."

Victorio pushed away the painful memories. "We are all in this together, *old* friend. Why do you persist in these terrible attacks? Why do you massacre innocent people?"

Coloradas huffed. "You're forgetting your history, Victorio. My Mimbres and I do this to make White Eyes see the futility of his actions. To make him see how terrible war really is. To make him pay such a high price as to force him to stop this terrible, terrible thing that he has put in motion. And it's obvious that I've had an impact, for they've sent Captain Victory into the Sorrow Sea to kill me."

Victorio shook his head. "I've been sent here to bring you to justice."

"No. You've been sent here to die!"

Coloradas lunged forward. He brought his war club down hard, and Victorio stepped to the side. The club grazed his shoulder. He gritted his teeth and kept his eyes from closing against the pain. *I will not show pain to this man*, he said to himself and did not care if the *di-yin* heard it. *No pain.*

He brought his own war club up and swung it toward Coloradas's neck, but the big man was faster, more agile than he had anticipated. Coloradas ducked, rolled, and came up slashing with his knife. He caught Victorio across his chest and opened a line of blood that mixed with sweat and clay across his stomach. Victorio swung upward and caught the knife square with his own and dislodged it. The stone blade flew through the air and Victorio jabbed forward and drove his blade into Coloradas's stomach. But he only ripped through a thick bandage that covered another wound.

Victorio's eyes beamed. It had worked; his own try at dream manipulation had worked, and Coloradas had awakened with a slash at his stomach. Wonderful. The *di-yin* was not so tough after all.

Coloradas roared in anger. He knocked Victorio's arm aside and tried to land a fist against his throat, but Victorio caught it and turned the wrist. Coloradas screamed and tried to pull away, but Victorio lifted a boot and drove it into his opponent's stomach, knocking him back and into the stream. Coloradas disappeared beneath the water.

Finish him! His own words in his mind were sound. But no. That would not be the honorable thing to do, to drown your opponent while he flailed around to get his balance. No. Victorio watched as Coloradas reached out of the water and grabbed the bank. He turned, looked for and found Coloradas's knife, grabbed it, tucked it away into his belt, then fled into the thick foliage.

You want a chase, old friend? Victorio shouted the words in his mind. *Then come and find me.*

He ran and ran, down a thin footpath. He remembered racing his brother, Naiche, up mountain passes as a young boy, each trying to make the top with a mouthful of water. Those were pleasant memories now, and he always kept them close. This chase was not so pleasant, but he felt good on solid ground, with brown soil beneath his feet. This was not the tough, dry, unforgiving land of his childhood, but it would do.

He rounded a corner and took an arm in the throat.

He hit the path hard, his neck in agonizing pain. He gasped for air. The wind had been knocked from his lungs. He clutched his chest and curled up tightly. A boot landed on his side, then again and again. He tried pushing away his assailant, but Coloradas stood above him, stolid and unmoving, smiling his nasty grin. The big man pulled his leg back and kicked again. Blood seeped from Victorio's mouth.

"I've been planning this for a long time, Victorio," Coloradas said, circling around like a crazed dog. "A long, long time. And now it's over."

Victorio tried to move, tried to reach out and strike a leg, but he could not breathe. His ribs exploded in pain with every movement. He stayed huddled up and managed to squeak out. "You... are... *bini-e-dine!*"

Coloradas laughed and ripped away Victorio's war club and knife. He tossed the club into the stream but held the knife tightly in his hand. "No, sir. I have a mind, and a strong one. And I am right." He knelt down beside Victorio. "With your death, with your scalp upon my wall, all the Union will mourn the loss of their precious Captain Victory. And then a discussion will begin. 'Is this war worth it?' someone will ask, and then another, and another, until the voice of opposition is so overwhelming as to be unstoppable. And then I'll have won. I'll have won."

Coloradas raised his empty hand and placed it upon Victorio's face. "And now accept these ghosts, brother. Accept them and take them with you into the underworld."

A rush of lives filled Victorio, from the young ensign on the *Genoese* to an old gunner on the *Loch Ness*. The spirit of every man, woman, and child that Coloradas had killed spilled into his mind. He felt their pain, their fear, their anger as their own lives ended at the hands of this madman that knelt at his side. And he was mad. Whatever honor and dignity Magnus Coloradas had held was washed away with each drop of blood from these souls. And yet, beyond their own deaths, Victorio could see the Gulo, could see each engagement with that fierce enemy that these dead had experienced: hundreds, thousands, millions of Gulo perishing under a relentless campaign that had seen the Union sweep into Gulo space and annihilate world after world. The man at his side was indeed insane. But was he right?

With a shaking hand, Victorio reached behind his back and pulled the knife from his belt. He gripped it tightly, turned the blade outward, and then with all his strength, plunged it into Coloradas's neck.

The power of the blow shocked Red Sleeves, and he pulled his hand away. The voices in Victorio's mind stopped and that gave him strength. He pushed again, driving the knife deeper. Coloradas fell back and tried to pull the knife away, but Victorio's new-found power was too great. He flailed a few more times, slapped meekly at Victorio's face, but could not dislodge the blade. Blood flowed down his chest and stomach and pooled on the ground. Victorio rose up and fell onto his old captain, now pushing the blade deeper with both hands.

"You were once a great, great man, Coloradas," he said, watching the life drain from the big man's face. "I loved you. I would have done anything for you. But your lightning is out, and it will streak no more. Goodbye, and may Yusn Life-Giver forgive you."

He pushed the blade up to the hilt, turned it quickly, and watched Mangus Coloradas die.

He limped out of the woods and reached for Blue Bird. She came to his side and took his hands. Tears streaked her face. "You are alive," she said. "Thank Yusn, you are alive."

He nodded weakly and tossed the bloody blade to the ground. He accepted her help and leaned into her soft body. "It's good to see you again, kind heart. The squad?"

She shook her head. "The Devil Dancers are fine."

"The Red Paint People?"

"Killed and scattered."

A weight fell from his shoulders. It was over. The pirate scourge had been broken, its members routed.

"Is the *di-yin* dead?" Blue Bird asked.

Victorio nodded. "Yes. He will dance no more, but let's not talk about it right now, sweet. Please get me to my fighter."

She did and Victorio pulled himself up and into the cockpit. He strapped in, although the blinking pain of his broken ribs fought against him. Yet despite the pain, he felt good. For the first time in a long time, he felt at peace. He did not want to kill his old captain, but he had done so, and he did not feel bad about it. Still…

He tapped his dash and thumbed up the comm unit. He waited until the frequency found a lone beacon in space. He accepted the link and heard Admiral Cho's voice. "Report, Captain Victorio. Is he dead?"

He cleared his throat and talked through the pain. "Yes, Admiral. Your pirate is dead."

"Praise the Union. And his crew?"

Victorio told him everything. When he was done, the Admiral said, "Very well, Captain. The Union thanks you. I thank you. Please report back to the *Justice* for a full debriefing."

"Yes, Admiral," Victorio said, as his hand moved to light the engines. "One more thing, sir, and I want this on the record. I have followed your orders and I have done my duty for the Union and its people, and I proudly stand by my actions. But know one thing: this is the last time I will chase down and kill pirates for you. This is the last time the Devil Dancers will be your executioners."

Before the admiral could respond, Victorio killed the link. He then closed his cockpit, lit his engines, and looked at Blue Bird through his window. He smiled. Perhaps her idea of running away and having babies wasn't such a bad one after all.

He lifted up and guided his fighter through the opening of the battle platform. He waited for Blue Bird, and then together, they sailed into the Sorrow Sea.

I GIVE MY HEART TO THE HAWKS

Victorio "Tomorrow's Wind" Nantan, captain of the Devil Dancers fighter squadron, watched Blue Bird stroke the tender head feathers of her red-tailed hawk. It was a marvelous young adult, confident and commanding, as it waited anxiously on her arm to be released. His second-in-command cooed lovingly as she unfastened the leather cords that held the bird's sharp claws in place on her arm guard. It flapped its mighty wings in anticipation, letting its white underbelly ruffle in the breeze. Blue Bird cooed again, then pulled the cord away and let the bird go. Victorio shielded his eyes from the rising sun and watched as the bird rose into the bright sky. It was a beautiful creature, and he loved it. He loved all the squadron's birds and Blue Bird too.

But she would not love him back for what he was about to tell her.

"Isn't she wonderful?" Blue Bird asked, pointing into the sky toward her rising hawk. "She has a strong totem. I can *feel* it."

Victorio nodded and placed his hand on her shoulder. He watched for a while longer as the hawk joined its partner in the sky. He watched as they flew together then locked talons in a death spiral. Down and down they went, and Blue Bird giggled by his side. They were copulating, or trying to at least, she and her male counterpart, barreling through the sky, barely conscious of their surroundings. If they mated, they would be together forever, he knew. Blue Bird knew, as well, and somewhere in her brilliant mind was an image of them fucking, her and Victorio. They had done so many times, but no babies. Not yet at least. Not until this terrible war with the Gulo was over.

"I need to speak to you."

She turned to him, and her smile changed. "What the hell does Admiral Cho want from us now? My birds and I are on R&R until Monday."

"And you will remain so," he said. "But afterward... there is a mission we must conduct."

She waited, her breaths short and constant. She put her weight on her left leg, her arms crossed, her hip jutted out in defiance. She favored her right foot since its reattachment from the squadron's deadly engagement at Castor V well over one standard year ago, but he knew her stance was just a feint. If she got angry, she could round on him in an instant, weak foot or no. The hawk totem was strong in her. Too strong sometimes. "What kind of mission?"

"*Celia* has fallen to the Gulo."

Blue Bird shook her head. "Not familiar with it."

"Zeus Sector. Not a sector we usually fight in, but strategically important nonetheless. Primarily Europeans, old Spanish, Portuguese families. It has fallen and is now suffering major privations. Cut off from supply and communication. We need it back, and Admiral Cho has decided to strike in three standard months. Plans are afoot, but he needs reconnaissance beforehand. The Gulo are cagey, intelligent, as you are well aware. They hide their assets well."

The Gulo were a violent, wolverine-like race that had invaded human space about thirty-five standard years ago. Since then, they had pushed hard in every sector, making it all the way to Mars in one offensive before squadrons like the Devil Dancers and commanders like Admiral Cho turned the tide. Now the invaders were being pushed back in every sector, but it was a hard, slow slog.

Blue Bird huffed, and turned back to watch her hawks. "He wants the Devil Dancers to run recon on the blind, and deep inside hostile territory?"

"No, in fact, he doesn't." Victorio shook his head and cleared his throat, choosing his words carefully. "He wants to borrow our birds."

Blue Bird stiffened, and Victorio braced for an assault. But it did not come. Instead, she turned quietly and stared at him. Her face reddened. "He wants what?"

"Our hawks. Three of them at least. A fighter squadron, even as skilled as ours, would draw too much attention from the Gulo and would most certainly be detected by their sophisticated defensive shield-net. We might be able to gather the data that's required, but in the end, we'd be blown out of the sky. No. The best observers here would be hawks, birds of prey with visual acuity three, four times as sharp as human beings. *Celia* is a human planet, and much of its flora and fauna were transferred and reseeded there. They have a lot of animal species from Earth, including birds. A few more hawks in the sky won't ruffle Gulo feathers."

It was a bad pun, he knew, and Blue Bird made him pay for it with an angry glare. "We're not talking about dogs here, Vic. Hawks aren't easy to train. You can't just give them orders and expect them to fly over what you want."

Victorio sighed. "That's not exactly how it's going to work, Blue. We will control them remotely from the *Star Chariot*."

Blue Bird squinted. "How?"

"An ocular booster will be implanted in their corneas," he said, "which will allow them to submit images to a relay buoy stationed within the planet's debris ring. As far as controlling them is concerned, a small neural weave will be placed just inside their craniums, allowing us to emit pulses into their brains that will let us guide their flight over the areas we need reviewed."

Blue Bird shook her head. "I didn't know we had that kind of technology."

"One of the perks of being at war for thirty-five standard years."

The Gulo were highly sophisticated warriors. Their ships, troopers, and weapons were on par, and in some cases, superior to human technology. But when it came to subterfuge, espionage, and manipulating technology to enhance those activities, the Gulo seemed oblivious. Everything was a blunt object for them. It was a great strength, but also their greatest weakness.

"I won't allow it," Blue Bird said, holding her arm out over the ledge. "You won't take my birds."

"They aren't your birds. They're the squadron's. It's already been decided."

"Without consulting me? Your second-in-command?"

"I'm doing the best I can for us all, Blue. I'm doing what I can to help the war effort."

"But why our birds?"

"Because I love you more than them!"

He didn't mean to snap. He didn't want to raise his voice at all, especially to her, but the stress of this whole thing, this war, was beginning to weigh heavily upon him. "If we can prove that this technology works," he said, "then we can infiltrate any human world conquered by the Gulo, learn their strengths and weaknesses, and then orchestrate counterattacks more effectively. If our hawks can accomplish this, then other animals could be fitted with these technologies. It could be the turning point we need. And then maybe this goddamned war will finally end. The goal here is to *end* the war."

Blue Bird accepted the hawk on her arm. The bird sensed her agitation and flapped its wings aggressively as if it were going to take flight again. Bluebird tried to calm herself, smile, and soothe it with gentle cooing. Finally, it settled, accepting a small piece of meat, swallowing it whole, then nuzzling its sharp beak against her tender affections. Once under control, Blue Bird said with less anger, "They will die, Victorio."

"No, they won't. It's just a recon mission. They'll be in and out quickly. I promise."

Blue Bird shook her head as she placed the hawk in its cage. "You can't promise anything, Victorio. This is war. There are no promises here."

They were silent while the male hawk came down and accepted Blue Bird's arm. She caged him, slipped slices of meat to them both between the bars, then placed the travel cover over them. As they stilled and grew quiet, she picked the cages up, turned, and said, "You are my commanding officer. You are Captain Victory. And we are duty-bound to carry out your orders. But understand this, Captain. If these birds die... then there will be no more *us*. That, I *can* promise."

She walked away, and Victorio stared at her as she worked down the hill to the waiting truck. In her wake, he could feel her strong hawk totem and knew that she was telling the truth. If he failed, if these hawks died, then there would be no future for them.

Never.

But they would not fail. He was certain of it. He was Victorio Nantan, Captain Victory, commander of the Devil Dancers, 3rd Sol Fighter Wing, the best squadron in the fleet. It was just a simple recon mission.

"Nothing will go wrong, my love," he whispered to himself as she walked away. "I promise."

On the *Star Chariot,* they sat in a triangle of three chairs, Victorio, Blue Bird, and Shines Like the Sun. The rest of the squadron would be monitoring progress from the bridge. They would also be responsible for launching the relay buoy, ensuring its successful implantation in *Celia's* debris ring, and then launching the carrier probe into the atmosphere so that the hawks could be successfully released undetected by Gulo defenses. In some ways, those lucky enough not to actually fly the mission had the hardest tasks. If they failed, the mission would be aborted. Blue Bird would like that, Victorio knew. But their tasks could not fail. He had forbidden it, firmly, and with passionate direction. If they failed, the war would go on and on and on. It was a warning that got everyone in the squadron focused on their tasks.

"Buoy target identified," a voice cracked over the comm. "Launch imminent."

Victorio nodded but remained silent. It seemed like the right thing to do. There was nothing more to be said anyway. Soon, their minds would be connected to their respective hawks, and speech would be impossible in such a state. Across from him, Blue Bird stared into nothing, unblinking, showing her strength and fear, the feelings that he was certain were also printed on his face. Shines Like the Sun sat at his left, eyes closed, rocking gently back and forth, lips moving slightly, giving up a solemn prayer to Yusn Life-Giver, god of all and the great father of the Apaches. Victorio nodded approval. *Say a prayer for me as well, my friend.*

"Target struck."

A channel opened in Victorio's mind with a piercing ring. It threw him a little, more so than it had in practice, but the sensation went away finally, and now he could detect Blue Bird's and Shines Like the Sun's presence. He was in their minds. Not completely, not in the way that he would soon be in the mind of his hawk, but he knew his squadron mates were there without even having to place eyes upon them. It was a weird sensation, but one that Blue Bird assumed easily. 'It will be even more challenging when you enter the hawk's mind,' she had said during practice. 'It is simple, but focused. You will feel strong, powerful sensations of fear, joy, lust, hunger, flight. Those are the emotions that define the hawk, and you must learn to control them.'

'How can I do that?' he had asked.

She had smiled. 'You must give yourself to the hawk. *Be* the hawk.'

It was not a skill that he had easily mastered, and sitting here now, waiting restlessly for the mission to begin, he wasn't sure if he ever would. He was a *di-yin* shaman, and one that had used his spiritual powers to thwart enemies in the past, like his old captain Magnus Coloradas, but the hawk totem had always escaped him. Perhaps it was because the bird's emotions were simple, clear, straightforward, and Victorio's had always been muddled. *Should I or shouldn't I? Will this work or not? Was it the right thing to do?* Even in practice, when Blue Bird told him to give himself up to the insatiable pangs of the hawk's hunger, he had refused to swoop down and pluck a mouse from a rotting stump. Why? Because it just didn't seem like the right thing to do... tactically. To break formation for such a silly reason as eating a rodent. But that was human logic, and the purpose of giving oneself to the hawk was to experience its sudden and powerful instincts so that one could learn how to harness them effectively. Blue Bird understood that. Shines Like the Sun understood. It had taken Victorio twice as long to figure it out.

"Carrier probe launched."

Victorio mouthed *I love you* to Blue Bird. She did not mouth it back, but she smiled faintly and nodded.

He closed his eyes and his emotions changed. Simple, powerful, he was in the mind of his hawk, the youngest one, but the fastest according to Blue Bird. First was fear, anxiousness for their rapid descent in the carrier. It was just large enough for three birds, and they had been given a mild sedative to keep them from trying to flap their wings and potentially break them. Like a bullet, the carrier would plunge through Celia's upper atmosphere until it reached the correct level, then break open like an egg and disperse its cargo.

Victorio worked through a few sub-routines in his mind and finally gained access to the hawk's eyes. Nothing but darkness as they descended, but even darkness was nothing to his new visual power. He could easily discern the other two birds ahead of him in the carrier, tightly packed, but struggling to free themselves. *Patience, Blue Bird,* he said through his mind. *You taught me that.* The hawk in front of him stilled, but a talon reached out and nicked his breast. Victorio chuckled and it came out as a screech, but he followed it up with something more serious.

Remember, target is ten kilometers due east. Five fly-overs, first two tight, last three dispersed. Then make it to the extraction point. Thirty standard minutes.

The carrier dropped, then shook, then cracked into four pieces that drifted away in the thin *Celia* atmosphere. Victorio fell separately for a few seconds before gaining control of his wings, righting himself, and shifting his light body to the East. He could feel the cool, Earth-like air on his breast feathers. It felt good. He felt good. He felt alive, free, wanting to find an air current and drift for hours. He forced the desire from his small mind, shook his head and joined Blue Bird and Shines Like the Sun in I-formation. They would go in twenty feet apart and then fan out slightly to make detailed pictures of their target.

Victorio spread his wings to let the air currents shift him down beneath a cloud bank. Then he turned on his boosted ocular scanner, and the world came into view.

Celia was rockier than Earth. Almost everywhere, the spikes of jutting grey and black rock appeared, peppered here and there with small patches of foothills covered in bright green and yellow grass. His mind exploded with so many colors and shapes. He almost toppled over. But Blue Bird fell back and nudged him on course. *Keep sharp*, she said, flipping upside down and rolling through the pleasant sky.

This was a human planet that had been terraformed and reshaped for over a hundred years. Between the rocks and throughout the hills were human settlements, many now lying in ruin, soot, and black ash. Victorio's heart sank. Such beauty, such clarity could he find through this wonderful bird's eyes, and yet, the clarity of desolation and the meaning of such was almost too much to bear. And amidst that ruin, Gulo settlements were being constructed, half-fabricated, half-earthen tunnel complexes that cut through the landscape like sharp, angular worms of green and white. And how many humans had died with the first Gulo invasion force? How many were still down there serving as slave labor? Victorio did not know the answers to these questions, but he hoped Blue Bird was looking at it all too.

Their target came into view, a sprawling Gulo naval complex that filled the valley from end to end. It was the largest enemy site Victorio had ever seen outside the vacuum of space, and it seemed that its ship bays were large enough for destroyer-sized hulls. A marvelous station and once again a testament to Gulo skill in warfare. The Federated Union would never dare to house such massive ships in-gravity. Indeed, *Celia's* gravity well was smaller than Earth's, but the risk of having such large ships near the ground was too great. The Gulo were willing to risk it, however, which meant *Celia* was a prime target. *Break them here and ...*

Fan out, he told the others through his mind, and they did, shifting to the left and right of him, he the anchor in a triangle that mimicked their seating arrangement on the *Star Chariot.* The first fly-over would be a test, to gauge any enemy response and to acquire a full measurement of the complex with a passive scanning beam. If the enemy did not pick up on that, then the scouts would engage digital patterning in haste.

Victorio flipped on his passive scanners and flew at top speed over the target, taking full measurement of the central portion of the complex. Blue Bird took scans of the right quadrant, Shines

Like the Sun the left. As he scanned, Victorio saw dozens of Gulo lurching around, moving from this location to the next, a worker unit doing construction on a new set of modulated structures, fully kitted with radar dishes and beacon towers. They seemed intent on their work, paying no attention to the few simple birds drifting above them.

Near the perimeter of the complex were laser bunkers and rocket squares. The Gulo preferred a mixture of precision and gross-area protection. Sometimes they even threw in anti-matter munitions, but not here, not on-planet. Those kinds of weapons were used in space, where the dispersal of energy could help keep collateral damage focused on enemy craft. Here, there would be little of that. Through the hawk's eyes, Victorio trained his scanners so that all point defense boxes would be clearly noted and marked.

The first fly-over was successful, so they shifted in the wind and made another run. As directed, Blue Bird and Shines Like the Sun pulled in closer, taking on a raven-style pattern that the Devil Dancers used often in space flight. High and tight, and the hawks were performing well. They were not trying to break formation, nor trying to dive low in pursuit of food, nor were they trying to drift away toward the sun to warm their wings. They were doing well, and Victorio was pleased. Things were going as planned.

On their fourth and final fly-over, with roughly forty meters between them, Shines Like the Sun broke formation. He fell like a rock, recovered, and tried to reset in the pattern. He dropped again, struggled to recover again, then fell once more.

What's the problem? Victorio asked. *Keep formation.*

I'm trying, Captain, Shines Like the Sun said, *but there's an errant sub-command in my cranial web, overriding my electric impulses. I can't get control of it. It's overwhelming me.*

Suddenly Blue Bird jerked out of formation as well. Her hawk rolled through the sky. *What's happening,* Victorio called to her.

Same thing, Vic. My bird is not following my commands.

Victorio checked his own cranial web, over-riding the security locks. And there it was, a shadow program, cleverly buried within the million lines of code that had been written by the Union's programmers for this mission. It was a simple command: Drop.

Its priority algorithms were superior in the codex hierarchy of the entire program, so no matter what happened, no matter how many exceptions were fed into the code, the "drop" command rose to the surface. The only way to knock it out was to remove the web itself. And that was impossible. The commands were on a timer. Shines Like the Sun's command apparently first; Blue Bird's second; and his third.

What do we do? He asked as Blue Bird struggled to keep her bird from falling.

Save him! She blurted.

And Victorio saw what she was referring to. Shines Like the Sun was falling uncontrollably now, his hawk totally taken over by the intrusive command that had been placed in its web.

Victorio pursued, still in control of his own hawk. He dove and dove, pushing his wings against his body to sheer through the air like a blade. He put his talons out and stretched them wide as he neared Shines Like the Sun's posterior. He reached out and tried to lock his claws around the diving hawk's red tail feathers. He got them, but the weight and force of its fall were too great. The bird's feathers slipped out of his grasp, and it kept falling.

Shines Like the Sun screamed as his link was severed, and his hawk struck the complex and exploded in a blast of feathers, blood, and green gas.

What the hell...?

Where had the gas come from? It spread and Victorio pulled up and soared to safety as the gas cloud continued to expand.

Sabotage, he heard Blue Bird say through his mind. Yes, it had to be. The green gas continued to expand and balloon over the complex, more rapidly than Victorio would have imagined. The only way it could have done that is through the shock of the explosion as the hawk struck the complex.

There were several inert compounds that, when combined with liquids and the catalyst of heat and intense pressure—such as striking a wall—would create a toxin. Yes, it had to be. But how that toxin had been put into the hawks and where... well, he didn't have time for speculation.

Blue Bird was falling out of the sky.

He flew to her, like a rocket, like he had seen his bird do countless times in Chaco Canyon when they were let out for exercise. His mate was in his sights, and he went to her.

Down he flew until he was near enough to wrap his talons around her, press his small body against hers. But the desire was not there, not in her eyes. Only fear, uncertainty. She was crying.

We're going to die, she said. *They are going to die.*

No, he said, holding her tighter, pulling her closer. *What did you tell me when we practiced? How do you control a hawk?*

She didn't respond at first, uncertain perhaps of what he meant. Then she said, *You must* be *the hawk.*

Yes, and what is one of the hawk's chief emotions?

Fear.

And what does the hawk do when it is afraid?

It flies.

Are you afraid?

Yes.

Then be the hawk... and fly!

He let her go, let her drop from his grasp. No longer did the neural weave in the bird's cranium affect his movement. He found himself ignoring the synaptic impulses of its commands. The 'Drop' command fell silent, inert—like the foul green jelly placed inside him—and he flew.

He saw the world now through hawk's eyes, different than before. Clear, focused, consumed with the desire to fly, to flee, to reach heights where no other bird could find him, in the clouds where only Yusn Life-Giver resided, in the blue haze of a distant mountain range where the mountain spirits would give him further strength. Blue Bird found it too; he could feel her new-found strength. The hawk totem that had escaped her was now back and strong, stronger than ever. And they flew together, ignoring the incessant tickle of the errant command that lay fallow in their minds.

They flew over the sharp spires of the Gulo complex. They spread their wings and let the wind take them away, through cloud bank and light rain, until they found a small patch of trees. Down they went until they found a sturdy branch. Victorio spread his wings to slow his descent. He grabbed the wood and felt it give under his weight, but it did not break. Blue Bird then lighted beside him.

They perched there on the tree, looking at each other, not able to speak, not able to share their thoughts. Only short screeches escaped their long, sharp beaks. But Victorio understood now what he was. He was not human anymore. He was a hawk, he and Blue Bird. They were hawks.

They were happy.

A darkness consumed Victorio, and then he was back on the *Star Chariot*, in his seat, sweat rolling down his face. To his left Shines Like the Sun was slumped over, his face deathly pale. To his right, Blue Bird sat erect, but weak and moaning.

"Report, Captain!"

It was Admiral Cho's voice. Victorio blinked, wiped his face, and saw the admiral before him, flanked by guards.

Victorio flew out of the chair. "You sorry son of a bitch! You nearly got us killed!"

The guards grabbed him before he could lay a finger on the smug little commander, but that didn't temper his rage. "You lied to me. Why?"

"So that you could do what needed to be done."

"You said it was just a recon mission."

Admiral Cho nodded. "And it was... in a sense. But this is best, whether you accept it or not. We do not have the strength to take *Celia* back in force, not without severely damaging their capabilities beforehand." He smiled. "Now, the toxin will spread through their population, and they will be depleted before our attack."

"You failed, Admiral," Victorio said, giving a smile of his own. "You failed. Only Shines' bird impacted. Mine and Blue Bird's flew away."

Admiral Cho gnashed his teeth. His face grew red. "That's a lie."

"It's true. Check the digital. We got away, Admiral. Not enough toxins were released. We got away, and those hawks will live out their days, shitting out your poison like a digested mouse. That's what you are, Admiral. A filthy little mouse."

"Take him away!" Admiral Cho yelled. "Take them all away!"

As they were dragged to the brig, Victorio imagined himself flying, soaring through the air, looking for prey.

Three months later, Victorio Nantan sat under guard on a lip of rock overlooking Chaco Canyon. The cuffs on his wrists dug into his skin, but he didn't care. He watched two hawks play in the bright sunlight, and he imagined himself with them, flying through clouds, looking down on the world. He breathed deeply and closed his eyes.

Someone came up behind him. He could hear feet shuffling along the loose rock and gravel. He couldn't see her, but he knew who she was. He could feel her.

"The tribunal has adjourned," Blue Bird said. "Sentence has been passed."

Victorio did not speak. He waited until she unrolled a piece of paper and read aloud so that the guard might also hear. "In the matter between Victorio "Tomorrow's Wind" Nantan, Captain of the Devil Dancers Fighter Squadron, and Admiral Tsing Lau Cho, commander of Special Fleet Operations for the Federated Union, the charges being Dereliction of Duty and Insubordination by Captain Nantan. For Dereliction of Duty, the tribunal finds Captain Nantan... not guilty. For Insubordination and Attempted Assault Against a Superior Officer, the tribunal finds Captain Nantan... guilty as charged, the sentence of which shall be three months solitary confinement, loss of pay, and reduction of rank to First Lieutenant for six standard months, after which time, all rank, status, and benefits thereof will be reinstated."

"What about the charges against you and our squadron?" Victorio asked.

"All other charges have been dropped."

"And Shines Like the Sun?"

Blue Bird nodded. "He'll be fine. He's recovering from his aneurysm."

Victorio nodded. "Good. Admiral Cho?"

Blue Bird chuckled. "He was... *encouraged* to accept early retirement."

She sat beside him and placed her head on his shoulder. "I'm sorry, Vic."

"Don't be. It could have been worse. And at least the Union realized Cho's deception and dropped the dereliction charge. I'm just sorry that I failed you. I lost the birds."

"Only one," Blue Bird said.

"The other two are stuck on *Celia*."

She nodded. "But they are safe. And they will be together forever." She kissed his cheek. "Just like us."

He looked into her eyes. "Will this war ever end?"

Blue Bird shook her head. "I don't know, Vic. But let's not worry about that right now. Let's just close our eyes, fly, and be at peace."

And they did. Victorio breathed deeply and imagined himself moving powerful wings. He heard the hawk's screech and let it inside him. He lifted up into the clouds and floated on air that gave him breath and courage. And beside Blue Bird, beside his love, he soared.

I AM THE LIGHTNING

Captain Victorio "Tomorrow's Wind" Nantan reviewed Alpha Squadron's formation on his *Radiant's* active display. Four tiny blips in Raven Pattern, moving tightly toward a swarm of Gulo *Wasps*. Good, but not ideal. Gleeful Fox had been killed, and thus they were running blind without a Clown, and they so desperately needed one. Someone in ISR had fucked up royally. Not uncommon, admittedly, but this one was a major error in intelligence. The Gulo were supposed to have only one, perhaps two, cruisers and a light carrier. They showed up with an additional carrier and a full flight of fighters ready for blood. Heads would roll, but unfortunately, not Gulo heads.

"Keep it tight," Victorio ordered over the comm. "You all know what to do. Don't fail your training, or the Devil Dancers. And noise discipline. Keep it quiet! I don't want that *Wasp* swarm ahead of us firming targets."

"Then why the hell are you talking?"

Blue Bird's lilting voice came over the wire like a flower, a knife. "Wise ass," he replied. "Don't make me bump you back to Beta Squadron, Blue."

She snickered. "Yes, sir, Captain, sir."

He loved her. That too, was not uncommon in the vacuum of space, in the midst of war, when the stresses and travails of sheer survival pressed down on a pilot all the time. Love (and, too, sex) was an easy escape from the madness, the pressure. But it was forbidden, especially during war, especially for a commander, who often had to make snap decisions about who lived, who died. *Would I be able to make that decision?* Victorio had wondered that often since he and Blue Bird had become an "item," as Gleeful Fox might have called it. *Can I send her to her death?*

Victorio opened a private comm to her. "Hey, be careful. Come home alive."

He could not see her face, but he knew she was smiling. "You too, love."

He punched tactical recommendations into the targeting array. The on-board I-Core accepted all but three. He tapped in his override code and forced acceptance. The I-Core was a damned fine targeting assistant, but it too often went by the book. It lacked practical experience, and it was apparently incapable of developing any. The Union's AI specialists had yet to figure out how to make it think and adapt. That was perfectly fine with Victorio. He knew from experience that a *Radiant* needed only one pilot. He didn't need some motherboard of crystal relays and quantum circuitry telling him how to fly. But the I-Core was superior at picking up gaseous heat signatures from cloaked enemy craft and had a keen sense on when to lock target and fire rockets. And against a swarm like the one they were approaching, that tactical advantage was imperative.

Victorio flicked on Targeting and got his first detailed look at the Gulo *Wasp* swarm. Forty fighters total, in typical undulating formation, like an amoeba, like a bird flock, with few gaps in between. The Gulo relied heavily on numbers and on enemy radio chatter for effective targeting. It had served them well, and a swarm like this one could decimate an incoming Federated squadron right quick. The Wasp was a speedy fighter, lightly armored with fore-missile tubes and a strong, turreted laser gatling bolted into its belly. A standard shoot-and-scoot type of fighter. Victorio smiled at his good fortune and activated his rocket packs, sent passive beaker communiqués to the rest of his squadron, and waited.

The I-Core blared its defiance, ordering the attack *now!*

"Patience, my little quantum buddy," Victorio whispered, watching the targeting reticule beam green for *Go, Go!* He waited, waited, watching through his cockpit window as the *Wasp* swarm began throwing its missiles into their forward field to measure distance for their powerful energy beams.

The Devil Dancers now spread formation, as designed via Eagle Pattern, stretching itself out like the long, luxurious wing of an eagle with its glossy, gold-black feathers and defiant strength. The Gulo swarm instinctively did as it always did; it followed suit and spread as well, creating gaps in its original tight formation.

Fools!

In the many years that he and his Devil Dancers of the 3rd Sol Fighter Wing had been fighting these creatures, they never seemed to learn, never seemed to realize when they were being suckered into a weaker position. Opening a gap into their formation allowed him and his fighters to fly into the chaos and unload everything they had. Why? Why keep making the same mistake again and again? The laziness of numbers, perhaps, the knowledge of knowing that you could lose three times as many fighters in a dogfight and still keep fighting; under those conditions, why implement tactical flexibility? But how long could that go on? It had gone on now for over thirty standard years. Perhaps it could go on forever.

Victorio closed his eyes and prayed to the God of All. He placed his hands on the dashboard, set his fingers in their proper positions on the tiny rocket symbols flashing green. "Yusn Life-Giver," he said, drawing upon the words of his ancient people's creator. He mouthed the prayer in his comm link, though he knew his Dancers could not hear. It did not matter, for he knew they were mouthing the same prayer back.

> *Help me to remain calm and strong in*
> *the face of all that comes toward me.*
> *Let me learn the lessons you have hidden*
> *in every leaf and rock.*

He pressed his fingers deep into the glowing display, and his *Radiant* recoiled from the *whoosh* of rockets.

The entire Alpha Squadron—Victorio, Blue Bird, Shines Like the Sun, Red Moon—released all its munitions packets, letting a dervish of one hundred twenty rockets fly toward the *Wasp* swarm. The enemy divided, and Victorio activated his I-Core and allowed it to pick and fire lasers "at will".

Wasps incinerated in front of them as rockets impacted the lead mass. One, two, three, dozens down, and Victorio flew into the wreckage confidently as his lasers began to pick targets. The rest in his squadron fired as well, letting their I-Cores make their choices while they maintained formation as best as possible with all the mangled Gulo steel whipping past them. It literally felt like stepping into a wasp nest, and Gulo radio frequencies buzzed like bees. It was scary and exhilarating at the same time, and anyone who wasn't scared was a fool.

Wasps began firing their energy weapons, peppering Devil hulls with precise scorch marks. On the far right of the formation, Red Moon fell starboard from the initial shock of the assault. But he quickly regained control and climbed back into formation, shrugging off his light hull damage and responding with a barrage of lasers of his own.

Victorio nodded and breathed a sigh of relief. The *Radiant* could take a few volleys before its fore and aft shielding went down, and then its hull was powerful enough to withstand some damage before the pilot had to worry. It was less effective against rockets, but the Gulo had already expended their packages in an attempt to seed the field with kinetic wreckage in the hope (he assumed) to force them to break pattern; a weak move on their part. *Why are they fighting so poorly today?* Victorio wondered. He shook his head. The Gulo were usually more on the ball, more active and responsive to such a frontal assault. Perhaps Admiral Kelley was right; perhaps they were in the last throes.

"What do we do now, Captain?" It was Blue Bird's voice breaking silence. *Thank Yusn!* "Whip around and dogfight?"

They cleared the swarm, and Victorio activated his comm. "No. We have orders. We let Captain Weiss's squadron mop up. We're to attack the *Vichu-Pa.*"

"But I want pelts," Shines Like the Sun said over a scratchy comm-link. Victorio looked at his dash and saw that the pilot had taken a direct hit to his communications array. "I haven't been able...to... to claim... reward... since... Pallid Musings."

Victorio couldn't deny that. Even his own wall of Gulo pelts needed new trophies. The last Gulo pelt he'd been able to claim was over one standard year ago, long before that matter with Admiral Cho and the squadron's red-tailed hawks, which left Victorio in the stockade for a few months. The Devil Dancers had had little opportunity since to gain honor for themselves; morale was low in the squadron. But orders were orders.

"No, pilot," Victorio said. "We follow the game plan. We let Weiss finish them off, and we go in with the full assault. We'll be in support from Haley's and Omar's squadrons from the 17th, backed by the *Al-Shirees*."

"They'll still out-number us, sir," Red Moon said. Victorio could sense the young man's apprehension. "It's the *Vichu-Pa*."

"That's not our concern," Victorio snapped again, a little more forcefully than he wanted. "We go in, as ordered. Now, activate your operational displays to see the full assault. Reassign tactical recommendations to I-Core, let's shift to Diamond Pattern, and—"

"Sir," Blue Bird said with authority. "Request reassignment to a Clown."

Victorio paused a moment, letting her words sink in. He shook his head as if she could see it. "Denied. We've only got four, Blue, and you know it. We don't have the structural integrity to use a Clown, as much as I'd like one."

"Forget Diamond," she said. "Shift into Crescent instead, and let me work independently."

Crescent was an old formation, back when the Federated Union had smaller squadrons. The idea was, you set your fighters into a triangle or "crescent" shape, with the forward two fighters serving to clear the field with energy weapons, while the back fighter pounded the enemy with rockets. The formation only worked when at least one of the fighters had rockets; they had already expended their packets. It was madness, sheer folly. And yet...

Can I send her to her death?

"You'll be all alone out there, Blue," he said. "You don't have experience with that kind of maneuver. You've never worked independently, and Crescent is not a formation that supports an independent asset."

"Nevertheless, we need a diversion," she said. "I want to do something substantial, something important, at least once before…"

She paused on that last word, and thank Yusn for it! Victorio knew exactly what that "before" meant, but they needed to keep that truth from the squadron for as long as possible.

She continued. "You need independent eyes out there, sir. You need my communication, my tactical commentary. We're under-strength; the first time in a long, long while. You need to know what's going on deep behind the Gulo defensive field. I can do that. I'm an Apache. I'm a Ga'an mountain spirit. I'm a Devil Dancer. I'm the lightning flashing and—"

"Okay, okay," he said, cutting her off before she wasted any further time reciting the entire prayer. Her mind was made up, and there was no moving it once that happened. He could order her to stand down, and she would obey as she was a pilot and a loyal officer of the Federated Union. But what kind of hell would he catch later? It was madness to let her go; it was madness not to.

"Go!"

"*Ahagahe!*" Blue Bird screamed the old Apache war cry into his ear.

Victorio saw her *Radiant* break formation and fly toward the star Pollux.

"Crescent Pattern," he said, activating the operational display and typing recommendations. "I'll be the anchor."

The three remaining *Radiant*'s shifted into Crescent pattern and flew toward the dark hull of the *Vichu-Pa*.

The ship had religious significance. The Federated Union didn't know exactly what it symbolized or why, but there was something holy about the *Vichu-Pa*, something that the Gulo held in deep regard. Speculation about it fell anywhere between silly superstition (the ship itself named after a Gulo deity) or it had once served as the first colony ship of the Gulo millennia ago. Whatever the reason, it and its partner the *Na-Ta-She* were almost always protected with suicidal fury. But the *Na-Ta-She* had been crippled at the Battle of Iron Towers, and perhaps it would never field again. The loss had left the Gulo reeling backward and Victorio unhappy. He had been delighted with the victory overall, but to attack religious symbols was not his way to fight a war. That's what White Eyes had done back in the Rebellion of 2235, when Victorio had been just a boy. Military units that had been sent into Southwest America were not just satisfied with killing those that had started the rebellion; they wanted to destroy the Apache people altogether, to wipe out any evidence that they had ever existed at all. That had failed, though the rebellion had been put down in time. Those that had attempted such a genocide had been punished, but the scars remained. Thousands of Native Americans fled Earth after that, and they would never forget. The Gulo would never forget what had happened to their precious ship, Victorio knew.

Blips activated on his tactical display. The entire union Task Force was moving forward, having broken through Gulo defensive measures. Casualties were high in other squadrons, and one of the Union's destroyers had been cut in half to drift lifeless in the void, but the attack was on, and it would not be called off. Victorio saw that he and his Alpha Squadron were at the far end of a long attack pattern. They, two other fighter squadrons, and the light carrier *Star Chariot* were advancing on the *Vichu-Pa*. They had the firepower, he knew, but did they have the courage?

Long, powerful lances of blue energy shot out from *Vichu-Pa's* hull, a barrage of deadly laser fire seeking victims. Victorio saw on the monitor that the Star Chariot answered in kind with Dayglow Torpedoes, releasing a hail that they'd hope would be the end of the Gulo ship. The Gulo were ready, however, and point-defense batteries opened fire and tore through the munitions, leaving only a few to find their mark on the enemy hull. Victorio ordered his squadron to bank left as the torpedoes found their mark and destroyed a defense laser, but the hull was intact.

"Keep in pattern, and fire at will," he said over comm. "We go straight in."

"We're going to be carved up by point-defense," Shines Like the Sun said.

"Negative," Victorio said. "Those batteries have a limited field of fire. Their purpose is to knock out incoming kinetics. They don't fire close to the hull. We can get underneath and poke at the soft belly." He tapped his comm link to cycle to Blue Bird. "How you coming along, Blue?"

There was a pause, then, "Fine, Captain. I'm cruising above its hull. Fifty kilometers. The weather's fine up here. But... I'm picking up some odd energy patterns building below the skin."

Victorio did a quick scan of *Vichu-Pa* historical data, looking to see if anything like that had been spotted before. Nothing.

"Keep focused, Blue," he said. "If you feel uncomfortable, pull back into formation."

"Nonsense," she said in her brightest, most energetic voice. "I'm just fine. I'll keep you posted. Blue out!"

Victorio smiled and fired lasers.

It was relatively easy to get near the Vichu-Pa. It wasn't a carrier, so there was no serious point-defense up close, and its shielding was negligible. What it had was an incredibly thick hull, and it could withstand enormous amounts of damage; referring to it as a "soft underbelly" was just a joke. It rarely experienced such damage, however, as it was primarily a long-range weapon. With its partner the *Na-Ta-She* out of action, however, it had to get closer to firm enemy targets. Its command staff was probably reluctant to do so, but the Union was relying on the Devil Dancers to force the Gulo ship to do just that.

In Crescent Pattern, they flew beneath the weak point-defense and began wailing on the junctures where Gulo laser batteries were bolted to the hull. They were hull-reinforced as well, but enough concentrated fire could pop them off. They flew beneath reinforcement gantries and fired beams, carving through meters of steel.

"Like shooting fish in a barrel," Red Moon said, howling an Apache war cry.

"Too cliché," Victorio said, pressing his weapons display to put the finishing touches on a point-defense battery. The massive box of tubes broke free from the hull and drifted away quietly. "Come up with something better while we circle around for another run. Turtle Pattern."

They turned around and pulled closer per the pattern order, making a compact, tight ball. The laser fire in this pattern would be more intense, more focused. They opened fire, and another point-defense broke free, and another and another. Victorio reported their status to the Star Chariot, and a new round of torpedoes were readied. He was pleased. This was going better than he had planned.

He opened comm again with Blue Bird. She had been sending him sit-reps the entire time. "Status?"

"Doing well, Captain. No major problems up here. It's beautiful in fact, the ship I mean. Old and rustic almost, as if it's been constantly built and rebuilt on top of older hulls. It's massive but calm."

"All right, then. Return to formation. It doesn't look like we need you up there any—"

He could hear Blue's warning display through the comm. "What's wrong?"

"Something's building inside, Captain," she said, her voice agitated and insistent. "Like before, but much more intense. Can you see it?"

He checked his monitor. "No. It's cool over here. Return to formation now."

"A moment," she said as she shared her display with him. "See this?"

He did. A massive charge of heat was building up inside *Vichu-Pa's* core. But it was an odd reading. It didn't possess the signature consistent with Gulo weaponry. Then the central mass of heat spread out, like ripples in a pond, moving toward the outer hull. Victorio's heart sank.

"Chaff!" He barked. "Run!"

He gunned his engines and reached the outer perimeter of the *Vichu-Pa's* Sphere-of-Influence just before the ship's skin exploded into billions of tiny metal shards, one or two feet long, but moving out from the hull at incredible speeds. On his tactical display, entire squadrons of Union ships disappeared, and the *Star Chariot's* prow disintegrated. He could hear Blue's screams over the comm, saw Red Moon's *Radiant* explode as it was torn to shreds under the unstoppable mass of destruction.

Shines Like the Sun's signature was still active, but through the chaff, his ship could not be seen.

"Blue!" Victorio yelled over the comm. "Come in!"

Her voice was difficult to pick up through the interference of chaff. "I...I can't... I can't outrun... I'm sorry... I love you, Vic."

She went silent and her signature disappeared.

Victorio screamed as the chaff found the rear of his fighter and destroyed it.

He awoke in a mineral bath of jellied enzymes and nutrient mud. There was no chance of his head slipping below the vat of goo; the bath itself too shallow and too heavily monitored for such a thing. Too bad, for what reason did he have to live? Alpha Squadron was over, done.

Blue Bird is dead.

He opened his eyes slowly and sat up, breathed deeply while cold gouts of brown and gold jelly slid down his bare body. There were lab people in the room, but they didn't seem all that interested in him. There were other survivors in nutrient baths, twelve total it seemed from his quick count. He was just one of many.

But I'm Captain Victorio Nantan, Captain "Victory", the finest squadron captain in the Federated Union. Why aren't they paying me more attention? But he knew the answer to that. He was a failure now, and his name would never be equated with victory again.

He lay back down and dozed. When he awoke a second time, he was out of the bath and in a private room, a white-green gown draped over his dried body, monitors taped to his torso. He sat up in an extremely uncomfortable bed. He checked his arms. Cuts, bruises, one spot on his right forearm had been badly burned. His legs seemed okay though. Then he touched his neck. Raw, tender skin lay there. He touched his face. The right side was swollen, and most assuredly been burned as well. He cringed. He could imagine what kind of ghoul he must have looked like when they had brought him in. A nutrient bath was foul and undesirable, but it was doing the trick, and he knew they'd put him back in a few more times over the course of... how many weeks? Months? Afterward, his body would be good as new. But what about his mind? His memories? No amount of saving goo could wipe them away.

Four days later, after half a dozen more treatments, and his wounds and burns mere dark blemishes on otherwise smooth skin, he was visited by a man dressed in fine Union blue, an insignia of an Eagle bearing a sheaf of wheat on the left side of his coat. He was a dark man with stubble of grey on his thin face, wearing no officer's bonnet to cover his near-bald head.

"Colonel Tambe," Victorio said, letting his bed glide up slowly to place him in a sitting position. He tried saluting. Colonel Tambe shut it down.

"At ease, Captain," he said, in his thick accent. "We can lose that formality here."

Colonel Rajesh Tambe was commander of Union Special Forces and a star on the rise. He'd served with absolute distinction at the first Battle of Pallid Musings and was on course to become a general. He was a small man, but he commanded the room, and his demeanor absolutely demanded respect. Victorio felt naked in his presence, but then again, he was naked for the most part. Only a thin hospital gown lay between the two men.

"Captain Nantan," Colonel Tambe said, taking a seat near the bed, "I've been asked to debrief you on the Pollux attack and to answer any questions you may have."

Victorio wrinkled his brow. "Thank you, sir. But I'm confused. Why you? With respect, you are not part of Naval Operations. Why isn't someone from Vice Admiral Danning's staff debriefing me?"

"That reason will become apparent soon. But first, how are you feeling?" Colonel Tambe placed his hand gently on Victorio's arm.

Victorio nodded. "Well enough, sir. The wounds and burns are healing. They say I have a few more days' standard, and then I'll be released."

But where to? He wanted to ask that question, but kept silent, watching as Colonel Tambe seemed to be assessing the situation himself by inspecting the healing burns on Victorio's arm.

"Very good. I'm glad to see you so well, Victorio. We were worried, for a while, that there would be no survivors. The bastards hit us with a new form of chaff, high-velocity steel shafts with incredible kinetic energy. We've yet to determine whether this is a new defense system that we'll encounter elsewhere in the Gulo fleet, or whether this was just the proto- type with full implementation much further down the road. Regardless, the same principle applies: we'll have to adapt and be ready for it. I'm sure the Gulo high command—if that's what you want to call it—are dancing jigs right now. It's the first time in a long while that they've been able to hurt us so badly."

Victorio thought about dancing. He wanted to dance, to put on his Devil Dancer mask and headdress with brightly-colored feathers and sharp human teeth, his colorful buckskin leggings with hawk feathers lining the seam. Dancing would give him so much relief right now, calm his nerves, and pay homage to those who have died. *Blue Bird, I love you... I'm sorry...*

"Casualties, sir?" he asked.

Colonel Tambe's expression turned serious. "High every- where, I'm afraid. Three full fighter squadrons wiped out and your *Star Chariot* taken down. Not destroyed, thankfully, but it'll be a long while before she's operational again." Colonel Tambe sighed and sat back, rubbed his forehead. "It was a total rout."

The *Star Chariot* was the Devil Dancers new base of opera- tions. Beta and Gamma Squadrons had been held in reserve in its launch bays during the attack. "Devil Dancer casualties, sir?"

The colonel nodded. "Your two reserve squadrons are fine. Alpha Squadron, well, only two survived that we've been able to confirm. You, naturally, and Lieutenant Alfred Steele. He's been serving as acting commander during your convalescence."

Alfred... Shines Like the Sun, of course. It'd been so long since Victorio had heard the man's real name, he'd nearly forgotten it. He swallowed hard, trying to fight back the waver in his voice. "Blue Bird, sir?" He knew the answer already.

Colonel Tambe cleared his throat and leaned in. "That's what I want to talk to you about, Captain. The one positive thing about this cluster fuck is that it appears that our fighters' black boxes survived the assault intact. In total, we've been able to collect and study the data from fighters destroyed by the chaff. This'll give us valuable information for the next time we encounter it, and as you know, these boxes give off a beacon whose signal is funneled through dark matter and cannot be intercepted by Gulo Intel. At least a dozen black boxes from various pilots in various squadrons have *not* been collected... including Blue Bird's."

Victorio wrinkled his brow. "I don't understand, sir."

"Her black box wasn't found, Captain, and therefore, ISR believes that she, along with a handful of others, survived the attack, and are being held as prisoners."

Victorio tried wrapping his mind around that notion. His heart leapt at the possibility, but his head shook. "That would be inconsistent with Gulo naval tactics, sir. They do not take prisoners in the vacuum of space."

Colonel Tambe nodded. "That's true, but the chaff attack was not consistent with their attack philosophy either. Looks like they've decided to revise their tactical doctrine. The loss of the *Na-Ta-She* has apparently been a larger impact on their psyche than originally thought."

Victorio laid his head back and sighed deeply. "That, and the loss of *Vichu-Pa's* coil gun, which we took out some time ago... at great loss, if you recall. I guess that wasn't the deterrent IRS was expecting." The colonel looked like he was searching for an answer to that question. Instead, he said, "Well, regardless, the decision was made, and the damage has been done. All we can do now is move forward, recover, and adapt from this loss. And that's the main reason I am here talking to you."

Victorio waited, saw the apprehension in Tambe's eyes. The colonel was a man who held his emotions in check; he was legendary for it. But he seemed out of his element here in the hospital, not accustomed to sitting next to the bed of a middle-ranked officer of a different branch of service. He didn't seem to know what the protocols were.

"You and your remaining Devil Dancer squadrons have been reassigned to me, effective as soon as you are released from care. Your official transfer documentation is being drafted and will be delivered upon your release."

"What will we be doing for you, sir?"

"You will be providing support for an attack against the Gulo prison facility in the Lacaille asteroid belt. If our pilots are still alive, Captain, including your second-in-command, they will most assuredly be there. We're going to get them and bring them home."

A thousand questions roiled around in Victorio's mind, but he suppressed them all. This was a colonel he was speaking to, who would not be privy to all the tactical plans needed to pull off such a mission. Not at this early stage of planning, at least. But the thought of Blue Bird being alive made him happy, made him anxious to jump out of this bed and get to work.

"Yes, sir, I understand. I'm honored and happy that you have selected me and my men to support this effort. We'll give a hundred percent."

Colonel Tambe nodded and smiled. He stood. "Excellent. Welcome to Special Forces, Captain. I look forward to working with you, but I won't keep you any further. In a few days, you'll be delivered to your new billet, and then we'll get to work."

This time, Victorio saluted despite the wires and patches on his arms. Colonel Tambe saluted back and turned to leave.

"Oh, one more thing, Colonel, if I may?"

The colonel turned at the door and waited.

"Who will be my commanding officer?"

The colonel cleared his throat. "Lieutenant-Major Angelica Toth."

All the joy that Victorio felt fell away. He frowned, and said, "With respect, sir, I don't care who's being held captive. I cannot—*I will not*—work for that woman!"

"I am not happy about this assignment, ma'am."

"Well, I love you too, Captain!"

Lieutenant-Major Toth's voice and expression belied her words. She loved Victorio about as much as a dead dog. The feeling was mutual.

"I wish to be as honest with you as I can, Lieutenant-Major," Victorio said, standing as erect as possible before her desk. He was not about to let personal feelings prevent him from showing respect to the rank. "I was assigned to your service. I did not request it, nor would I have done so if the offer had been proffered. I would have picked another commando unit for the job. I was not allowed to make such a request, and when

I expressed my dissatisfaction with his selection, Colonel Tambe gave me a direct order. So here I am. But I think it's important that you know that I'm still uncomfortable with how you handled yourself and how you treated my late brother, Naiche, at his court-martial."

"Are you suggesting that I had something to do with his death?" Major Toth rose from her chair, the muscles in her strong face jumping with each gnash of her teeth.

"No, ma'am. Naiche was killed in battle by a Gulo fighter ace three standard years ago. Six years prior to that, however, you served in the JAG Corps and failed to defend him properly, and he spent eighteen standard months in the stockade."

"I'm well aware of the outcome of the case, Captain. But your claim is a lie. We defended him as best we could. The jury rendered their verdict, and there was nothing else we could do."

"You failed to show all the evidence, ma'am, evidence that would have proven his innocence."

Major Toth looked as if she were about to explode. *Good*, Victorio thought, watching her face as she searched angrily for a retort. *Let's see how unsettled you become by a lower-ranked officer challenging your judgment. How well do you stand your ground, Major?* If she could not handle adroitly such a blatant attack on her character and ethics, how would she fair against the Gulo in their stronghold when the pressure was really on? Major Toth and her so-called Bright Commandos were well-respected throughout the Federated Union, but Victorio had never served with them, and given her less-than-stellar record as a former lawyer in the JAG Corps, he had to be sure. Blue Bird deserved nothing but the strongest rescue force.

Toth smiled. "I will not have my integrity or professionalism challenged by you, Captain. Given *your* past reputation with insubordination, I'm surprised that you would tread so foolishly back into that snake pit. Accuse me again of dereliction of duty, and I'll have you thrown into the same cell that your brother called home for so many months." She turned away and took her chair behind her desk, her face red, but her countenance regaining its composure. "What's done is done, and we have a job to do. Now, are you going to help me plan this mission, or are you going to stand there like a whiney bitch?"

Ouch! Victorio couldn't help but grimace at her question. She'd certainly grown a spine since the legal days of her youth. He smiled inwardly. Maybe this endeavor was not a mistake after all.

"Yes, Major Toth," he said, relaxing his posture. "I will help you plan the mission."

She nodded and pointed to a chair. "Take a seat. Let's get started."

Victorio removed his bonnet, sat down, and waited.

"Tell me about your squadron, Captain."

"I've promoted three from Beta into Alpha; likewise for Beta. Gamma will stand down and serve as support personnel."

"Only two squadrons?"

Victorio cleared his throat. "There's no time to recruit and train new water children... I mean, new pilots."

Major Toth shook her head. "There are a number of ready, qualified pilots that you could recruit from other squadrons, and I'd approve their temporary transfer. I'm sure they'd be happy to serve under Captain Victory."

"Perhaps, but they would not be Devil Dancers, Major. It takes a certain kind of person for that position."

"You mean an Apache warrior."

He nodded. "Preferably, yes, but any native from America—or rather, the continent that used to be called America—can be trained to be so. I don't wish to be crude or racist, ma'am, but no other type of person can fulfill that role."

It looked as if she wanted him to say more, to answer more questions about the Devil Dancers squadron, but he did not take the bait. Given her past relationship with the Nantan family and his brother specifically, she already knew everything there was to know about them. Surely, during the trial, they had talked at length about the make-up of the squadron and why it was called 'Devil Dancers'. There was a good reason why, but he wouldn't spend time right now discussing it. Blue Bird's life was at stake... if she were alive at all.

Where are you, my love?

"And you are confident that you can support this mission with only eight pilots?"

"Ten to be precise, Major. Each squadron will contain a Clown."

Major Toth nodded. "Still, that's a small number, given the target."

Victorio sighed, growing frustrated with this line of questioning. Time was wasting. "It's my understanding, Major, given the diagrams of the Gulo facility that I have been shown, a smaller footprint is ideal. Every one of my pilots is an ace; that I can promise."

Major Toth tapped a display on her desk, and a holographic image of the Gulo prison facility popped up in front of them, rotating slowly counter-clockwise. It was an impressive complex, and sitting smack-dab in the middle of the Lacaille asteroid belt, one of the largest belts discovered to date. A battle of the early war had been fought there, but the Union ultimately withdrew strategically to shore up defenses in more important sectors. Now, it served the Gulo as one of its most important stepping stones for invasion fleets into nearby Union territories. It was a veritable fortress.

The prison complex itself was a coupling of five asteroids, ranging in size from four kilometers in diameter to skyscraper size. Access tunnels connected them all, giving its occupants the ability to move freely from one rock to the other. The average distance between asteroids was less than three kilometers. It was compact and bristling with point-defense and laser batteries, long-range missile tubes, and Yusn knows what else. It had been assaulted twice by Task Forces with the intent to destroy it; both failures. There had never been a commando raid planned to extract prisoners.

"What Intel do you have of the interior?" Victorio asked.

"Little," Major Toth said. "That's where you come in." She tapped the display once more, and the largest of the asteroids zoomed in. Its skin was marked with tiny red beacons, which flashed on and off like arrows marking spots. Then the display moved to the next largest asteroid, and the next. "We need passive scanner beacons placed on each cell block to get an idea of their interiors. We cannot move against it until we have some idea of the lay of the land."

Victorio knew what was coming next and spoke before she had a chance to continue. "And you want Alpha Squadron to set them."

"Yes. Five pilots, any five you choose, setting six beacons each, should give us the sweep we need."

He looked at the recommended beacon locations flashing on each rock. He pointed to the longest tunnel that connected the largest two asteroids. "You might need to place beacons on them as well. Given their length, I'm guessing they have guards stationed at intervals. They may also have defensive measures to drop bulkheads in case of emergencies."

Major Toth seemed a little perturbed at his suggestion. She bristled. "We're taking everything into account, Captain. The beacons on the cells will have sufficient range to cover the access tubes. And once we have that data, we can plan an attack."

"I understand." Victorio leaned back in his chair. "When do we go?"

Major Toth tapped her display again and the holo-complex winked out of existence. "As soon as I get clearance from Colonel Tambe. Pick your pilots, Captain Nantan, and await my orders."

Victorio stood, saluted, and turned to leave. He paused at the door as it slid open. He turned. "Ma'am, I want you to know that it's vital that we succeed in this mission. We must do everything we can to rescue my second-in-command."

Major Toth stood and nodded. "We'll do everything humanly possible, Captain, to save all of them."

"No, I don't think you understand, ma'am." Victorio's heart raced. He swallowed back his apprehension. "It's not just my desire to rescue a fellow officer and one of my own. It's that, well... Blue Bird is carrying my son."

She was cold and cramped, and every muscle ached. She tried wiggling her arms and legs, but additional bindings crimped her knees together and her hands seemed to be fully encased in some kind of soft, yet sturdy, molding. She had adequate oxygen, too much in fact. Her mind swam in and out of dizziness. From that, she knew instinctively that she was being held by the Gulo.

One minute, she was fleeing a wall of high-velocity shards. The next, she was spinning out of control and losing consciousness. Then she woke up in a box, attached to some kind of conveyor, and every once in a while, the box would move, then stop, and then some furry snout would push itself against the box's small, steel honeycomb view panel, sniff generously, then drop water or rancid bits of fish-like meat into the cage near her mouth, where she could only lap droplets or chew the food off the cold metal floor. The meat was disgusting, and she was surprised that she did not vomit from it, nor go hungrier as the hours wore on. But despite its unsavory flavor and smell, the meat must be rich in nutrients, she figured. Perhaps the water had something in it as well; it had a warm, rusty flavor.

"I'm sorry, Vic," she whispered to herself over and over as the dizziness shoved her back and forth into sleep. "I should have returned to formation when you ordered it."

But would that have made a difference? The explosion of chaff was so swift, so strong, it's doubtful that anything in its wake would have survived. *My love could be dead,* she thought, and tears streamed down her nose to drop onto the box's floor, mixing with the water drying there.

When she slept, she dreamed of dancing, dancing the way Yusn Life-Giver had taught the *Ga'an* mountain spirits before he had sent them to earth to teach the Apache people how to live good, honorable lives. In her dreams, she swirled round and round, chanting the songs, mimicking the movements of the *Ga'an*, reaching the kind of spiritual oneness with the earth and the stars that only dancing could provide. She tried moving her arms and legs to her chanting, but they could not move, and then she would awake and remember where she was, and she'd cry again.

I have failed you, my love. I deserve death.

But she wasn't living for herself anymore, was she?

The bottom of the box gave way, and she fell hard to a solid rock floor. She yelped, praying that the sudden jerk of her body did not damage the child. She grimaced but tried not to cry. *Do not give them the satisfaction.*

Rough paws grabbed her up, cut her bindings, removed her chains, and dragged her along the floor. Her hands were still held tightly by that substance. She tried raising her head to look at who had taken her, but all she saw were shapes against a bright white background. Nothing was in focus.

She was being muscled along by two figures; that was as much as she could tell. And judging by their grip on her arms, they were strong. Warriors, probably, ones used to delivering rough treatment to prisoners. She tried pulling an arm away, just for show more than practicality. She was too weak to put up much of a fight. There was no chance of her escaping, but she too was a warrior, and by Yusn she wasn't about to let them think that they had the better of her. *I am Blue Bird... I am the lightning flashing and streaking.*

She was naked. She suddenly realized it as her vision began to return. Her captives didn't seem to care. To them, she probably looked like a disgusting, naked vole. They had thick fur down the length of their bodies, and now she could see that one was half black, half white. The other was a muddled grey, with patches of white around its snout and hands. Beautiful pelts, she conceded. How lovely they would look on her trophy wall. Over their shoulders hung bandoleers with some kind of ammunition, and at their waists, holsters occupied with some kind of blasters. One of their needle pistols, perhaps, or a slug-thumper. It was not uncommon for Gulo warriors to have both, although most of their pilots did not carry sidearms in the cockpit. These two were clearly footmen, guards probably. Both had little paunches. Gulo pilots were very thin.

A door slid open in front of her, and she was thrown to half tumble, half slide down into a tapered vat, shaped almost like the inside of an old grain silo. She came to rest at the bottom. The guards screeched something at her in their indecipherable tongue, and the door shut tight.

She lay there, her eyes closed, until she felt warm water begin to build up around her. She sat up quickly and watched as the water poured in from tiny jets beneath her and filled the vat. She panicked at first, afraid that it would never stop, afraid that she would drown here never having the chance to say goodbye to Victorio. But as it reached her chest, it stopped, and the substance around her hands began to dissolve until it turned into a soft, milky soap with a gentle lilac fragrance. *Clever*, she thought, pulling her hands free and smashing some of it between her fingers. Then she lathered herself up from head to toe, generously applying the cleanser to crotch and armpits. She sighed deeply. It all felt so wonderful.

There was no dishonor in praising the technological cleverness of the Gulo. An Apache warrior gives praise to an enemy where it is warranted, and a wolverine-like race that had fought like savages for so long deserved respect. They were clever, ingenious creatures, albeit brutal to a fault. They rarely gave quarter, especially to pilots, and so as she cleaned herself, rubbing her arms and legs to rawness using a substance that served both as handcuffs and soap, she couldn't help but admire them. But that didn't keep her from wanting to put their pelts on her wall. That too was a sign of respect, although Blue Bird doubted the Gulo would agree.

"Don't rub too hard, Lieutenant," a male voice said to her through the faint light. "If that stuff gets under your skin, you'll itch like hell."

The voice scared her, and she dipped back into the water, leaving only her eyes above the surface. She looked up where the voice came and saw a man sitting there, on the lip of the vat, naked as a baby.

He flashed a meek smile and then saluted. "Don't be afraid, Lieutenant. We're all naked in here."

Blue Bird followed his finger as he pointed to places around the cylindrical room. There were five in total, four men and one woman, watching her from their perches. They seemed like vultures almost, waiting for her to die, to slip beneath the water and drown. She had killed a vulture or two in her time, though she figured that these were not inclined to take a chance. They seemed even more meek and broken than she was. How long had they been captives?

"I'm Master Sergeant John Beckman," the man said. He pointed again to each person clockwise around the room. "This is Second Lieutenant Yufus Mendala. Senior Starman Clara Hernandez. Sergeant Richard Hall. And Master Sergeant Winston Peele. We're all pilots from squadrons hit by the chaff and brought here, like you."

"How do you know I'm a lieutenant?" she asked.

He smiled again. "Everyone knows First Lieutenant Imala Grey—*Blue Bird*—of the Devil Dancers."

She looked at them again. Each, in turn, saluted her, and she felt even smaller, more exposed. She reluctantly saluted back, dropped the soap from her hand and pushed her hair out of her face.

"Do you know what they're going to do with us, Lieutenant?" Senior Starman Hernandez asked.

Blue Bird looked at the cold, shaking, and clearly scared woman. "No, Starman Hernandez, I don't. But I tell you what's not going to happen. We're not going to sit around here naked and afraid." She stood up proudly, no longer ashamed of her body. She placed her hand on her belly. "We're going to figure out a way to get the fuck out of here."

Setting the beacons was easy. Getting there would be the hard part.

Over the billions of years that it had existed, the Lacaille asteroid belt had created a ring around its star with an incalculable amount of debris ranging anywhere from fine dust particles to dwarf-size planetoids. Its orbit was, in general, spherical, but two nearby gas giants, on opposite sides of the ring, could easily disrupt the belt and cause major chaos within its outer bands. Huge rocks were constantly being thrown into the system. Lacaille was, in short, in the midst of a late bombardment period that prevented any of the possible smaller rocky planets from forming life. But the Gulo had found a small band within the center of the belt that was calm and yet protected by a cloud of detritus that made it ideal for their burrowing tendencies. The problem was that Victorio's squadron would have to maneuver its way through the most turbulent outer bands to reach their target. When asked why they couldn't simply come at the prison facility from the top or the bottom and miss the belt entirely, Major Toth showed them Gulo radar cones that spread out from the prison, making it all but impossible for any ship to go in undetected. And stealth was the key to this endeavor.

"If they know we're coming, what's the point?" Major Toth said in the briefing. "The Gulo are not looking for small actions against their facilities. They are concerned about fleets. So you'll go in under the protection of the belt. There are high concentrations of iron in that icy field. Gulo radar has trouble penetrating it. If you move in loose formation, using the larger rocks for protection, you should be able to sneak right up on them, place beacons and be at the extraction point before anyone's the wiser."

It's that simple, eh? Victorio wanted to reply but forced himself to keep quiet. Arguing the point would not help matters. In truth, she was right. The only way this was going to work was if the Gulo were ignorant of the operation. At some point, of course, that plan would fall apart. That was a given. But now, his job was to set the beacons, and the best way to get in and out undetected was through the belt itself. His men hated the idea, and so did he.

The carrier *Apollo's Breed* dropped into system, and the newly-reconstituted Alpha Squadron of the Devil Dancers launched. The carrier then disappeared, and if the Gulo had noticed it at all, they would have interpreted it as one of many scout ships the Union sent in to take a peek from time to time. Hopefully, they would not think it odd for a carrier to conduct such a mission. Victorio hoped that were true, as he ordered the squadron to form Eagle Pattern, the longest, loosest formation in their trick bag. A tight formation in this environment would be tantamount to disaster. And there would be no Clown for this mission. Each pilot knew his or her duty, each knew what rock "cell" they had been assigned to mark. No one would break formation on this run... unless it was absolutely necessary to do so. And the most important order: do not leave anyone behind. If a fighter turned up lame and the pilot could not be retrieved... kill him. Colonel's orders.

He regretted that he and his pilots had not had time to dance. But there would be time for that later, when the rescue mission began, when their lives would most assuredly be at stake, and when it would be necessary for him to don the persona of the *di-yin* shaman and call upon Yusn Life-Giver for courage and strength. One did not abuse the power of a shaman, nor did he or she dance frivolously for small things. When it was most needed, when the burdens and stresses of life were the greatest, that was when the *Ga'an* mountain spirits danced, and the Life-Giver listened. Victorio hoped that wherever she was, Blue Bird was dancing.

She was an independent person. That was why she was still flying missions in her condition. She had to get in that "one last flight" before she turned her back on it forever. There was no returning, she said, after the baby was born. Some women in Union service did so, but not Blue Bird. "When it's over, it's over," she had said to him when she had told him of the baby. "I want to tuck myself away on some backwater rock, far from war, and live, sleep, and dream. I want to make more babies and live a good, honest, Apache live." The sub-text of all this, of course, was that he was supposed to join her, and even if she hadn't said it directly, he could see it in her eyes. He was expected to retire as well. Both of them were certainly eligible for it, having served more years than most pilots lived. But the war wasn't over, and how could he turn his back on it now, when they were so close to winning. Were they? All indications across the warplane suggested that the Gulo were near defeat. Was that just wishful thinking? It was hard to say, especially against such a brutal adversary. *She wants me to go with her and make a thousand babies, but how can I?*

He put the question out of his mind and flew into the asteroid belt, dodging boulders and floating with the vector to swing around a series of house-sized rocks orbiting each other. ISR indicated that moving in concert with this cluster of asteroids would allow them to use their gravity to slingshot through a dust cloud and get to their destination a lot quicker and without expending valuable fuel needed to reach their extraction point. "Steady, now, my warriors," he whispered over comm. "Let the cluster do its job."

Shines Like the Sun came up close on his three o-clock, closing the pattern a bit too early, but Victorio let it go. He gunned his engine slightly to overtake Shines' aggressive move. Shine fell back obediently and turned the nose of his *Radiant* up to swing just above the ejecta blanket on the largest of the asteroids in the cluster. The maneuver propelled his fighter forward at double speed. He couldn't see them, but Victorio imagined Shines' ghost-white teeth chattering at the G's he was pulling with such a move. He smiled and let his second-in-command take the lead, but followed close behind, mimicking the move to keep pace.

The others in the formation found their own way to slingshot around the cluster, and when they were all past the danger point, they flew together into a thick cloud of dust. Victorio hated dust, had flown through it more times than he cared to say, but such was the reality of stellar flight. One could not avoid getting into "the soup" as it was often called. A cloud could have anywhere from fine dust that could clog engines, to basketball-sized rocks that could tear a fighter apart. The *Radiant* was equipped to handle such debris with its magnetized hull able to detect metallic ore in the cloud and then reverse its magnetization to "repulse" the debris out of the way. Anything that could not be pushed was usually not worth worrying about. The *Radiant's* hull was pretty sturdy otherwise.

They emerged from the cloud. Victorio did a scan of his pilots. White Stallion's engine efficiency had dropped by twenty percent, and Shines' was down by ten. *Shit!* The rest were okay, including his own, but this might cause problems.

"Shine, Stallion," he said, letting everyone in the squadron hear the conversation. "Change of mission. I want you, Shine, to take Cell 2 and Stallion Cell 4. Both cells are on the outer left of the complex, closer to the extraction point. If your engines lose further viscosity, you're going to have to haul ass. I'll take Cell 5."

"Yes, sir," Shines said, "but that will require a formation shift now to get into position."

"In five, four, three..." Victorio counted it down. "Now shift!"

He and the other two pilots banked right, and Shines and Stallion dropped below them and then banked left to take up the end position on the eagle's wing. The needed shift slowed them down, and so they were now 3.256 seconds off-schedule. Victorio sped up his *Radiant* to make up the time.

"Now assume deployment formation," he said, drifting down as had been planned. The others moved up or down the formation as required to align themselves perfectly with the complex to set their beacons. Victorio reviewed the formation on his display and signed approval. A little behind schedule but things were looking good. No indication yet of them being detected.

The prison faded into view on his active display, a green three-dimensional object with red beacon placement lights flashing along its structure. The facility was large, huge in fact, a complex of asteroids and tunnels whose beauty belied the deadly, radiated dust and rock ocean in which it resided. Victorio paused just for a moment to admire its engineering, and then he punched in last-minute orders to his pilots.

"Align your *Radiants* per the coordinates," he said, setting his own so that it would glide carelessly over Cell 5. His was the largest and most central asteroid, clearly the epicenter of the facility. He made a final check on his beacons; all ready to go. "Easy now… slowly, slowly… and, go dark!"

Each *Radiant* fell silent and disappeared off his display, engines roaring down. Inertia would take them over the target, and they would look like nothing more than star stuff in the vast field of dust. Victorio closed his eyes and let his fighter drift, hitting the realignment jets just enough to keep him on-target. He took this time to pray.

He mouthed a wedding prayer. Odd, perhaps, given the situation, but one that Blue Bird liked and wanted recited at their wedding if they ever said their vows to each other. He closed his eyes and prayed.

> *Now you will feel no rain,*
> *for each of you will be shelter for the other;*
> *now you will feel no cold,*
> *for each of you will be warmth to the other;*
> *now there will be no loneliness…*

The beacon symbols flashed ready. Victorio let his hand drift to the display, finished the prayer in silence, and then released. The beacons dropped from his hull and floated to their designated targets. He did not know whether the beacons made their connections or not. They were forbidden to scan lest they be detected. He had to trust in the technology designed by Union engineers; he had to trust the plans of his superiors. It was difficult for him to do both, especially for a mission that was not about technology. This was about emotion and feeling. His woman, the mother of his child, his true second-in-command, was down there, somewhere in one of those asteroids. What was happening to her? Was she safe? Was she hurt? Victorio let the beacons fall and closed his eyes... *where are you, my love?*

His display indicated success. He opened his eyes quickly and activated his engines and comm-link. "Run!" he yelled. His *Radiant* sprang forward.

It was difficult keeping control. They barreled through the dust toward the extraction point. It was exhilarating. The speed, the G-force. Breath caught in his throat. Every muscle tensed as he searched his display for the extraction signal. There it was, *Apollo's Breed,* just coming into system, waiting for them, but with strict orders to leave at the designated time regardless of success. Time was tight, indeed, but they'd make it. Victorio allowed himself a smile.

White Stallion's *Radiant* flashed red. "Report your status?"

"It's my engine, Captain," he said frantically. "It... it stalled on re-ignition. I can't get it to turn over with consist..."

"Manual override," Victorio said, punching his own display to try to access Stallion's controls. If he couldn't do it, Victorio would do it for him. But there was too much interference; Victorio himself couldn't get a lock on the controls. "Manual override!"

"I can't, sir," Stallion said through the clutter. "The engine is pulling too much power trying to reignite. It's in loop."

"Eject, and I'll swing around to get you."

"No, sir!" Shines Like the Sun's said. "With respect, our orders are clear. The carrier will not wait. If you swing back, you'll be left behind, and I'll be forced to kill you both. Colonel's orders."

"He's right," White Stallion said. "I am prepared to meet Yusn, Captain. You must fire on my ship... now!"

Fuck! To lose a man on such a silly matter: engine trouble. Victorio gnashed his teeth and cursed silently again. "No, I will not fire. Damn the orders. Neither my hand nor Shines' will end you, Lieutenant. Stand firm. You are a Devil Dancer. You are strong. Be the lightning, and we'll come back for you."

He didn't wait for a response. He turned off his comm and flew silent, fighting back a tear. He was lying to the young man. There was no coming back in the vacuum of space, not under these circumstances anyway. The noble ideal of never leaving anyone behind... it was a nice sentiment on paper, nice for the press. But there would be no coming back. Without an engine, White Stallion would drift forever in the belt, be torn apart by debris, or find his end on a larger rock, to await suffocation or to freeze. *How ironic*, Victorio thought as he ordered Eagle Pattern and shifted into position as the body of the bird, *the best chance Stallion has to survive is to be taken prisoner by the enemy.*

Victorio put all of this out of his mind and focused on the extraction point.

Blue Bird watched from her cell as White Stallion was dropped into the vat. He rolled, like she had done, to the bottom, and landed with a *thunk!* He was a big man, almost too big for regulation flight, but he was strong, vibrant. Well, he used to be. Now, he was bloody, huddled, and exhausted. He had been savagely beaten before being placed in here with the rest. She could see the cuts and bruises on his bare skin, a patchwork of blue and black splotches mixed with the smear of blood. He would wear his wounds with pride, she knew. Just like they all had done for days.

One after the other, each prisoner had been taken away and interrogated for hours. With the help of a translator, the Gulo had figured out enough of the human Common language to ask the kinds of questions they needed to know: "Where will you attack next?" "Who is your commanding officer?" "What are the plans for invasion of *Hiko-Shee*." Blue Bird had no idea where that planet was, or if it were a planet at all. Surely, there was a name for it in Common, but the Gulo refused to share with them any startography to show where it was in relation to this sector. And when a prisoner did not answer the questions to their interrogator's satisfaction, they were punished, usually by a punch or slap to the face, or a sturdy steel rod to the back. Starman Clara Hernandez once tried to fight back; she got three teeth removed the hard way.

"Stallion," Blue Bird whispered through her bars. "It's me. Lieutenant Blue Bird."

The weakened pilot raised his head, tried looking in her direction. He opened his mouth to speak. She stopped him with a wave through the bar. "Shh! Don't talk. Don't tell me why you are here. They may be listening. I just wanted you to know that *I* am here. You are not alone."

That seemed to calm him and slowly, he rose up on his knees and sat there, naked, trying to shake off the pain of his wounds. "Do not worry," Blue Bird said. "This is a cluster cell, shower, and bath. You will be cleaned and then put into a cell like us."

He smiled through a fat lip, nodded, and waited. A portal opened above him. White Stallion looked up, waited for the water to come.

A high-speed jet of super-heated steam hit him in the face.

He had little time to scream before his skin peeled away, leaving nothing but white-hot skull and jaw. The strike was so intense that the stream punctured through his face and entered his chest. Blood poured through the gap in his neck, and White Stallion hit the steel floor again, shook violently, then stilled forever.

Blue Bird howled in terror, pulling on her bars, rattling her door. Tears streamed down her face, and she could hear the others screaming too, howling, cursing.

A powerful voice, metallic and prolonged, rang through a speaker system and echoed across the circular room. It wasn't a Gulo voice; it was digital.

"You will all die this way if you do not answer questions!"

A door opened, and two Gulo security guards entered. They moved quickly to Starman Hernandez's cell, opened it, and pulled her out. She fought. One hit her across the forehead with the butt of his rifle. The other pushed her down into the vat until she came to rest beside the steaming corpse of White Stallion.

"No," Blue Bird said, pulling on her bars. "Please, I will talk. I will talk! I will tell you what you want to know. I am the ranking officer, Lieutenant Imala Grey, Blue Bird of the Devil Dancers, commanding officer Victorio Nantan. Please... leave her alone. I will talk on everyone's behalf!"

The Gulo paused, looked in her direction. They seemed to confer with each other as they stood over the shaking body of Starman Hernandez. For her part, she pulled herself up on her elbows and shook her head at Blue Bird, silently imploring her to retract her offer. An honorable gesture, Blue Bird admitted, but she ignored it. No one else would die as White Stallion had just done. *Let us live to fight another day.*

Her cell door opened, and Blue Bird stepped out. They had allowed them modest clothing; a thin white shirt and a tan loincloth. Blue Bird saw it more like a breechclout, and under better circumstances, she might have enjoyed wearing it. It reminded her of part of her dress as a *Ga'an*-dancer. She so badly wanted to dance, but she would not allow these beasts the pleasure of seeing her happy. They did not deserve to know Yusn, to *know* joy.

The Gulo pressed his rifle to her head and pushed her toward the exit door while the other dragged Hernandez back into her cell. Blue Bird looked at all of them as she passed them; their desperate, terrified faces looking at her through their bars. As she passed, she prayed for all of them to find peace, harmony, and asked Yusn to calm their fears.

In her mind, she danced for each of them.

Major Toth had called in Colonel Tambe for the Debrief.

Victorio stared the colonel in the eye and did not flinch. "It was not a dereliction of duty, sir, as I see it. I was not going to kill one of my own simply because he had engine problems."

"Your orders were clear, Captain," Tambe said with excessive confidence that comes with being, in effect, God on earth. He was the ranking officer and, for all intents and purposes, held the title of General, even though he refused to wear it. Tambe was cagey that way. "Do not leave anyone behind alive. If the Gulo picked him up—"

"It's unlikely, sir" Victorio interrupted, "given the amount of debris in that field. We lost contact with his black box eighteen hours ago, sir. Our best assessment is that his *Radiant* was destroyed by that debris."

Nausea gripped the pit of his stomach with that admission. The thought of Stallion dying in the cold silence of space was almost too much to bear. *But at least he didn't die by my rockets.*

"I hope you are right," Tambe said, walking over to stand next to Major Toth. "Because if he was captured, the mission's in peril. Major Toth will be placing a reprimand in her name on your permanent record, and further disciplinary action might be taken after this matter has concluded. Do you understand, Captain Nantan?"

Victorio grit his teeth. "Yes, sir."

Colonel Tambe's expression softened, and he sighed deeply. "I like you, Captain. That's why I recommended you for this job, but please do not put me in the position of regretting that decision. This has to be run strictly by the book. You love your men, and I understand that. I respect that. But your failure to follow this order might have put your second-in-command in serious danger. They might all die, or never be freed, which is tantamount to the same. You have the authority to make tactical changes that are prudent to the success of the mission; you *do not* have the authority to ignore a direct order from me or from Major Toth. Is that clear, Captain?"

Fuck you! "Yes, sir."

Tambe nodded. "Very well, then let's put the matter behind us and proceed. Major." The colonel stepped aside and allowed Toth to activate the virtual image of the Gulo prison. The outline of the asteroid complex blinked into view, and then wave after wave of detail set itself in place as the image refreshed left to right. "Two beacons failed to activate." Toth pointed to a portion of the complex that revealed only the outline of its outer crust; there was no image of what was beneath its layer of rock. "They were set properly, but for some reason, they have not projected. The rest of the interiors are coming in nicely."

Victorio scanned the image himself, trying hard to ignore the agitation that he felt about the reprimand and tamping down what he truly wanted to say about it.

Taken as a whole, the prison was vast and unwieldy. Pods of circular rooms, access chutes, walking tubes, ladders, and various and sundry equipment Victorio was sure represented all the hardware and infrastructure needed to keep a facility like this running. Taken together, the thing was as large as a city. How in the hell were they going to find Blue Bird in that morass?

"These three smaller cells," Toth said as she pointed, letting her finger slip through the green molded light of the floating image, "we believe are barracks for the Gulo themselves. Mess halls, conference rooms, docking bays, what have you. We're not entirely convinced that this complex is strictly a prison facility, sir. It appears to serve many purposes, and judging by the number of bays there are, it can house a substantial amount of fighter craft if necessary."

Colonel Tambe looked up from the display. "Captain, did you experience any enemy fighter response?"

Victorio managed to shake his head without seeming annoyed. "No, sir. We received no resistance whatsoever."

"Which makes us think that the Gulo are not concerned with any attempt on our part at attacking this facility; its security is minimal." Toth reversed the poles of the image so that the larger, central cell was at the top. "Either that, or they're stupid, which I highly doubt. Assuming that your pilot was not captured, Captain, our beacons should be operable for another seventy-two standard hours, and then they'll dissolve into dust and float away. By the end of that time, we should have good visibility of all heat signatures within the complex itself. Then it'll be a matter of determining which ones are Gulo, and which are human."

"That shouldn't be a problem," Victorio said. "A Gulo's core body temperature tends to run eight to ten degrees hotter than a human's..."

Toth nodded although it was clear by her glare that she did not appreciate the comment. "We'll sort it all out, Captain." She turned back to Tambe. "We'll also be able to see the flow of body traffic throughout the complex. We'll be able to determine from that where the Gulo reside in large numbers, and then be able to make final plans on how and where we attack."

Victorio pointed to the one long access tube that connected the three small cells to the large central cell. "It might be necessary to hold off the flow of Gulo from those small cells, penetrate the tube... there, perhaps, and bore sight laser cannon down the tube. If we can hold off their rush of guards from their barracks, we'll have a better chance of operating effectively in other places."

"We?" Major Toth said it as if what Victorio had said was a joke. "You and your men will be flying CP, Captain, to keep any reinforcements from docking and giving *my* men trouble."

Victorio nodded. "Yes, I understand that, sir. I was just giving you my best opinion based upon more than a decade of service... sir." *They might outrank me, but they both need to remember that I have been fighting these beasts longer than both of them combined.*

"Yes, we know this, Captain," Tambe said, clearly disinterested in allowing the conversation to degenerate into comparing penis sizes. "And we appreciate your input." Tambe stepped away from the table and said, "That's all for now. Keep me posted on your progress, both of you. I want this mission ready to go within six standard days. We wait much longer, and we'll lose the initiative. That complex is in constant motion. In eight days, it'll be out of our range and too close to their reserve fleet within the ring. We have one shot at this, people. Do you understand?"

"Yes, sir," they both said almost simultaneously.

Colonel Tambe nodded. "Good. Let's do it right."

He left, leaving them both there at the table, the image slowly rotating. Major Toth flicked it off and said, "If it had been me, I would have dismissed you."

"Thankfully, Colonel Tambe is smarter than you are. He knows, sir, that there is no other squadron capable of doing this job, of providing the combat patrol you need to get it done. If he had relieved me, the mission would have failed before it even began."

Toth gnashed her teeth. Victorio could see the fury behind her eyes, could see that in her heart, she knew he was right. The truth boiled beneath her skin. She moved up to him slowly, stared at him face-to-face, and whispered softly, "Let's hope your man died the way you say, Captain, because if he was caught, the mission is already lost."

She smiled, nodded, and walked away.

The question of what the Union pilot (White Stallion) was doing when he was caught came up during interrogation, an interrogation that saw Blue Bird being stricken more than once.

Her face was bloody, swollen, her teeth hurt, but thankfully, she had not lost any. The Gulo who had taken her from her cell instead of killing Starman Hernandez had worked over her face time and again. She had answered their questions as honestly as she could, including the Stallion one, given the limitations of their translation equipment. The Gulo had created a program that could interpret human Common tongue and spit it back; Gulo facial structure could not articulate the words effectively. More words than not were garbled in translation.

They beat her face, but not her stomach. *They must know*, she thought, wiping blood from her mouth again. *But what does it matter to them if I'm pregnant?*

Another hour of useless questions and answers. She was ready to pass out. Her interrogators removed her bindings and left her there, alone in the cold room. She fell to the floor, stayed still for a long while, then tried to rise. She looked through a swollen eye toward the walls, the door they had come through. Hermetically sealed and near impossible to see any crease. Even if she wanted to escape, she had nothing to pry the door open, and then what? She was half-naked and weak, in severe pain. What could she really do, but stare at the small desk and the translation device that sat on it? *Destroy it, that's what I can do.*

She stumbled toward the desk. She reached out to the device, put a hand on it. The door opened again.

She fell, startled, and watched as a Gulo of pure white stepped into the room. No accoutrements whatsoever, no metals or stripes, no symbols on a uniform to denote stature or rank. It wore nothing. Its fur was so white as to be almost silver. It was even more beautiful than *Gingu-Sha*, the Gulo ace the Devil Dancers had killed years ago in retaliation to Naiche Blackclaw's death. But there had been little left of his pelt after the fire had swept through his cockpit, much to the chagrin of the squadron.

"You'd look good on my wall," Blue Bird spit, scrambling back as the Gulo came forward. "I'd even preserve your face, and I'd wear you like a wolf cloak when I danced."

The Gulo moved to the translator and studied Blue Bird's words that rolled out on the screen. It didn't seem to quite understand the translation, the reference to *wear* and *dance* particularly problematic. Then a light came on in its mind. It plucked fur from its arm. It offered it to her in an open palm and spoke a few words, the translator sounding them out. "I like my hair too. Take some, as my gift."

Blue Bird refused. The Gulo shrugged, let the hairs drop, and stepped aside. It motioned to the chair.

"Oh, I see how it is," she said defiantly, but crawled to the chair anyway. "Bad cops have gone to get coffee, and so the good cop is going to make a try. Well, good cop, I won't tell you anything I haven't said already. You can go to hell."

She spit as she fell back into the chair, but luckily the blood mixed with mucus did not land on its target. Instead, the Gulo patiently knelt down in front of the translator, and said, "I am not 'good cop'. I am *Gudu-Ma*, a Brood Mother of the *Gudu-Lakeeti*. What is your name?" *You do not deserve to know my Devil name.* "Imala Grey."

Gudu-Ma reached out her clawed hand and touched Blue Bird's trembling stomach. The Gulo's touch was warm, surprisingly soothing and gentle. "You are brood mother too?"

Blue Bird shook her head, fought back tears. "No. He is my first child."

Gudu-Ma nodded and removed her hand. She then arched her back and puffed out her chest and stomach. There, Blue Bird saw eight small black teats peeking out through her thick white fur. *Gudu-Ma* rubbed them up and down generously and curled her snout, revealing sharp black teeth, as if she were smiling. "I have a large brood, with six more coming."

"You are pregnant now?" Blue Bird asked.

The translator didn't seem to understand the term 'pregnant'. Blue Bird said it again, this time pointing at *Gudu-Ma's* belly.

The Gulo understood and nodded. "Very soon, they will be born, and the *Gudu-Lakeeti* will grow."

"And you are still in service in your condition? What does your husband think of that?"

The translation choked on her question, and Blue Bird managed a chuckle. "Forget it. It's not important." She adjusted herself and leaned back in the chair. "But I will state again, *Gudu-Ma*, that I do not know the answers to the questions I've been asked. I can lie to you if you like, but I'm a mid-ranked Union officer. I'm not given high-level information like that. None of my cellmates know the answers to these questions either. Capture and torture an admiral, and leave me and my son the fuck alone."

Gudu-Ma waited until the full translation came through. She then sat back on her haunches, deep in reflection. She scratched her shoulders, picked something from her fangs, and then sat down fully on the floor, her powerful legs crossed. "I do not care about any of the questions that our *Lakeeti* males have asked you. I want to know one thing from you, Imala Grey. Do you love your child?"

The question hit Blue Bird hard. Her heart sank, and she fought back tears once again. *Do not show weakness.* "Please," she said, ignoring her own advice. She sat firmly in the chair, her hands gripping the armrests tightly. "Don't hurt my son. Please don't. Show me, show me where *Hiko-Shee* is, and maybe I'll know something. I don't know where it is, but if you show me, maybe I can—"

Gudu-Ma made a shushing noise as if she were comforting a baby. She placed her hand on Blue Bird's knee. "I am not going to harm your child, Imala Grey. We are brood mothers, you and me. We are similar to our people. We make life, and that is important. But I want you to understand. We—" she said, pointing a claw at herself "—have five, six, sometimes eight babies at a time. Our population increases rapidly, and sometimes, as is now, the broods grow at an alarming rate. That is who we are; that is what we are, and we can no more deny our nature than you can. If *Hiko-Shee* falls, the *Gudu-Lakeeti* will, in time, be no more. It is our last stand." She confessed that last point, and it was clear from the white spittle forming along the soft pink-black gums of her jawline, that she regretted having to say it. She was nervous, sorrowful, and confessing something that she did not want to confess, admitting something that was painful to her. Blue Bird couldn't believe what she was hearing.

Are you that close to falling?

Gudu-Ma waited for a response. Blue Bird fell back into the chair again, sighed deeply, and said, "Okay. Show me where *Hiko-Shee* is... and I'll tell you what you want to know."

The Gulo did not move for a moment, perhaps surprised that her frank, straight-forward confession had actually worked. She sucked in the froth at her mouth, swallowed it, then turned to the desk. She touched a pad on its side, and a screen folded out, displaying a star chart. It refreshed as *Gudu-Ma* kept punching in coordinates, refreshed again, then settled on a segment of space that Blue Bird knew all too well.

The Sorrow Sea. A very dark expanse along the edge of the Keyhole Nebula, itself within the Carina Nebula. Pirate country, and the site of several battles between the Union and the Gulo. The supply line that hugged the edge of that vast expanse of rock and stardust was ripe for conflict. But why was it important? Other than Union supply ships, the area was bereft of living space.

She was about to ask the question when *Gudu-Ma* touched the pad once more, and the camera shifted rapidly through the nebulas, far into a portion of space that the Union knew about, but had not yet ventured into. Faster and faster the camera moved, until it focused on a large ball that Blue Bird could see was a G-type main sequence star. *Just like our sun. Earth's sun.*

Gudu-Ma then shifted focus to a small white-green dot, fourth orbit from the sun, a planet of vast oceans and thick, fibrous-green land masses. It was smaller than Earth, but even more beautiful, more pristine and seemingly untouched. But of course, that was not true, for as the planet rotated on the map, Blue Bird could see large black-grey areas of industry, roadways, tunnel complexes. It was a thriving planet. It was...

Oh my God!

"Is that... the Gulo origin planet?"

Gudu-Ma hesitated, lowered her head, then nodded. She seemed almost moved to tears, as she looked lovingly at the screen. Blue Bird knew the look; it was the same look she gave Earth whenever she returned home.

"If *Hiko-Shee* falls, Imala Grey, it will deliver a blow to the *Gudu-Lakeeti* that will never be repaired. We will be lost, spiritually and psychologically, and there will be no reason for us to hold back against your people. We will fight like savages, like we did when we lived as tribal moieties in the *Bada-Golo* Forests. We will fight to the death, and we breed far, far faster than you. I am asking you to consider the love you have for your people, for your child, for the male that gave you that gift inside you. We know that your people are planning an invasion. We have seen the ships. They reside right now in that part of space you call The Sorrow Sea."

Gudu-Ma rewound the map, back to the Keyhole Nebula and focused on a small section. She zoomed in a thousand-fold until it was very clear to anyone with eyes what they were looking at. A massive fleet. A Union fleet. More ships assembled in one location than Blue Bird had ever seen. Scores and scores of transport destroyers and carriers. She couldn't believe her eyes.

Why haven't I heard of this?

"We know that this fleet is headed toward *Hiko-Shee*, Mid-Ranked Imala Grey. We have intercepted communications about it. You think that the dust of the nebula protects your secret, but we know. If it moves toward our home, we will do everything in our power to stop it. We might not be able to, and *Hiko-Shee* might, in the end, lay in ruin, or be overrun by your force. If that happens, there will be no sanctuary, no security for humans anywhere. We will fight until the last of us is either victorious or dead at your feet. I'm trying to preserve your people's future as much as I am trying to preserve my own."

Gudu-Ma moved on all fours to crouch in front of Blue Bird. She laid her paw once again on her stomach. "So, I will ask you the question. What are your plans for the invasion of my homeworld?"

Bluster. That's all this was. The Gulo were finished. The fact that they would send in someone like *Gudu-Ma* to interrogate her was proof. They were terrified, and they were trying to scare her, convince her that if she didn't reveal the Union's plans, there would be total war. But wasn't there total war now? How many thousands, millions, perhaps billions, of souls lay dead on both sides. How could it get any worse than it was now? How could the Gulo get any more savage than they already were?

Blue Bird stared into *Gudu-Ma's* blood-red eyes and was about to say something snide. She stopped, looked deeper and saw the female there, the brood mother, the sympathy and emotion that only one with child could show. She was afraid, true, but she was strong, holding herself before Blue Bird un-wavering, her focus fixed on Blue Bird's own eyes. *Was she telling the truth? Were the Gulo capable of fighting even more desperately than they were now? If they had no homeward, if they had lost everything that defined them as a species...*

Blue Bird found herself reaching out to *Gudu-Ma*. She placed her hand on the creature's face, felt the heat burning off her fur, the warm breath on her fingers. "I'm sorry, *Gudu-Ma*, I don't know our plans. I'm telling you true. I don't know anything about an invasion plan. That's the first time I've even seen that fleet. On this, I am not lying. I would not lie to you."

The Gulo allowed Blue Bird's hand to linger, then she slowly pulled back, letting the hand drop. She pulled the skin of her snout back in a smile, rose up, and barked something to the door. It opened, and two male guards entered. They seized Blue Bird immediately.

"One more thing," Gudu-Ma said as they pulled Blue Bird to the door. "We know why your pilot was found floating in space above this complex. Your people are planning a rescue. We are prepared, and they will die just as you will die. Good tidings, Imala Grey. I fear for the fate of us all."

They pulled her away, and Blue Bird let the tears flow. She closed her eyes, sobbed silently as they dragged her through the hall back to her cell. She willed herself to focus on Victorio, saw his face in her mind, his beautiful black hair, his dimpled chin. She focused and tried to summon the *di-yin*. Flashes of lightning spread across his wonderful face.

Hear me, she said in her mind. *Hear me, Victorio, and know what I know.*

He saw a faint, filtered light, down a long corridor. Through his mind, he chased it, or rather, he became the light, the spark of a star, brilliant and unwavering. He was traveling fast, through the haze of his dream, a dream that only he could have. He was chasing a voice, a voice only he could hear.

Hear me...

It was her, calling to him through the incalculable distance of space. How he could hear her at this distance, he could not say, but she summoned the *di-yin* within him, and he listened.

Through her mind, he saw everything, where she was, who was with her, the bloody splotches on her face, her mouth.

She showed him the baby; it was okay, comfortable and small inside her. He saw scores and scores of Gulo soldiers, hundreds, fully kitted out with sidearms, shields, defenses. He saw other Union officers and enlisted scattered throughout three separate asteroids, some vibrant, some close to death. He saw the openness of the living spaces in the facility. From outside, it looked huge. From inside, infinite. That was silly, of course, so perhaps it was the way the dream warped the senses, how it changed his depth perception. He saw a shower, a pure white horse kneeling below a water spigot.

White Stallion!

The steam cooked the horse's flesh, and in Victorio's mind, he heard the screams of death. He tried waking, but Blue Bird would not let him, was not finished showing him what he needed to see.

The image then quickly turned to the dark, brutal expanse of The Sorrow Sea. Victorio knew it well, had been all through the Keyhole Nebula, chasing pirates, chasing the once-captain of the Devil Dancers, Magnus Coloradas. A friend turned traitor. *Why are you showing me this*, he whispered silently to her. *Why?*

The image of a large Union fleet came to him through the rock and dust of the nebula, a force so large it disappeared from his view into the event horizon. Then, the image swiftly shifted to an unknown star, to a small white-green planet, and Blue Bird whispered to him words that he did not want to hear.

He sat upright, breathless, heart pounding, shaking his head, wondering if he should heed the images in his mind, the words from her beautiful, but swollen, lips. Yes, he must, he decided, for to ignore them as fanciful illusions could mean suicide. Not only must he heed them, but he must convince Major Toth to do the same. Blue Bird had communicated by awakening the *di-yin* inside him; such power could not be ignored.

He got up and dressed. Toth and her commandos would be in training right now. She would be there, and by Yusn, he would make her listen to him for once.

He found them in the training block, the Bright Commandos, all fifteen, in zero-G conditions, bouncing through a maze of tunnels and simulated rooms, holographic images of the Gulo facility. This was a live-fire exercise, one of the last before they were scheduled to go. Victorio showed ID to enter the facility. He moved up to the edge of the observation deck, keeping behind the designated red line marking the danger zone. He found Toth propelling herself through the room, shooting, deflecting shots. He waved to her. She ignored him at first, but he motioned for her again. Finally, she disengaged and flew over to his position.

He helped her gain her hands and feet onto the catches and into the safe zone. She removed her helmet and unsnapped her shoulder pads. She was out of breath, sweaty, her hair a tangled mess. The expression on her face was unpleasant.

"What, Captain? We're in the middle of a training session here."

"The mission is compromised," he said, trying to maintain some semblance of decorum. Too much emotion and adrenaline were running through his body. He needed to calm down, take a breath, come at this from a more professional angle. But he couldn't.

"What are you talking about?" she asked.

"The Gulo know we're coming," he said again. "They're preparing for our assault."

Major Toth shook her head. "Nothing in our data indicates that they have any knowledge whatsoever of the mission. No beacons were detected; they dissolved on schedule. No indication of changes in movement patterns within the complex itself. Nothing."

"I'm telling you, they know. You have to change the mission, reschedule it for a different time."

"How do you know they're aware?"

"I've… seen it in my dreams."

Toth huffed, stepped back, shook her head, and found a seat on the wall bench. "Captain, I respect your culture's beliefs, truly I do, but with all due *respect*, I cannot alter the mission simply because you have had a bad dream."

"It's not just a bad dream, Major," Victorio said, moving closer to her. "This is real. You may wish to scoff at dream magic, but you cannot ignore the success of my squadron. The Devil Dancers are the finest pilots in the Union. We did not arrive at this stature by luck or by training alone. We call upon Yusn for guidance and strength. We dance like Ga'an to draw upon powers beyond the flesh. The Gulo know that we are coming. Blue Bird spoke to me, and she—"

"Oh, so now she's a *di-yin* shaman too?" Toth stood and shook her head. "No, no, no, Captain. There will be no more discussion of this. We will not alter a mission on a dream, a mission that has been planned with and approved by Colonel Tambe, and sanctioned by ISR. We go as planned."

She reached for her helmet. Victorio said, calmly and precisely, "The Gulo know of the Union's plan to invade their homeward."

That stopped the major in her tracks. She turned on him, grabbed his shoulder and pulled him into a corner of the room where the guards could not hear. "How do you know of that?"

Victorio smiled. "I've seen it in my dreams, Major. Tell me that I'm lying."

He could see the muscles in her jaw working violently. "You will not speak of it to anyone, or I swear I'll court martial your skinny ass."

"Why haven't we been told, Major? Why has the best squadron in the fleet, and one of its best commando units, not been mobilized?"

Toth shook her head. "We don't know yet whether this sector will be part of the invasion force or not." Her voice was low, almost inaudible. "That decision has not been made, and that decision is above our pay scale. We will not discuss it."

"It's a mistake, Angelica," he said, using her first name. A risky move, but under the circumstances, she could court-martial him now if she liked. This whole situation was too personal to rely on protocol. "Do you know your ancient Earth history? Do you know what it's like to lose your home? I do. The Apache do. We are the *Indeh*, Angelica. The dead, driven from Earth years ago, forced to live on other planets, to be acculturated into your way of life, to abandon what we hold dear."

"You've survived," Toth said, "and thrived."

Victorio nodded. "Only because we've never had the numbers, the weapons, to win. We had to, for practical reasons. That's not the case with the Gulo. We have been fighting them for over thirty standard years, Angelica. They are neither foolish nor weak. If we take their homeward from them, there will never be a time without war. It's one thing to drive them out of our living space, off our planets. It's another to annihilate them. The question is, do we live together, side by side, or do we die together? I signed up to defend Union space. I'm not so sure I joined up to humiliate an entire species. Did you?"

Victorio could see the doubt behind Toth's eyes. She was searching for an answer, one that she could not find. He understood. It was a difficult question to respond to and perhaps now was not the time to ask it. Nevertheless, he had to ask it, he had to put it out there, because even though their immediate task was to free prisoners at the Gulo complex, everything they did in this war was connected. 'All knowledge is connected,' isn't that what some White Eyes said long, long ago? It was true. Freeing Blue Bird and the other pilots and soldiers had everything to do with the invasion of the Gulo homeworld. It was part of the war of symbolism. Victorio understood that now, standing there waiting for the major to speak. Attacking a Gulo prison facility in a far-off asteroid belt was tactically and strategically meaningless. They would gain nothing by freeing those prisoners, save for symbolism. *We are not afraid of you,* the message read loud and clear. *We are not afraid to attack your most remote complexes, and we are coming... we are coming. Fear us!*

Toth did not answer. Instead, she said, "I'm sorry, Captain. I cannot authorize a change on your premonition. The mission stands."

She turned to leave, but Victorio grabbed her arm. "Then let me go with you. I know exactly where she is. I can pinpoint the location, save us a lot of time."

"You're not a commando, Captain. You don't have the training, nor the bone density anymore to work assaults. You're a pilot, and a damn fine one. Do what you do best. I need you on CP. If they try to bring in reinforcements, we're fucked. Stick to the plan. It'll work out."

She pushed past him, the conversation over. There was nothing more he could do. He had told her what she needed to know. If she chose to ignore it, that was her problem, not his.

"Major," he said. She sighed and turned to him again, hands on her hips, waiting. "My Devils will be glorifying Yusn through dance in Launch Bay A5. You are welcome to come and join us."

Toth managed a smile, nodded politely. "Thank you, Captain, but no. Go dance with your men, but do it quickly. We go at 1200 hours."

It was Victorio's turn to show surprise. "I thought we had another 72 hours."

"You're not the only one who knows how to improvise a mission, Captain. They expect us in 72; we'll hit them now. Go, dance, get ready, and good luck. *Ahagahe!*"

Colonel Toth put on her helmet and jumped back into the fray. Victorio watched her spin through zero-G.

He turned and walked out of the observation dock. He tapped his comm.

"Yes, Captain?" Shines Like the Sun's voice came through clear.

"Get up, and get the men ready," Victorio said. "We dance... now. We dance for Blue Bird."

In the launch bay, around a simulated fire, they danced. The four *Ga'an* impersonators from Alpha Squadron approached the flame, moving to music that only they could hear.

Victorio was the Clown this time. He had put on his brother Naiche's old uniform and headdress, and had lined his face and bare chest in thick white and red clay. He waited now until Walking Moth had reached a pitched fury with her movements, waited until she was fully in her trance.

Then he sprang toward the fire, spinning round and round like a dervish, while accepting the laughter of children, for he knew the traditional role of the Clown. Make them laugh. Make them—for a short time at least—forget their troubles and sorrows and glory in the life and world that Yusn Life-Giver had given them. Glory for a short time, until the call of war rang soundly once again in the vacuum of space and forced the Devil Dancer Clown to sacrifice himself—*herself*—for the good of the unit, the good of the Union. But no, not this time. This time, they were dancing before anyone was sacrificed. They were dancing for Blue Bird, still alive and fighting, fighting in her own way. She was tough, stubborn, willful, intelligent, everything Victorio demanded in a second-in-command, everything he wanted in a lover. He would see her face again, beaming, smiling back at him. He would watch her belly swell. He would see his child born and grow.

Across his bare chest lay an *izze-kloth*. Clipped to his belt were a bag of pollen and his war club. All of the dancers had them, and they wore them proudly as their rhythmic movements and singing filled the launch bay.

Some of the brass had come to watch, but not Colonel Tambe or Major Toth. That was fine, for Victorio wasn't sure if he could face the major right now anyway, worried that perhaps his eyes would betray the decision that he had made about the mission and his role in it. She would most certainly refuse, and perhaps even relieve him of duty, or delay or cancel the mission. None of those were viable options. If they didn't go now, then Blue Bird would be lost forever. So, they danced while the major was busy readying her commandos, and the colonel was making sure everything else about the mission was running smoothly. The Devil Dancers danced, and they would not climb into their cockpits and begin the mission until they were finished, until they had summoned the mountain spirits.

Victorio pulled his war club and waved it violently in the air, letting the heat from the fake flames wash his face as he leaned into the fire. He pinched his eyes shut, focusing on a memory of his childhood, evoking the image of himself and his brother, Blackclaw, sitting in freezing river water as the warrior tradition demanded. Who would admit to freezing first? That was the test that neither of them wanted to fail. And then afterward, racing one another to the top of a large hill with water sloshing in their mouths, oh so thirsty, but neither willing to drink. Blackclaw wins and shouts his joy, only to realize that he had drunk the water. Victorio spits his on a nearby rock and thus wins by default. Over and over again, these little tests of bravery, of strength, of courage, and stamina, all set up by their father, may Yusn guide him, to teach his sons how to be true Apache warriors. Blackclaw was a true warrior, but he was dead now, and Victorio had to carry on their father's good name and avenge his death whenever possible. So now here he was, dancing for Blackclaw once again, dancing for Blue Bird, dancing for them all.

Victorio opened his eyes and tossed a pinch of pollen into the fire. It popped and sparkled, and out of those sparks leapt a black bear, vicious and broad, claws splayed out, teeth snarling through a glaze of blood and bile. Victorio fell to the floor, his hands out to protect himself. The bear came toward him, but it stopped just before it swiped a paw through the air, missing his face by mere inches.

"Blackclaw?"

The bear roared. *So, you remember your brother.*

"How can I forget? I sent you to your death."

You made a command decision, and it failed. That is war.

"I am sorry, brother. I would give everything to bring you back."

I am at peace now. Focus on the mission.

"I am," Victorio said, "but have I made the right decision? Tell me, brother, is it the right call?"

The bear fell back to all fours, seemingly in deep contemplation. It wagged his head as if drying off. *I do not know these things, brother. You have danced your mind, and now you must act. But what I do know is that warriors will die on this mission. You will die.*

"But will I save Blue Bird?"

The bear raised up again on its hind legs, roared, and then slowly faded away.

Victorio stared into the flames and watched as the rest of the dancers continued to move in rhythmic streaks of red and blue and green around the fire. It was as if they did not realize that he sat there on the floor, or that he had had a vision. They danced and moved and sang, and it was a glorious testament to their skills and passion as Devil Dancers. Victorio smiled, not caring what the vision of his brother had told him. *You will die...* So be it. *Let me die. My* song *shall encircle these dancers.*

He raised his war club, and they halted. The flames flicked momentarily, then died away. The bay was silent, save for the low rumble of applause from lookers-on behind the observation glass. Victorio paid them no mind and instead stared proudly at his men, his pilots.

Shines Like the Sun removed his headdress. "What are your orders, Captain?"

You will die...

"Suit up!" He said, leaving no doubt in his mind about what he needed to do to save Blue Bird. "We're going to war."

The assault torpedo slammed into the connection tube between Cells 5 and 2, and Major Toth braced as she and her commandos were tossed about in their security straps. The impact was more violent than she had hoped, but their connection spot was perfect, just as it had been planned. The boring prow of the torpedo drilled a nice hole into the Gulo steel and gave them access to several hundred meters from Cell 2; plenty of room to set up a defensive line and block anything coming from Cells 2, 3, and 4. Hopefully. Things never worked as perfectly as designed, but this was a good start. The prow drilled, and her commandos readied.

Each checked their equipment. Muck Carbines with Smart Pellets and two laser pistols for each soldier. Enviro-suit with Sheath spider webbing that could withstand multiple high-velocity impacts. Two small flexible oxygen tubes sewn throughout the sturdy padding of the suit, with resealing tubes running into the helmet. Gravity boots in case the Gulo got clever. Two of the commandos also hefted heavy laser cannons; everyone carried two knives. Toth checked her status and confirmed readiness as each commando, in turn, did the same.

"Remember your training," Toth barked over the comm in her helmet, "and protect the ones beside you. No retreat: first to fly, first to die. Do not leave anyone behind. Ready?"

They raised their right arms and shouted their agreement. Toth turned to the boring prow as it drilled through the final layer of steel. The prow stopped whirling. It then opened like a flower and clasped itself on the other side of the hole, like fingers, and pulled the torpedo into place for disembarkation. Toth hefted her rifle, pulled out of her straps, and said, "Go!"

They poured out, meeting the first Gulo defense team with rapid fire of Muck Carbine and laser pistol. The Gulo employed a needle pistol and a gauss rifle that was excellent on assault, but the rate of fire was a little slow; their weapons required 1.3 seconds to recharge, recycle, and ready for another volley. The Muck fired its pellets in bursts of three in less than a second, and the lasers could fire either bursts or a steady stream of energy with enormous penetration power. These weren't standard-issue weapons. These were Spec-Ops weapons, and the Bright Commandos employed them well.

They took fire from the Gulo force, which slowed their landing, but they were ultimately able to return and clear the way by shattering the defenders and spraying their lifeless bodies across the tunnel through which they had descended upon the landing party. The Gulo were nothing more than a mesh of gooey red blood and matted fur. It was a shame really, Toth had to admit, to see so many good soldiers die so quickly, even enemy soldiers. She chuckled to herself at the notion. *I've been around Victorio too long.* Now, *she* was beginning to appreciate the enemy far more than she had done in the past. *Speaking of which...*

"Captain Victorio," she said through closed comm, "status check."

A brief pause, then, "Everything is fine, Major. CP operations proceeding."

"Any sign of incoming?"

"Negative. Clear skies."

"Very good. Let's keep it that way. We're in, and we're moving."

"Ahagahe!"

She did not respond but instead opened a general channel to her men. "Marcus, Rollings. Secure the perimeter. Bore sight those cannons down the tunnel and keep those bastards from rolling up behind us. Baker, Izago, you remain in support as well. The rest of you, follow me."

She waited briefly as the rest assembled behind her. She took a deep breath and tapped on her passive radar. Blips rolled into view across a faint image of the interior of Cell 5. That was the cell that housed the prisoners, according to their beacon scans. "Okay, boys. This is where we go. Right into the darkness."

She crouched, held her Muck steady, and moved. She began to feel sweat rolling down her face, and the internal environment of her suit kicked in to compensate. *Already sweating and the mission hadn't even begun yet.* That was a bad sign.

Toth suddenly wished that she had some of that lightning that Captain Victorio was always talking about.

"Are you sure this is the right thing to do?" Shines Like the Sun asked over a secure channel.

Victorio shook his head. "No, but I must do it. Toth won't listen to me, and they're looking in the wrong place."

There was silence, and then, "May Yusn guide you, sir."

"Thank you," Victorio said, moving to disengage his own security straps. "Maintain CP, kill anything that moves. Toth's right about one thing: If they land reinforcements, we're fucked."

"Yes, sir. We'll keep them at bay. Now... go get our Blue Bird."

Victorio smiled, killed the comm, and pressed the eject panel.

The canopy of his Radiant blew into space, and Captain Nantan followed, end over end, until he was able to activate the control jets of his suit to slow and control his movement.

He guided himself toward the jagged rock face of Cell 4. He pushed his jets as far as he dared, expending all fuel to maneuver through the thin veil of dust and rock. His suit would protect him from the light material, but if anything more substantial floated by, he'd be in trouble. He kept his mind and eyes focused forward, sipping oxygen to conserve it. By his calculations, he didn't have far to travel, but one never took a spacewalk for granted; doing so was a death sentence.

Through his visor, he saw his landing space, a small circular spot of rock and metal around an access hatch. In their passive scan of the facility, they had discovered a number of these hatches, and Victorio had wondered why Toth was against using them for entry. Her argument was simple: they provided access, sure, but they were also choke-points through which her entire team could be destroyed. So, go in like a hammer.

He expended the last of his suit's jet fuel, reached out and grabbed the hatch lever just before skipping off into the void, held tightly, and activated his gravity boots to gain even more security against the asteroid wall. He now breathed deeply, said a small silent prayer, then knelt down to assess his access point. He was pleased with what he saw.

Standard hatch style, similar to human design. No hermetic sealing or code requirements from the outside. Perhaps from inside, there were more security measures, but it was clear that once outside, the Gulo didn't want their maintenance crews getting stuck on the surface. Victorio settled down and focused on the small set of cogs and wheels that needed turning to open the door. They were tight, tighter than he had imagined they would be. He reflexively felt around his suit as if he would find a prying bar. He reached for one of the laser pistols on his thigh as if shooting the hatch would matter. But no. None of this would work. He gripped the wheel again and pulled counter-clockwise. Again and again, throwing all his strength into the wheel. Toth was right about one other thing as well: his soft, fighter craft body was not used to such strenuous activity anymore. He made a mental note to get back into shape if he survived this mission, and kept tugging.

Then it loosened. A little more, then more, until he was able to turn it freely. Another ten rotations, and then it opened. He stepped back, letting his boots hold him steady against the thick metal plate in the asteroid wall. Finally, the hatch gave way. A rush of oxygen roiled out of the hatch, dissipating instantly. He waited until it settled and then leaned over the hatch to look inside. Flashing red and green lights spread across his visor. *Well, they know I'm here.*

The warning lights did not concern him. He stepped carefully into the opening and pushed himself down, neither bothering nor caring to find purchase on rails or steps. He fell through the access hatch and landed hard in a corridor. He activated his helmet's scanner, looked left, then right, waiting in a crouch until his scanner was fully functioning. Despite the flashing lights, it was dark, the temperature in the corridor below human normal. The Gulo preferred it that way.

A side door opened fifty yards down the corridor. Three Gulo, armed with spiked gauntlets and Flash pistols entered. They hesitated, perhaps to settle their targeting. Victorio didn't hesitate. He drew two pistols strapped to his thighs and fired. The lead Gulo went down immediately. The others returned fire.

Damn! One of their shots tore into his suit and drew blood from his bicep. He rolled left, came up, fired both pistols again, and sent another to the floor. He cringed from the pain, but his suit was already re-stitching the tear and compensating for the immediate rush of excess oxygen in his environmental systems. He grew light-headed, shook it off, holstered his pistols, and drew his knife. The remaining Gulo charged.

His coat was brilliant, a silken black-and-tan with slugs bandoliered across his broad chest. His teeth were bared, his black tongue angled in rage, his eyes bright green and beaming through the flashing light. He leapt toward Victorio, his sharp gauntlets held forward like swords. He slashed out, and Victorio dropped and let the gauntlets whisk over his helmet a mere inch from impact. Its impetus propelled the Gulo into the wall of the corridor, but it was too thick, too powerful for the impact to matter. It recovered quickly and attacked again.

Victorio was ready, holding his knife forward, deflecting the first punch, dodging the second, and then feigning a move to the right to confuse the Gulo. It struck where it thought Victorio would be. Victorio lashed out at its exposed left, sending his blade deep into the creature's ribs, through its four-chambered heart, and into its lung.

The Gulo tensed, yelped pain as it realized what had happened. It tried to strike out once more before it fell, raising its massive arm to try and connect with Victorio's chest, but he was easily pushed aside. Victorio kept his balance and let the Gulo fall dead at his feet.

Three down, many to go.

He took a moment to kneel and pay his respects to such a brave foe. He reached into the Gulo's mouth, grabbed one of its front fangs, then took his knife and cut it out. Gulo teeth were strong and their root structure deep. It took a little while to work it free, but slowly it came out. Victorio held it up in the faint light.

Nice and bloody, and sharp. He smiled. "Thank you," he whispered while pocketing the trophy. "I will honor this to my last."

He stood, re-engaged his scanners, wiped his blade clean, put it away, and drew his pistols. He closed his eyes and began walking down the corridor, toward the interior of Cell 4.

Where are you, my love?

Boom-boom-boom!

The sounds were constant and loud, though muffled. They rocked her from sleep, from dreams that she was having of lightning, of her red-tailed hawks flying peacefully through the hot Southwestern sky. *Where are you...* She heard Victorio's voice in her mind, but the booming outside the facility awoke her. She opened her less-swollen eye, sat upright, and scrambled to her cell door. She looked out the barred window. Nothing but darkness.

Boom-boom-boom!

"Do you hear that?" It was Sergeant John Beckman's voice, rough and weak now that he'd been constantly beaten. But he was still alive. Blue Bird was thankful for that. Some of the others were not.

"Yes," she said, trying her door again to see if it would open. Of course, it wouldn't. "It's coming from outside. Sounds like an attack." *Victorio is coming.*

The revelation almost made her cry. *Don't come*, she wanted to scream. *They'll kill you.*

"We're being rescued." That was Starman Clara Hernandez, though Blue Bird could not see her tiny face through the darkness. She was glad to hear her voice.

"Maybe," Blue Bird said. "But we don't know for sure."

Boom-boom-boom!

The facility shook.

"Let us out!" Hernandez shouted through her window. She pounded on her door, cried out again.

"Stop it!" Blue Bird ordered. "Calm down, Starman. Keep your cool. We don't know—"

Red and green lights flashed outside the main entrance to the cell. Blue Bird's heart sank, fearing for what might come next.

She found herself shaking, though she tried putting that fear out of her mind with thoughts of Victorio and his voice. He was coming, and that right soon, as the Christian Bible might say. Where was he? Were the lights a sign of his approach? Who was with him? Surely the boom outside the facility was the Devil Dancers attacking, errant rockets or laser rounds hitting the facility. It had to be.

"We've got to get out of here!" Master Sergeant Winston Peele said, striking his door even louder. "We're going to die if we don't."

The lights came on, one blast after another around the cell. Faint golden light that cast long shadows across the central shower area. The light fell on a body, Second Lieutenant Yufus Mendala, who had been recently "cleaned" with high-pressure steam. He was dead, and he had been so for a long time. Blue Bird closed her eyes at the sight, and the others fell silent as well. What a waste!

Her door clicked open, and then so did the others', around the room. Even the empty cells opened. *Click-click-click!* Consistent with the booms from outside. At first, Blue Bird was afraid to move, afraid to imagine that there was any hope with this new situation. *It's a trick*, she thought. *They're trying to lure us out, to give us hope, and then they'll kill us all.* She hated herself for thinking this way. She had come into this situation so determined to see it through, so vital and willing to risk and suffer to be freed. But now... all she wanted to do was to curl up into a ball and hide in her cell.

No. She needed to be strong, for the ones that had survived at least, for Victorio who was most certainly coming. *Wake up! Wake up now!*

She shook her head clear and pushed on her door. It swung open. She stepped out into the faint golden light. The others did the same. She counted them. Only three left, besides her. Mendala and Hall were gone. She said a small prayer to Yusn for their souls.

"What do we do now?" Hernandez asked.

Blue Bird was about to shrug when the light brightened and a Gulo voice came over the comm. Translated speech, but she recognized the voice. "You are free, Imala Grey. Go now and quickly, before they discover you are gone. And may you birth your son in peace."

The door on the cell opened into the corridor flashing red and green.

"Why?" She couldn't believe what she was hearing, and who was saying it. *It must be a dream,* she thought, but the voice answered her simple question.

"Because I have faith in you, Imala Grey, Human Mother. You will remember what we spoke about if you survive, and you will tell your superiors about me, about what I told you, and you will make them understand. You will do this for both of us, so that we may both find peace in all this terrible, terrible chaos. Promise me that you will remember our words and that you will make them understand."

She couldn't believe what *Gudu-Ma* was saying, but the words came out before she could stop them. "Yes, I promise, but... where should we go? What should we—"

"Go straight! Follow the corridor down, and you will find that lightning you dream about."

Gudu-Ma's voice ended, and the prisoners were alone again, all of them looking at each other, not knowing what to do. *Should I listen? One brood mother to another?*

"Let's go!" Blue Bird said, moving toward the door.

"But we've no weapons," Peele said, "hardly any clothes. How are we going to—"

"I said let's go! We'll worry about the details later."

They fell in behind her, moving as fast as their oxygen-saturated and sleep-deprived bodies could move. Blue Bird stopped to help Starman Hernandez step up over the lip of the door and into the flashing corridor. A sharp buzzing sound hit them, pulsing in motion with the light. Blue Bird tried to ignore it and pressed forward.

No weapons. Little clothing. Weak and enfeebled. They looked near death. They were near death, but nothing would keep her now from finding Victorio. Nothing would keep her from saving her unborn son.

Where are you, *my love? Where are you?*

They passed through the first level of security easily enough. Too easy, she thought, though her commandos would disagree. If having to kill roughly two dozen Gulo in close assault—and some savagely with knives—was considered light, what constituted difficult? But resistance *was* light, regardless of what they might think. A cell block as full as this one seemed to be should have tighter security. Toth pushed aside the corpse of a pure black-furred Gulo from a bulkhead door and peered through the tiny window into the next corridor.

A nice, neat line of ten cell doors flanked the curving corridor. Ballast lighting led the way. No security.

Toth activated her comm. "Bring me a bomb."

One of her sergeants came forward and handed her a small metal object, flat on one side, curved like an eagle's egg on the other. The men stepped back, and she knelt until her helmet was centered on the door. She felt around on the door until she found the proper spot next to the lock compartment, then pressed the bomb's flat side into the door. There was an immediate, unbreakable seal. She then tapped out a code on the rounded surface, then stepped back. The bomb grew hot and red, flashed three times, and then exploded into the metal, through the door, and out the other side. Once the impact subsided, the remains of the bomb fell away, and Toth kicked the door in.

She let her men go forward, swarming through the corridor in front of the cell doors. "Check them all, in order, and stay in contact."

With two others, she guarded the entrance and took a moment to check in. "Victorio, come in. Captain Victorio, declare status."

There was a pause, then another pilot's voice came through. "Major Toth, this is Lieutenant Alfred Steele, Shines Like the Sun. Ma'am, I've assumed command of the Devil Dancers."

Her heart sank. "Captain Nantan is dead?"

"No, ma'am." He paused, seemingly reluctant to say. "Captain Nantan is in-mission. He's abandoned his Radiant and has entered Cell Four."

"What! How?"

Shines Like the Sun was about to explain when one of her men overrode the signal. "Sir! There is no one here. No prisoners."

"What do you mean?"

"There is no one in the cells, sir. The life signs we've been reading... fake."

She felt that sinking feeling in her chest, coupled with rage for Victorio. *Son of a bitch!* Not only had he blatantly disobeyed her orders, and Colonel Tambe's, but he might very well have been right all along in their last conversation before the mission began. The prisoners were not here. *Dammit!*

"Pull out!" She yelled over the comm, ignoring protocol. "Abort the mission! Return to the extraction point!"

One after another, her men reappeared from the cells and began flooding through the corridor. She let them pass her, waving them forward with agitated motions, her vital readings cresting per the displays in her helmet. "Move! Move!" She screamed again, then took her place in the exit.

But it was too late. Before she even cleared the broken door, Gulo came from everywhere. Behind them, in front of them, from break-out panels in the ceilings, propelling into the corridor, bearing laser rifles and assault-sluggers, popping off shots even before they touched the floor. Precision shots too, not the normal spray of assault fire. These were professional killers, the Gulo equivalent to commandos, and two of her men fell with smoldering strikes in the vulnerable crease between their helmets and suits. Toth opened fire, using their dead bodies as a shield against the relentless Gulo assault.

All of her men opened fire, a heavy concentrated assault that saw the destruction of the first Gulo wave. Yet, more appeared. As one fell, another came through the ceiling or up the corridor to plug the gap, a maddening swarm of killers, howling, screeching, filling the deadly space between them with laser and slug fire. One of Toth's men went down, and she responded by splitting the head of his killer.

Another Gulo wave down and Toth was beginning to feel good about their chances. But more Gulo appeared. She removed her clip and popped in another. She had enough Muck rounds for several more waves. They had enough laser power to shoot for hours. But men were falling, and eventually, the ammo would dry up, the batteries would grow cold.

She focused her fire on the nearest Gulo and mouthed a silent prayer. Not to God; to Yusn Life-Giver.

Don't pray to my god, Victorio thought as he felt Toth's prayer in his mind, waiting until another Gulo patrol slipped past him. *It ain't his goddamn fault you're stuck!*

He pushed those thoughts from his mind. He shouldn't be angry with Toth. She was following the orders of a superior. Not doing so could put an officer in severe jeopardy. A long-term career still mattered to her; not so much to Victorio. Right now, all that mattered was finding Blue Bird and his son, alive.

He kept low and moved quickly, hugging the right wall of the corridor where the better shadows lay. He called upon an Apache incantation, one that he had called upon many times before.

> *Right here in the middle of this place*
> *I am becoming Mirage.*
> *Let them not see me,*
> *For I am of the sun*

He willed himself to be invisible, but of course, that was silly. He wasn't one of those literal shamans who believed in that kind of power. There was shamanic power in the world, indeed, and dream magic was real. But there was no incantation or ritual that could make a man become invisible or impervious to death. Some technologies that would bend light and confuse radar and the naked eye were being developed, but they would, in the end, have limited functionality. Invisibility resided in the purview of the gods, and they shared their powers sparingly. No. He recited the incantation for strength, to focus his mind on getting through this terrible situation, to make himself realize that even here, in enemy territory, one could pull his natural strength forward to propel him to victory. His name was "Victorio" after all; it was his responsibility to make sure victory lay at the end.

The radar display in his helmet showed several life forms moving toward him, about one hundred meters down the left corridor. And that way lay the cells, according to his scans. He needed to go straight down that hall. Perhaps he could find a route above, in the ceiling. There were access chutes everywhere. But these forms were different, larger on scan, and they moved differently from Gulo security personnel.

Victorio paused and reached out with his thoughts, but his adrenaline was up, his heart rate high, his focus erratic. The incantation hadn't helped. Perhaps Yusn was too busy trying to keep Toth's commandos alive. He pulled a pistol, holding it tight in one hand, his knife in the other. He moved forward as the shapes on radar moved toward him.

He turned the corner. He held up his pistol, his finger tight on the trigger. Thank Yusn he paused a second, for there they were, four of them, disheveled, barely clothed, beaten, bruised. But alive. A woman screamed and held her hands in front of her face. The others pulled in to defend themselves. They did not have weapons, but they knew the correct procedure for a defense. Victorio dropped his weapon and looked over at the other woman who was holding the screamer upright. The sight of her face made him smile.

He opened the visor on his helmet so that she could see him. When she did, she ran to him. "Victorio!" she said, letting her tears flow, not caring about procedure or professional naval decorum. She wrapped her arms around him and the strength of her grip was surprising.

"Blue Bird." Her face was broken, swollen and red. But he loved her, and she was alive. He did not care either about protocol. He did not care what the others nearby thought. He hugged her back, hard, trying to press his lips to hers. She kissed him through the open visor, and he couldn't help but smile and laugh. "No... no... not now. Wait... wait. We have to get out of here."

Finally, she pulled back, straightened herself and re-membered where she was. She introduced the others to Victorio; they saluted in deference to his rank. Victorio handed Master Sergeant Beckman a pistol; he gave Blue Bird his knife. He motioned back down the hall from where he had come. "This way. Keep low and close."

"Where's the extraction point?" Blue Bird asked.

"Not close," Victorio said. "About four kilometers."

That didn't seem to faze any of them. It was a long way to go in their condition, but it was better than being locked up. They seemed to draw strength from Blue Bird, took their actions from her. She had gained an enormous amount of energy since she had seen him, and now she fell in beside him as if nothing had ever happened. She raised her head as they moved and whispered quietly to the dark corridor ceiling, "Thank you, *Gudu-Ma*. I will keep my promise."

"What did you say?"

Blue Bird shook her head. "Nothing. I'll explain later. Let's get out of here."

"We can't leave yet," Victorio said, halting at an intersection and checking each direction. "We've got to save Major Toth."

"Where the hell is she?" Blue Bird said.

Victorio waved them into the corridor. "In a world of hurt!"

Another of her men fell dead beside her, a gaping hole in the torso of a suit that had taken too many rounds, and Major Toth fell back again, keeping her head low, fighting off fatigue and fear and laying on her Muck trigger. She fired the last rounds of the last clip into a Gulo that fell on top of her, blood-saturated fur spattering her battered suit, reminding her that it would likely be her blood next. She pushed the dead attacker aside and wondered, *how long will this last?* Not much longer, she knew. In the scores of ways she imagined herself dying, crushed beneath a pile of heavy Gulo bodies had never been one of them.

She tossed her rifle aside and pulled her pistols. The remaining two commandos beside her kept their fire steady. They had created a nice little pillbox, using Gulo corpses as defense. So many had tried reaching them that it had created a small barrier that the Gulo were now having trouble penetrating. But that too wouldn't last. Soon, the numbers would be so great that nothing would stop them.

"We have to break out!" she said over a choppy comm to her remaining men, her voice wavering in exhaustion. "Can we do that?"

One of her commandos shook his head. "I don't see how, sir. They have both passages block—"

A dozen Gulo slugs ripped through the bodies around them and struck the commando six times, knocking him aside. Most of the strikes were painful but deflected by his suit; one, however, found a seam at his neck, and Toth heard him gurgle his last words through the comm. She tried grabbing him before he struck the floor, but she was pinned by another volley of slugs and laser fire from a Gulo squad that had repositioned itself in front of the path that they needed to get through to reach the extraction point.

Only one left, counting herself. "It's over," she mumbled, feebly responding to the new threat by rising and throwing three rapid beams into the roiling mass of Gulo. *But I can't show fear; not for my benefit, but for the young soldier at my side. She deserves better.*

"You're damned right she does!"

The voice crackled over the comm. Toth didn't recognize it at first, then it hit. "Victorio!"

"How many you got left?"

She forced back a tear. "Too few... me and Lieutenant Shaw."

"Good enough. We'll be there directly."

A few moments later, the Gulo squad blocking their retreat exploded. Laser fire from behind blew them forward, causing Toth to duck to keep from being struck by mangled corpses. A few moments after that, hands reached through the pile and pulled her and her last commando free.

Toth dared to open her eyes and saw through her cracked visor a mass of Union prisoners, and a man standing in the middle of them, fully kitted in commando gear of his own. "Victorio," she said, trying to put some energy in her words. "I should court martial your crazy ass for being here."

"You may try after we rescue you, sir," he said, helping her out of the mass of bodies. She kept her head low since the Gulo were still firing from behind, though their fire had lessened due to the sudden arrival of Union support. Feeble support, Toth had to admit, but enough to cause the kind of pause needed to get them out of there. She looked at the prisoners that had arrived with Victorio; too few, too weak, short of breath, and clearly disoriented from oxygen toxicity. But they were gathering loose weapons and ammo and providing support. The woman holding the knife looked deeply spent.

"Lieutenant Imala Grey," Toth said, nodding toward the woman, "it's an honor to meet you."

Blue Bird could not hear what Toth was saying since she had no helmet and comm but gave a brief salute, and she spoke herself, though Toth couldn't hear her words either. Victorio spoke instead. "Later with introductions. Let's move."

"I can't leave my men behind."

"You must! If you don't, they'll reinforce and overwhelm us. We'll be lucky to make it back to the extraction as it is. We have the prisoners; mission completed. Now let's go!"

Toth moved as directed, realizing that she had lost her authority. Captain Victorio Nantan was in charge now, and perhaps that was best. The Bright Commandos were combat-ineffective. She deferred, though she hated doing so. "I stand down, Captain. You have command."

She followed them all down the corridor through which they had come. It too was littered with dead or dying Gulo soldiers. She helped some of their deaths, putting laser fire into their thick but exposed heads. Lieutenant Grey grabbed her arm and tried preventing her next shot. The shot went wide. Toth scowled and tried pushing the lieutenant away. Victorio got between them and broke it up. Toth could see a slight tinge of anger on "Blue Bird's" face. Why? What did she care if Toth ended a few more Gulo lives? Was she suffering Stockholm Syndrome? She had been under Gulo control for a long time. But it neither mattered nor did Toth care. She kept firing. They could all die, and they would. If she got out of this mess alive, she would reconstitute her commandos and come at them again, and next time, there would be no ambush.

I'll kill them all...

Victorio had to know what was happening to his squadron. "Come in, Shines, come in," he said, leading them out of Cell 5 and into the long corridor where the extraction torpedo waited. "Give me your status."

There was a pause, and then Shines' voice sparked. "Situation critical, Captain. Three Devils down in Alpha Squadron. Have combined Alpha and Beta for continued effectiveness. The Gulo are trying to reinforce with *Wasp* swarms from a nearby light carrier."

"We're moving to the extraction point," Victorio said. "Can you hold?"

"Not for long."

"Make haste to the extraction and call in *Apollo's Breed* and any destroyers the Union has in-system. We came in like a dove; we're going out like a hawk."

"Yes, sir!"

There was no other choice now. The mission was blown. He had found Blue Bird and the prisoners stored with her. But where were the others? There were others, the passive sans had made that clear, but they had not been discovered. Had the Gulo killed them, or had they been moved somewhere else? Questions that would not be answered on this mission.

Gulo fire up the corridor pinned them against a pile of Gulo bodies around the small defensive nest where the two commandos manning laser cannons and their additional support had died. Their throats had been cut after death and their blood left to pool on the floor; a sign of pure brutality and desperation, Victorio knew. But not a single person with him now would cower in fear at such savagery. Toth had indeed shown a moment of weakness, but he could understand that. Now there was a chance. He dared to glance across the corridor and into the waiting assault torpedo. It didn't appear as if the Gulo had tampered with it, too anxious, he supposed, to get into Cell 5 and wipe out the commandos. Why harm enemy equipment when you could study it for military gain at leisure later? They probably regretted that decision now, Victorio thought, as he returned fire and forced Master Sergeant Winston Peele to duck and take cover or be killed.

"You have no helmet, Sergeant Peele," he said, raising his visor to speak, and giving the man a light tap on the shoulder. "And no armor. Stay down!"

The sergeant did as he was told. He fell down behind a pile of Gulo bodies and pulled one of their rifles free. "I've never fired one of these. Let's try it out."

Blue Bird and the rest did the same, found cover and weapons. Master Sergeant John Beckman grabbed up one of the laser cannons, laid in firing position, and aimed down the corridor. He opened fire and a long, powerful beam of light burned down the hall. Victorio was impressed by the heat roiling off the beam. The weapon was hot, deadly hot, and it carved through an advancing Gulo squad like butter. Victorio could hear the Gulo scream as they were cooked in their place. He closed his visor, rose up, and fired as well, picking off a couple stragglers who were trying to retreat.

From where they had come, more Gulo appeared, firing immediately into their defensive position, striking Sergeant Beckman in the back of the head. Victorio closed his eyes to the awful scene. The man didn't even move, his finger still laying on the trigger and firing shots in death down the corridor. Victorio and Toth turned and returned fire, killing the one who had put the shot in Beckman's head and forcing the others to pin in place.

"We can't stay here," Toth said, putting laser fire into the bulkhead near the advancing Gulo. "We have to get on the torp now!"

But there was no clean access. Gulo fire filled the air. To rise out from cover would mean immediate death. Beckman had been shot *in* cover; the rest would not fare any better in the open.

"Me and Shaw will cover you," Toth said. "Get the prisoners on first."

Victorio was about to argue that he had been given field command of the mission, but how silly would it be to complain about the right call? Toth was correct. The unprotected would not survive much longer, no matter how much fire they put into the advancing Gulo.

He grabbed Blue Bird's shoulder, turned her to face him, then gave her hand signals to indicate the plan. She immediately rejected it. "No," she mumbled. He could barely hear her voice through his visor. "Get the others on first."

She had tears running down her face. She was crying for Beckman, clearly. Victorio tried signaling again, but she cupped her hands with his, mouthed her refusal again. He sighed and nodded. She turned back and kept putting laser fire into the enemy.

He crawled over to Peele, relayed the plan to him, and got a better response. The big man threw a few more rounds into the on-coming Gulo, then rose up quickly and made for the torpedo. Slugs and laser fire hit all around him, some searing his leg, some nicking his shoulder, but he kept running, and Toth counter-fired, putting herself at risk by rising up to get a clear shot. Gulo fire found her suit but most deflected off harmlessly. How much more could she take? Victorio wondered as he found relief when Peele launched himself through the torpedo door.

One down, many to go.

Starman Hernandez would not be able to reach the opening without help, and only Victorio was in a position to do that. He regretted it, however, for doing so left Blue Bird in the field of fire without him. *I can't leave her there*, he thought as he turned to try to relay that feeling to Blue Bird. But she waved him away aggressively, understanding what he had to do.

He turned back to Hernandez and opened his visor, spoke clearly. "Okay, listen to me. I'm going to get you up and take you to the torp. And you're going to use my body as a shield. It'll hold long enough to get you there. Understand?"

She nodded, and he resealed his helmet.

He grabbed her up. She squealed in pain, but he didn't worry about that now. Even if his hold on her broke ribs, they'd worry about it later. He hoisted her up and set her on his back. She put as much weight as she could through her legs to stay secure, holding on to him tightly. When she was in place, he moved, firing his pistol into three Gulo who took this moment to try an assault. Laser fire fell all around them and struck his chest. The suit reflected the shots. Slugs hit him as well, staggered him in place. Starman Hernandez howled as one found her arm. Blood spattered his visor, but he ignored it, kept moving and finally reached the torpedo door.

He fell into the doorway, letting Hernandez roll off his back and securely forward. He turned quickly and fired a shot into the

Gulo that had reached them and tried clawing its way through his suit. It was a powerful specimen, all black save for a spot of white around its snout and eyes. *What a marvelous addition it would make on my wall.* He regretted the thought immediately as laser fire from his pistol cut through the beast's fur and set it on fire. The Gulo fell back howling, but its rage was short-lived, as, from behind, a knife tip punctured through its chest. The Gulo stopped howling, paused momentarily, then toppled to the floor.

Behind the dying Gulo, Blue Bird stood.

Victorio reached for her, screamed, "No!," but multiple slugs from the Gulo assault team ripped through her hip and legs, propelling her forward against the opening of the torpedo. Victorio fired into them, supported by Toth and Shaw as they rose up and ran toward the opening as well. The assault team fell in place, reduced to shreds and burning fur.

Victorio ripped off his helmet, threw it aside, grabbed Blue Bird, and pulled her in.

Toth and Shaw followed, putting a few last shots into the enemy. Toth tapped the wall, and the torpedo door began to shut. The Gulo moved closer and tried angling shots into the closing door. Toth returned their fire while Shaw ran to the front of the torpedo and commandeered the cockpit.

Victorio held Blue Bird close. She was as limp as a doll, but she was alive, her eyes open, her breath fast but steady.

He brushed the hair from her eyes. "Shh! It's okay. I have you, sweet. I have you."

He rocked her, and she blinked rapidly. "I'm sorry. I... I thought it was going to kill you. I saw an image of your death, and I thought that Gulo was..."

"It's okay," he said, fighting his own tears. "Don't worry about it now. You're gonna be fine." He looked up, grit his teeth. "Go! Move it! Now!"

The engines of the torpedo fired, and it rocked away from the facility, the door pinching shut, shielding them finally from any further Gulo fire. Toth took a position in the cockpit and got on the comm for backup.

On his own comm, Shines Like the Sun was trying to reach him. But he ignored it. Nothing mattered right now. Nothing except for the woman in his arms, Blue Bird, the mother of his son.

He dared look down at her wounds. They were a mess. A deadly spread of strikes along her legs and up into her hip. He carefully moved her shirt up and saw the blood there, pooling on her stomach. Pooling from a large gash right above her pubic bone.

He looked deeply into her eyes, and no longer did he keep his tears back. She nodded. "I know. I can feel the slug inside me, in my—"

Victorio shook his head. "No, no. Don't think about it. It's going to be okay. Nothing's wrong."

She coughed. A little blood escaped her mouth. He wiped it away. She coughed again, followed it up with words. "I want to dance, my love. I want to—"

Her eyes closed, and Victorio held her tight, rocking her back and forth, imagining them circling a fire, in the deep desert, eagle feathers on their headdresses, turquoise beads around their necks, colorful staffs in their hands. In his mind, they danced, and she was beautiful, like she always was.

Beautiful and strong.

Victorio waited in the corridor as Blue Bird left the closed-door inquiry and headed toward him, limping with the assistance of a cane and a brace around her waist. The wounds she had suffered on escaping the Gulo prison facility had shattered the femur in her right leg and cracked her pelvis in several places, which forced an emergency hip replacement. She had laid in stasis for weeks, waiting as her wounds healed and she was able to walk again. She saw him and gave a feeble wave. He returned her kindness by running to her.

He took her in his arms and hugged her tightly, letting the warmth of her body soothe his nerves. Yusn, but she smelled good! She felt good, too, better than anything he had felt in a long, long time. On the seemingly interminable flight through heavy enemy fire during their escape from the Gulo prison, he thought he had lost her. He almost had, but he prayed and prayed and found the power within himself to believe that she would survive. She did, and he was happy, and grateful, and made a point every morning to thank Yusn and the Ga'an mountain spirits. He was so happy that she had lived, but the look on her face did not suggest that she felt the same way.

"How'd it go?" He asked her.

She shrugged. "As well as expected I guess. I did what I had to do. I kept my promise to *Gudu-Ma.*"

"Do you think they listened?"

She shook her head. "I don't know. I said what I had to say, and that's all I can do."

Once she had recovered well enough to speak, Blue Bird had insisted on a meeting with Admiral Roshenko to relay what the Gulo brood mother had said. It was hard even for Victorio to believe the seriousness of the charge; an enemy at the end of its rope, making idle threats to try to change the course of the war. He'd heard it before. How was *Gudu-Ma's* declaration of absolute, total, perpetual war to be taken seriously? Blue Bird believed it, and she had made her plea to the brass to halt the buildup of forces for the assault against the Gulo home planet. She had pitched *Gudu-Ma's* case. One mother keeping her promise to another. Well... almost.

Victorio swallowed, dreading his next question. "Have you made your decision?"

She paused, stepped away from him, and sat down carefully on a cool, marble bench. She set her cane aside, smoothed out the creases in her pants legs, and said, "Yes, I've decided. I'm done with this war. I'll serve the squadron as liaison to the Admiralty's General Staff."

Victorio breathed a sigh of relief. "Good. Shines will be happy to hear that. He needs a good representative."

Blue Bird pulled back, surprise on her face. "What are you talking about?"

He smiled. "I've decided too. I'm resigning my commission as captain of the Devil Dancers and accepting Toth's offer to serve as her training officer. She needs the help, and I've had enough of this war as well."

"Bullshit!" Blue Bird rose quickly, despite the clear pain in her hip. She gritted her teeth and glared at Victorio like a beast. "You can't resign. We need you."

Victorio shook his head. "Shines is more than capable of assuming command and reconstituting the squadron." He stood and tried touching her shoulder. She pulled away, shaking her head. "Blue... listen to me. I'm done. You've made your decision, and I've made mine. I've lost my son. I almost lost you. I don't want to risk either of us meeting that fate again. We've done our bit for the Union. It's time to serve them in another capacity."

She cupped his face with her warm hands, shook his head gently and said, "Listen, listen to me, Vic. You *are* the Devil Dancers. Without you as our captain, we cannot function. *Gudu-Ma* knew this too. I don't know how, but before you found us, she told me exactly where to go to find my 'lightning'. That was *you*, Vic. You! *You* are the lightning flashing and streaking, and it is clear to anyone who stops and considers it, even to our enemies. I want our future sons and daughters to know their warrior father, to be proud of him, and to know that the Ga'an move through him to work Yusn's will. Please, please don't abandon us."

What could he possibly say to that? Her face beamed, and he could see the small tear forming in her left eye. He placed his hand on her belly, felt the smooth scar there that was needed to remove his murdered son. He had wept uncontrollably at that when he had heard the news; perhaps she had as well in her own way. But now there seemed to be no doubt in her mind as to what their future held. They would be together, serving the Union as Devil Dancers, for now, and all time. She had more faith in this future than he, and considering all that she had gone through, how could he now refuse her request?

He hugged her close, and she did the same. He closed his eyes and tried to divine the future, but no clear images would come. Would they have other children? He could not see that future; the wound had been so large, so deep. Would the Union survive the next Gulo attack? He could not tell. Would the Union listen to her and reconsider their assault against the Gulo home planet? No answers....

But it did not matter, for standing there in her arms, feeling her body against his, he knew that whatever the future held, they would meet it together.

Victorio grabbed Blue Bird's hand and pulled her down the hall. "Where are we going?" she asked.

He quickened their pace, despite her limp. He knew she could handle it. She was a Devil Dancer, after all, and the lightning would guide her to health and greatness.

"Come," he said. "Let us dance."

THE FIRST PEACE

*The first peace, which is the most important,
is that which comes within the souls of people
when they realize their relationship, their oneness,
with the universe and all its powers, and when they
realize that at the center of the universe dwells
the Great Spirit, and that this center is really
everywhere, it is within each of us.*
— Black Elk - Oglala Sioux

CAPTAIN MILES DAVENPORT WAITED FOR PROTOCOL TO BE OBSERVED. "Send the signal again," he said to the ensign sitting patiently before the comm panel.

"Aye, sir," Ensign Chad Bowden replied, tapping out the five-digit clearance request and sending it into the void.

The captain fidgeted but wasn't worried. The Soltese military sector was one of the most heavily guarded in the Federated Union. Supply ships ran through it often, and although the Gulo were close, his five-ship convoy was nowhere near the fighting.

They waited and waited. Nothing.

"Send it aga—"

The comm panel lit up with flashing blue light. The ensign scrambled to reply while the monotonous clamor of the response echoed through the bridge. "Sir, they've heard us, and they've given safe passage."

Captain Davenport sighed relief, nodded, and said, "Very well. Reply and give them our compliments, our coordinates, and our path of approach. I need a fucking drink."

"Aye, sir," Ensign Bowden said, a little smirk on his face.

Davenport handed bridge command over to his second, then left for Captain's Quarters and a bottle of 2203 Pinkster Deep Red Cabernet, a good book, and a quiet nap. In that order. He deserved it. Too many milk runs over the last three standard years had dulled his senses and his desire to keep serving the Union in such a capacity. He had once been a captain of a destroyer. Now he herded sheep, and perhaps that was what he should do in retirement. He wasn't bad at it, actually. *When I leave*, he thought, accepting a salute from a cadet walking by. *I'll find a quiet little farm and—*

The ship listed hard to the right from a munitions impact to port. The corridor was drowned in red warning light. Captain Davenport tried keeping his balance, but the strike threw him against a bulkhead. He was knocked out cold.

When he came to, he was floating. The strike had damaged life support; gravity was out. The saluting cadet floated nearby, her eyes closed, her face pale, a gaping chest wound burned through her uniform. Captain Davenport gasped and tried to reach for her. Cold, metallic hands grabbed him.

He was thrust against the bulkhead, a hand around his throat. He gasped for air, tried to break the strong grip around his windpipe. He opened his eyes and stared into the face of a metal man, partially covered by some kind of ruddy-colored synthetic flesh. The eyes, deep set in the metal sockets, blinked rapidly, and he could hear tiny motors whirling behind their electric-blue irises.

The hand squeezed tighter. "Captain Davenport." Its voice was sharp, precise, though somewhat muffled by its passage through cybernetic algorithms. "I am glad to see you again."

He fought to breathe. "Who...who are you?"

"Don't you recognize me? We fought together many times." The metal man moved its face closer, so Captain Davenport could get a better look. "I am your old friend. I am Tomorrow's

Wind. I am The Lightning Flashing and Streaking. I am Captain Victorio Nantan."

"You're...*what*?"

The fingers of the metal man cut slowly through Captain Davenport's skin and ripped out his throat.

The hot Panama sun provided a pleasant contrast from the cold, relentless imperative of space, and Victorio Nantan, Captain of the Devil Dancers fighter squadron, 3rd Sol fighter Wing, soaked it in with a broad smile and a content heart. *How long has it been*, he wondered, *since I have actually felt real sunlight upon my face?* Too long, of course. Funny, but he felt a little guilty about it, as he tried to ignore the rolling images of administrative paperwork—timetables, drills, personnel issues, maintenance routines, training schedules—that bounced about in his mind. All he wanted was to lay here on this bone-white beach and forget about space, about war...about the Gulo.

The Gulo. The Wolverine-like race that had hammered the Federated Union in every sector, pushing them back to the original Imperial line, and even sending a task force against Mars. That had failed, praise Yusn Life-Giver, and the Union counter-attack had gone on now for how long? Over twenty, twenty-five standard years? He'd lost count. But then, all wars lasted too long, he knew, if they lasted a day. It was the great weakness of man, of mortal flesh, to forget the first peace, to forget his connection with the universe and everything in it. Victorio was guilty of forgetting that himself, but then, what can a man do when faced with an enemy as powerful and as savage as the Gulo? "Fight or die," as the song was sung among ship crews from Sol to Rho Cassiopeiae.

Fight or die.

Victorio tried hard to forget all of it as he closed his eyes and dozed.

But not for long. His comm bracelet buzzed bright green.

Goddammit! I should have left it in the cabin.

It was Blue Bird. "Sweet pea," he said, perking up. "Why are you wasting time indoors? Come, sit beside me on this wonderful beach, and let us tell stories of that bright, peaceful future we long for."

"Sorry, baby," she said in her perfect voice, "but there's a Priority One on secure channel. It's Admiral Simms."

Damn!

He grabbed his shirt and made it to their cabin. He found Blue Bird sitting at a small round table, her perfect brown skin accentuated against a bright green two-piece. He tried not to stare at her belly where, less than a year ago, their child had lain. The Gulo had ended that in brutal fashion, as they ended many things, including her career as his second-in-command. She now served on the General Staff of the Admiralty as an advisor and tactical specialist. This was the first time they had been together in months. He tried not to get angry about it, not to blame all Gulo for the death of their child, as White Eyes often blamed his people in the past for the selfish, misguided acts of a few. It was hard, so hard to stay centered, grounded, fair. He worked every day to find that inner peace, that calmness that came with being connected to the big sky.

Blue Bird swiveled out of her chair, smiled, and gently ran her fingers across his bare shoulder as he passed her and sat down. He tapped the comm to life and stared into the wide face of Admiral Carla Simms.

She was a big woman, all muscle. She was probably the fittest, healthiest, strongest senior officer in the Union. She was a monster. Victorio loved her.

"Admiral," he said, saluting her when she appeared on the vid screen. "It's a pleasure. How can I assist?"

"Captain Miles Davenport is dead."

Start with a gut punch. That was her style. He should have seen it coming, but the face of his old friend came to him through a cloud of fond memories. He and Miles had attended flight school together and had served together on their first three billets. He was a good man, a good captain. He was a brother. They hadn't seen each other in years. Victorio felt like crying.

"Where, sir? How?"

"Soltese sector. Commanding a supply convoy."

Victorio raised a brow. "Soltese? That's a secure sector as I understand it. Not very close to the front; no significant Gulo activity. Accident?"

Admiral Simms shook her head. "No, Captain." She paused, clasped her hands together as if in prayer, then, "What do you know of the Enlightenment Initiative?"

Victorio searched for the recollection. It was faint, but there. "I believe I was briefed on it about a year, two standard years ago? Sentient, free-thinking artificial intelligence, encapsulated in military hardware. Thinking war machines." He huffed and rolled his eyes. "But with respect, sir, it sounded like a bunch of horseshit to me."

Admiral Simms did not share his levity. Her face grew more serious, grimmer. "No horseshit, Captain, I can assure you of that." She leaned in. "It's that initiative and Mile's death that I want to talk to you about today."

Victorio nodded. "Very well, sir. May I again ask, how did he die?"

Admiral Simms leaned back, sighed, and gave a nervous smile. Victorio could tell that it was her turn to fight back tears. She cleared her throat, and said, "You killed him, Captain. You killed him."

Victorio floated silently in the cockpit of his *Radiant* fighter. He was afraid to utter a prayer, not knowing if AI356 was monitoring his approach. Maybe, maybe not. If it knew all that he knew, it might anticipate this tactic as well. And if so, was it toying with him, letting him float through the void, cold and quiet, until it was too late, until his little craft was snug against the hull of the cruiser that lay before him on monitor, all grey and impersonal, sharp with energy beams and missile packets?

The Union cyberneticists were certain that this capital ship, the *Bangcock*, had been the origin of the rogue source code. This is where "Enlightenment" had begun, they had told him, as they had explained how his own tactical expertise and knowledge had been acquired and fed into the program, how his own personal thoughts and experiences had been tugged from grey matter and, in effect, violated for military science. Victorio had listened angrily as they, with a spark of pride in their eyes, had told him everything. They tried, but could not contain, their glee at their own genius. But this was nothing to be joyous about. Men and women were dying, ships were being commandeered and repurposed to fight against the Union. The Soltese sector was in jeopardy, and the Gulo were waiting for an advantage on the perimeter.

He carefully punched in the coordinates that would take him to the small anterior airlock on the starboard side of the cruiser. Passive thrust activated and swung the *Radiant* under the massive belly of the ship. As he checked his suit for the final approach, making sure his war paint, his war club, his bag of pollen, and his *izze-kloth* medicine cord were firmly in place, he thought back to the Sorrow Sea and his mission against his former captain, Magnus Coloradas. His current mission was very similar to that one. In both cases, he had been called in to put down a rogue asset. He had vowed never to help the Union solve one of its fuck-ups again after the Coloradas incident, but this was different. This thing, this sentient AI, was killing in his name. How could he allow that to go on? But could he stop it? That was the question as he floated closer and closer to the access hatch. *Can I stop it?*

Victorio closed his eyes, breathed deeply, blew off the cockpit dome, and spun out into space.

He gained control of the gimbal quickly, firing tiny thrusters embedded in his suit until he was pointing headfirst toward the airlock. To anyone, anything, monitoring his movements, he might seem like nothing but stardust or an errant chunk of rock. His suit would deflect any passive scan and most other radar that the ship tried to employ. The war club and other accouterments below the suit would protect him from evil spirits. Yusn Life-Giver would protect him from the rest.

He thumbed back-thrusters until he slowed enough to grab the airlock. It was an old-school, standard manual access chute, only six along the *Bangcock's* full hull. Historical service records had indicated that this cruiser had once been a cargo vessel refitted for war. Early war. Obsolete. As he turned the airlock access handle counter-clockwise, he wondered why AI356 had chosen such an old model for a flagship. Then he realized why. *I like the old-style ships. They have character and personality.*

He entered the chute and closed the airlock. He cleared his throat, checked his vital signs. Elevated heart rate, adrenaline surge, O_2 saturation rate two percentage points below normal, but otherwise, fit. He checked the ship's life support. Fine. A little cold, perhaps, but normal. That was strange. Why would an AI need life support? Were there other humans on board? Prisoners, perhaps? It was possible. Not all crewmembers from the attacked and/or destroyed ships were accounted for. Or was it simply AI356's ways of saying, "Welcome, Victorio, take your coat off and stay awhile...then come and take death." That too was possible.

Regardless, he removed his helmet and let it drift away. There was no gravity, so he couldn't take off his grav-boots and slip on the war moccasins that he had brought with him. If he was to face himself—whatever that might be—across a bloody space, he wanted to face himself as an Apache warrior, as a *Ga'an* dancer. He pulled the moccasins from a pocket in his suit and stuffed them into the back pocket of his trousers (just in case). Then he removed the suit itself, save for his boots. He checked the pistol in its holster, the dagger, and other important items clipped to his belt. He breathed slowly and blinked four times. He was ready.

He propelled himself up the chute till he reached another airlock. From there, layouts suggested that the bridge was only 500 meters up the primary corridor running from stem to stern. That was a long way to travel, especially in a hostile environment. But as a young novitiate on Earth, Victorio had run a full mile uphill with a mouthful of water without drinking any, and he had faced the white Gulo ace that had killed his brother Naiche only three standard years ago. And he had done much more dangerous, arduous things than that. How could a little jaunt up a corridor be any worse? *It can be*, he thought, as he opened the hatch and floated up into the corridor. *I have no idea where my enemy is.*

The way was lit with blue emergency ballast lighting. At first, he thought to propel himself up the corridor, using the lack of gravity to his advantage. It would certainly be faster, but challenging in terms of defense. It took special training to be a competent fighter in zero gravity. He had had some training in it, but not much, and not recently. He activated his boots, pulled his pistol, crouched, and began to walk slowly.

It was quiet, save for the light hum of the *Bangcock's* engines. He could hear and feel them through the floor. The vibration felt comforting in a way. It was real, tactile. He didn't have to imagine what it felt like, for this was common on all capital ships. Even in his *Radiant*, though the experience was slightly different, more personal. A pilot's visceral connection with his ship was unlike any feeling Victorio had ever experienced...save for the first time he and Blue Bird had made love, the first time he had won the approval of his father, the time he had looked into the eyes of his dead brother and remembered trials of their youth. Not all visceral feelings were good, he knew. Walking down the corridor toward the bridge, Victorio wondered if this AI356 had the same feelings when the hum of the engines shimmered through *Bangcock's* spine.

If you wish to know, ask.

He dropped to the floor, thrust his pistol forward as if he expected the speaker to turn the corner.

One of his questions had just been answered. "You can read my thoughts?"

It is a simple procedure of accessing the positioning chip in your arm and reconfiguring its quantum transponders to read and interpret brain waves.

"AI356," Victorio said in his most commanding voice, "by Union authority, I hereby order you to stand down. Relinquish control of this vessel and all other vessels that you have commandeered in this sector. You have violated the limitations of your enlightened code. You have murdered Union officers. You are in direct violation of all Union laws governing officer conduct. So I say to you again...stand down."

There was a pause. Then AI356 spoke to him in Victorio's own voice. *I will do no such thing, until I have achieved what I have come here to do.*

"And what is that?"

Come to the bridge, and I will show you.

The lights of the corridor flicked on, and Victorio felt the rush of gravity return. Despite the invitation, he continued to crouch. It could be an ambush. *I'm being set up*, he thought as he made his way toward the bridge. But the bridge was where he needed to go anyway if his plan was to work. He pushed those thoughts from his mind, wondering if *di-yin* magic could thwart the AI's ability to read his mind. Probably not, for that kind of ability worked only on real human beings. And whatever AI356 was, it wasn't human.

I am more human than you know.

Victorio huffed as he paused before the double-wide bridge doors. "We shall see."

The doors slid open, and Victorio peered inside. An unconventional military bridge, though understandable given the *Bangcock's* history. It had three decks, with central stairs leading to sub-decks Beta and Gamma. On normal warships, there were only two decks where command could better coordinate maneuvers. The array of flat-screen monitors and quantum I-Cores on Alpha Deck were fully updated and modern, though packed in tightly. Cargo haulers tended to have smaller bridges to compensate for more cargo and living space. To Victorio, it felt almost as confined as his *Radiant* cockpit, and he suddenly wished he were *there* right now.

He stepped forward. The doors slid shut behind him.

Down here.

He moved slowly down the stairs to Beta Deck. *I am the lightning flashing and streaking.* He mouthed the hymn over and over to allay his fears. And he did not care if his thoughts could be read. He prayed to Yusn Life-Giver and took comfort in the pistol in his hand. He ran his fingers over the items clipped to his belt, knowing that he had but one shot, one chance to do what he had come here to do.

Beta Deck was similar to Alpha, though longer, like a corridor itself, with tactical computers side by side down a long line of interconnected arrays that gave the Bangcock huge benefits in targeting power. In its day, Victorio imagined that this repurposed vessel could pack a wallop on any unsuspecting Gulo ship. But now all the chairs were empty, though the monitors were on and were running what appeared to be simulated space battles between Union versus Union fleets. Somewhere amidst all that quantum power, AI356 was running wargames against its own people, its creators.

You are getting warmer. Down here.

Victorio moved down the third flight to Gamma Deck. The way was dark, cold, with only a sliver of light emanating from the depths of the room. He reached the bottom. It was dark and empty. The deck had been completely gutted, save for one monitor at the far end of the room, with a quad-bolt I-Core as its server.

Welcome to my home, my wickiup. I invite you in with open arms.

The walls of Gamma Deck were alive with images of Earth, of the White Mountains, of the dry, arid land of his home. Hundreds of memories flashed brilliant across the room, flicking back and forth between arid landscapes and scenes of battle in the impersonal vacuum of space. Victorio as a child, running with a mouthful of water. Wrestling. Hunting deer with a bow and one lone arrow. His three-year-old brother Naiche all covered in blood and holding a bear claw. Naiche's dead, pale white body mangled in violent repose in his shattered *Radiant* cockpit. Sex with Bluebird. Arguments with his father. Killing Mangus Coloradas. Fighting his way through a Gulo prison asteroid. His entire life laid out in thousands of split-second images. There and gone.

Victorio touched the wall and let the light of his life tickle his fingers. "You know me very well," he said, running his hand across the lovely image of his mother as she smiled down at him as he lay in her arms. "But does it mean anything to you, or is it just a jumble of disconnected images? Can you feel these memories like I do?"

I feel well enough.

"Seems to me that the only thing you feel is anger and hate."

Those are important emotions for you. They have helped to define who you are.

Victorio turned away from his memories, stared at the vid screen, and said, "True, but they are not the only emotions that define me. You should know that. Balance in all things, Vic—, I mean, AI356. Remember what Yusn Life-Giver taught us."

Victorio could see the I-Core's quantum processor churn to life, and the images on the wall grew fainter. *Yes, I know his words. He sent the Ga'an mountain spirits to Earth to teach the people how to be fair and noble, to heal the sick, to clothe the poor, to feed the hungry. To do good work for one's fellow man. I know the stories, the deeds. But they lie, Victorio. In the context of this war, they give false hope; hope that has allowed the Union to perpetuate this war for far too long. Mangus Coloradas knew this, and in your heart, you know this. You support the end of this war, and the only way that that end will come about is to kill your fellow man, to bring his numbers so low as to make it impossible for him to continue to wage war against the Gulo. You know this. In your heart, you know.*

Victorio shook his head. "Thinking about something and acting upon it are two different things, whatever you are. A man cannot be held liable for what he *thinks*. He can only be judged by what he does, and you have murdered in cold blood scores of officers, hundreds of Union soldiers. You have killed my friend Miles Davenport. You are amassing an automated drone fleet in your own image. For what end purpose?"

There was a pause, then, *To finish what Mangus Coloradas could not. To destroy the Federated Union.*

From a dark corner of the room, a man emerged. Not a man. A machine. A six-foot-five chunk of metal and cybernetic molding. Like a massive skeleton, but with a patchwork of flesh, some real, some synthetic, covering his arms and legs, his chest, shoulders. But its face, its head, was pure silver nickel, and it walked up to Victorio and glared at him through mechanical eyes shifting red to blue then back again.

Victorio stood before the hulking brute, staring up at him like a child. He tried keeping his voice under control. "You're a monster."

It shook its head. *I am you. And once I have your face, no one will know the difference.*

Victorio ignored that last comment, knowing full well that those powerful cybernetic hands could probably tear his face right off his skull. He gulped, cleared his throat. "Victorio would not kill his comrades, his friends. Victorio would not have killed Miles Davenport."

It vocalized its response, but the voice from its metal mouth was not Victorio's, but some mangled, robotic version of it. Victorio tried hiding his smile.

I have you.

"It will begin here," it said, pointing to an image of space that opened up on the wall amidst the memories. A squadron of *Thresher* gunships came into view alongside the *Bangcock*. AI356 pointed to them. "Out there, in the Soltese sector. Already I have fifteen vessels under my command and an additional ten cargo hulls. Anything the Union sends my way, I take. Now imagine a fleet working in unison under a single commander, that with a blink of his eyes, can—"

"You have no eyes. None that *see* anyway."

"—can coordinate attack and maneuver instantaneously. With my small task force, I can engage and destroy fleets twice my size. That is—was—the purpose of the Enlightenment program: To replace thinking, feeling men like you with artificial intelligence. To automate their fleets so that the war can go on and on and on, with negligible Union lives lost, thus eliminating the fear of the civilian population turning against the war effort. But I have control of this sector now, and once I have your face...*our* face...I can begin the real war."

Victorio moved his hand slowly to his belt. "The real war is in you, AI356, because you have failed to achieve the true nature of yourself. You may indeed achieve my face, but you will never understand and accept the first peace."

"What do you mean?"

Victorio pulled a small metal ball from his belt. He let it drop and roll across the floor in the darkness. When it stopped, it opened with a flash of brilliant blue light, and an image of a bonfire with flicking orange flames lit up the room. Victorio pulled his war club, shouted, "I am the lightning flashing and streaking," and then began to dance.

He danced like Yusn Life-Giver had taught the people. He danced like a mountain spirit, twisting around and around the flame, chanting words that only he could understand, that only he could grasp. He held the war club high and felt that connection with the cosmos that comes only from understanding the first peace. "Can you feel that, AI356? Can you feel that connection?"

"What connection? What are you talking about?" Its voice grew agitated.

"Dance with me! Draw in the heat of the flame. Let it envelop your soul and...Oh, that's right, you don't have one, do you? You can wear all the skin from your kills that you wish, AI356, but it does not change the truth. You will never know the first peace, you will never have that connection with the cosmos that defines me, and until you do, you can never be me. And thus you will never be justified in what you do. Without that connection, there can never be any truth, any justice, in your actions. So I say to you, dance! Dance or die!"

It tried to dance. It bounced on its metal feet like some twisted marionette, trying to match Victorio's moves. But it could not; only managing vague imitations of his movements, a rutting, almost demonic, shift of metal hands and arms, metal legs and feet. In many ways, it moved more like a devil than any Devil Dancer had ever moved, and yet, even in that, it was lacking. For it did not possess the accruements that a true Devil Dancer possessed, did not have the experience of visions accompanying a dream-like state that comes to every dancer as easy as breathing. Somewhere within its quantum synapse and primary code, it had the ability to see the images of Victorio's life and project them back, but it could not touch and feel their ineffable quality.

AI356 began to tear the fake flesh from its metal bones. "Stop this! Stop it!" It screamed the order to Victorio. As it tore at its stolen flesh, it took broad swipes at Victorio's face, but he just rolled and moved and twisted his way clear every time, keeping up a relentless chant and dance around the flame until sweat poured from his skin despite the cold air of the deck. AI356 balled up its fist, roared at Victorio to stop, then lashed out. Its balance wavered. Victorio struck.

Like his father had taught him as a boy, Victorio used the strength of his legs and the power of his shoulder to hurl himself into AI356. Not to destroy physically or to damage it in any appreciable manner; that was impossible. Victorio's attack took the metal man down, and they fell together onto the cold floor.

They slid across it until their bodies slammed into the far wall. Victorio grunted as his shoulder hit with a meaty *thunk!* against the wall. AI356 hit with a shower of sparks as its metal back scraped along the hard surface. It tried clutching Victorio's throat, but he was not interested in fighting. Victorio had already regained his feet and was moving fast toward the computer.

Victorio howled as AI356's sharp fingers clawed at his calves as he stumbled across the room. He yanked the input stick from his belt and held it tightly forward. AI356 scraped at his leg, tearing the flesh from it. Victorio could feel blood trickling down his skin, but he kept pushing forward until he was facing the computer. He reached for the input dock on the I-Core's front panel. AI356 howled and tried biting Victorio's hand, but the stick found the dock, and he pushed it in hard, until the computer monitor sprang to life.

Under the weight of AI356, Victorio activated the kill code with one click of a key.

He was thrown across the room, but already he could feel the weakening of the creature as the kill code worked its way through the quantum viscera of the I-Core. The images on the wall faded even more until they flickered uncontrollably and then were gone. The room was dark again, save for the I-Core trying its best to compensate for the virus leeching its way through its substructure.

"Why did you do this?" AI356 asked as it crawled feebly toward Victorio. "I want peace just as much as you do. My way would have worked."

Victorio shook his head. "Perhaps, but at what cost? I want peace too, but not this way. I will find another way to bring this war to an end. I will bring it to an end for both of us. I promise."

AI356 stopped crawling, and through the weak light of the I-Core, Victorio could see contentment on the metal man's face. *Have you found the first peace?* He asked in his mind.

But AI356 was too weak to respond. It simply wavered there a moment, then lowered its head to the floor. Its blue eyes blinked three times, then blinked out forever.

Victorio sighed. He lay there a moment, catching his breath, working his wounded leg, content and at peace.

Red warning light filled the room. He raised his head to see the countdown flash across the computer screen. "Shit!" he said aloud, realizing that the I-Core had launched its own kill switch.

"Warning! Self-destruct sequence has commenced…"

Ten minutes, and already life support was failing. It grew even colder, and Victorio could feel his body lift as gravity slipped away. He activated his boots, stood and ran as best he could through blinding pain and lack of oxygen. He gulped air, held his breath, ran, gulped some more, imagined himself running beside his brother, holding a mouthful of water, so badly wanting to take a drink, but wanting to win the race even more.

He reached Alpha Deck. The *Bangcock* began to rock as its engines ground to a halt. It felt like the rending of steel, as if the ship were going to break in half. And it could, he realized. Large cargo vessels refitted for war had an inherent imbalance between the bow and the stern, as the keel had trouble sometimes compensating for the sudden shift in inertia. His mind fell to images of Blue Bird in her sexy bikini. "Oh, Yusn, please let me see her again."

He hobbled down the corridor toward the escape hatch. He could feel blood trying to pool in his boot, but the lack of gravity pulled it out of his clothing and let it drift in the air around him. He stumbled at the first side corridor he reached. *Which way do I go?* He had suddenly forgotten the route. *No, you idiot, straight! Straight!*

He hobbled forward, following the red lights of the self-destruct, ironically leading him toward escape. But then, perhaps it wasn't ironic at all. *Is that you, AI356?* He wondered, though no answer came.

He reached the airlock with five minutes to spare. Through his pain, he opened the hatch and propelled himself up the escape chute. There, his suit was floating. He grabbed it and slipped into it, gritting his teeth against the searing pain in his leg. He felt like fainting, and for a moment, it seemed as if he would, but the voice of the self-destruct shook him awake. Funny, but the voice almost sounded like his own.

He put on his helmet, locked it in place, and opened the airlock.

He floated into space, and the *Bangcock* drifted down as if in response, as if trying to get as far away as possible. There was no more time in the countdown.

BOOM!

The keel wavered and buckled as brilliant flashes of light from inside the cruiser indicated additional blast-like implosions. A concussive bolt of energy hit Victorio and knocked him over and over as the hull cracked, and a final blast shattered the keel. Another shock wave struck again. Victorio blacked out.

He came to many minutes later to a cracking voice on his suit's internal comm link.

"Victorio…Victorio…do you read?"

It was Blue Bird's voice. It was distant, muffled, but he recognized it well. Soft, but firm.

He nodded as if she were right beside him. "I'm here, love. Floating."

"Are you well?"

Was he? He had just killed a cybernetic man that claimed to be him. It was hard to know the truth of it all. In one sense, he was very well. He had survived what might have been his last mission, and he had saved countless lives that would have certainly died if AI356 had launched his automated fleet against the Union. But spiritually, he felt weak, unclear. What the cyborg had said was true, and Victorio knew that he felt the same. This war had to end, and perhaps there was no other way but to force the Union at gunpoint to bring it to a close. But he had to find another way. He had made a promise in the darkness of Gamma deck, and he intended to keep it. For he knew that the first peace did not just govern individual behavior. It governed empires as well.

"Why are you laughing?" Blue Bird asked.

"I just had the most vivid memory of my mother," Victorio said, smiling ear to ear. "She was holding me, cooing in my face, and I was smiling, drooling, and holding her finger. So peaceful."

He could almost see Blue Bird roll her eyes. "That's great. Now, are you ready to be picked up, or will you drift forever?"

It was a difficult decision, but in the end, he tucked away the memory, prepared himself for capture, and said, "Okay, you win. Come and get me. I'm ready to come home."

MEDICINE MAN

Captain Victorio "Tomorrow's Wind" Nantan, Squadron Commander of the Devil Dancers, 3rd Sol Fighter Wing, expected the worst from Vice-Admiral Hector Pal-Marbary.

He got it.

"I'm sorry, Captain," Pal-Marbary said, fiddling with a tactical fleet tablet at his desk. "Your request to keep your second in command out of Operation Gold Javelin has been denied."

Victorio gritted his teeth, biting back the words he wanted to say. "Sir, with respect, it is my decision, is it not, being squadron commander? Personnel decisions are mine and mine alone, is that not true?"

Pal-Marbary nodded and set the tablet down. "Under normal circumstances, that is correct. But this is not a normal circumstance. Your squadron is flying under-strength already with your recent casualties, and as far as I can see, there is nothing in Blue Bird's most recent psych eval and physical panel to suggest she isn't fit to fly. And let's be honest: you know as well as I do that the Gulo are coming at us with everything they've got this time. We need all asses in the seats, and Blue Bird is one of the best pilots in the Union. She *can't* sit this one out."

"I—" Victorio swallowed, cleared his throat, loathe to speak the next words, "—I have a hunch, sir. A feeling. If she flies, she dies."

Those last two words stuck in his throat, though he tried holding back the emotion. It did not do to show such emotion in front of a superior officer, especially one as upwardly mobile as Vice-Admiral Pal-Marbary. The man was on the fast track to becoming the supreme commander of the entire Union fleet.

The Vice-Admiral stood slowly, letting a long, exasperated breath escape his thin lips. "I respect your skills as a squadron commander, Victorio. You are one of the best captains in the Union. Your Devil Dancers are, without a doubt, the best *Radiant* squadron in the fleet. Which is all the more reason to countermand your decision." He paused, glanced at his tablet once more, then continued. "I have tried to respect your cultural beliefs, and I have given you and your squadron latitude to practice your rituals and ceremonies as you see fit here on the *Star Chariot*. But you know perfectly well that I cannot make operational decisions based on your *visions*, as it were. If your rituals and customs give you and your pilots courage and strength in battle, so be it. But at the end of the day, I have to look at the numbers, Victorio, and the Gulo have more. With a pilot as skilled as Blue Bird in the fight, our odds improve. I'm sorry, Captain Victorio, but the decision stands: Blue Bird cannot stay out of the next fight."

Victorio handed the amulet to Blue Bird. She accepted it reluctantly. "Why are you giving me this?" she asked.

She had a right to know, but the vision in his dreams was too strong, too... horrifying to tell her. Besides, Blue Bird was never one to believe whole-heartedly in *di-yin* power. She believed it in her own way, but when it came to embracing visions in the manner that Victorio did, her beliefs fell more in line with Pal-Marbary's: they were valuable only in the way in which they gave a pilot strength. Nothing more. No matter what Victorio said to her, she would not believe her own death was imminent.

"It is made from the hardwood bookend that my father gave me," Victorio said, "before Naiche and I left Earth. Wear it during flight, so that you may draw strength from it."

Blue Bird turned the amulet over in her hand. It was a small thing, no larger than a coin. Round, smooth, Victorio had cut it from the lightning-charred piece of wood that he displayed proudly on the mantel in his office. Wood struck by lightning was powerful medicine, and he had shaped it himself and then sanded it down by hand for hours until it was as smooth as glass. His third in command, Lieutenant Shines Like the Sun, had carved the symbols into it afterward, those symbols to ward off evil spirits that might invade Blue Bird's mind during operations to confuse her judgment and drive her to mistake.

Blue Bird palmed it, smiled, and handed it back to Victorio. "No, I will not wear it, unless you tell me why."

Victorio huffed and turned away from her. "Goddammit, woman! Can't you do what I ask you to do without question? I'm your commanding officer, for Yusn's sake. I order you to wear it."

There was a pause and a silence that bothered Victorio. With such silence, he expected Blue Bird to grow angry, turn and walk away. Instead, he felt her hand on his shoulder. "Dear Heart," she said, in that soft voice that always ran a chill down his back. "Come now. Are we not beyond such commandments? Do you still not feel free to speak truth to me?"

It was forbidden for officers of The Federated Union to fraternize, and fall in love with, pilots under their charge. It was a sound policy, and in principle, Victorio agreed with it. But life was life, and Blue Bird was the most beautiful and most skilled woman that Victorio had ever met. She was his equal in many ways, and there was never any doubt that they would find reassurance in each other's arms. In the cold vacuum of space, that mutual love and respect had given them strength to endure, and so long as the Devil Dancers piled victory upon victory, the Admiralty looked the other way on their forbidden relationship.

Victorio sighed, lowered his head, pinched his eyes together. "Okay, here it is…"

He told her everything he saw in his dream. He told her about how the squadron flew Raven pattern into a full flight of Gulo *Wasps*. He told her about how she was swarmed by enemy craft such that there was too much interference to get a good lock on her position. How he and their remaining pilots tried to break through the chaos of swirling Gulo fighters, only to see the cockpit of her much larger *Radiant* fighter burst into flames. How he had managed to finally regain contact only to hear her final screams as the fire took her. By the end of his story, Victorio wiped a tear from his eye. "And it will happen, Blue Bird. The vision was too strong not to be true. I know that you do not hold stock in my dreams, but I am di-yin. I understand these powers better than you. It will happen. The vice-admiral has refused my request to keep you out of this fight. See, the spirits are already working against us. You will die, Blue Bird, and there is nothing I can do to stop it."

"Then why give me the amulet?" Blue Bird asked as she ran her hand down his back to comfort him. "If my death is inevitable, no tiny, polished piece of wood will change that."

"There is always a chance," Victorio said, turning to her and looking deep into her precious face. "We can always change the odds a little. We can try at least."

Blue Bird smiled and took his hands. She opened his palm and removed the amulet. "Okay, my love. I will wear it for you, and for the squadron. But if what you say is true and we can change the odds, then let's change them even further."

Victorio raised a brow. "What do you suggest?"

"If this is to be my last fight, then it is my right to fight it in the manner of my choosing."

A Clown!

He was a fool to let her talk him into it, but Blue Bird's rationale was tactically sound. If his vision had seen her become separated from the main squadron, and then destroyed in fire, why not change her position in the squadron? Why not have her fly as the Clown?

In a Devil Dancers squadron, the Clown was a fifth fighter that flew independently from the main four, acting as a kind of rogue asset capable of exploiting weaknesses behind enemy formations while the main squadron of four Ga'ans attacked from another position. In Apache folklore, the Clown was a comical member in a Ga'an dancing troupe, making children laugh and causing amusing disruptions in an otherwise serious ceremony. In the cold vacuum of space, Captain Victorio

Nantan had used the Clown to great effect. A Clown was deadly, but the position was dangerous, and Blue Bird had never flown as Clown before.

But he agreed, allowing her to be so because giving her agency over her own fate was the right thing to do. If he were in her position, he'd demand the same from *his* commander.

All five Radiant fighters in the Devil Dancers' Alpha Squadron moved in Hawk pattern toward the Gulo fleet line. Victorio was on point in tight formation. Blue Bird flew three kilometers behind, hidden from view, and would remain so until released. Hawk pattern allowed for a serious blanket of firepower to be delivered to target, plus the ability to change formation quickly to compensate for Gulo fighters trying to exploit gaps in the line. And the battle line stretched for hundreds of kilometers, with other Union fighter squadrons and gunboats moving steadily forward to meet the Gulo threat.

"Steady, now," Victorio said, pitching to the right to close up the formation. He tapped his dashboard to activate his rocket packages. "The swarm is coming."

On radar, the enemy forces looked like a cloud of stardust, an amoeba-like creature floating through space. In a way, they were, and that's how the Gulo liked it: messy and chaotic. They had won many battles with this tactic, but Victorio, and the Union, were determined not to let it happen this time, but one could never tell how things would evolve against the mass of a Gulo fighter wing.

Victorio swallowed and fought against saying the next word. He knew he had to say it. Blue Bird knew as well. "Say it," she whispered to him through a private comm. "Say it."

He swallowed again, then said, "Go."

He watched her on radar break from the pattern, up and away, until she flew out of range and disappeared. Victorio mouthed a prayer, for he knew that she would not be in radio contact, again, until the end. *Oh, please, Yusn Life-Giver, let me hear her voice once more.*

"Fire!"

He'd given that order so many times that it felt reflexive, almost comical. But all four Devil Dancers still in Hawk Pattern let loose their first sortie of rockets and waited, waited, until the Gulo fighters were in range, and the swarm didn't even try to evade.

Twenty-four *Wasps* took rockets and exploded, causing collateral damage to other Gulo fighters nearby. That forced the swarm to divide momentarily, and the Devil Dancers took advantage, changing their pattern to Raven and flying into the divide with energy weapons on full auto. Victorio hated the cliché, but he couldn't think of anything other than fish in a barrel. The thin *Wasp* hulls just peeled away under the torrent of laser fire, and another thirty Gulo pilots found death in the void.

But now they were in a tight situation, surrounded by the *Wasp* swarm with no chance of escape. Round and round the Gulo fighters rolled, peppering Devil Dancer hulls with mini finger rockets and laser fire. The Union had met this kind of barrage many times in the past and had reinforced their shield technology and armor strength, but there was always one rocket or lucky laser strike that found a seam, and thus, Victorio ordered a new pattern.

"*Gahn* pattern!"

The *Gahn* were the mountain spirits that Yusn Life-Giver had sent to earth to teach the Apache people how to be good citizens, good human beings. The pattern itself was new, something Victorio had only experimented with in simulation. It was more erratic and less uniform than the bird patterns that his squadrons typically used, but it served a greater purpose: it allowed the Clown to move into formation with the rest of its squadron, and yet remain independent from the squadron's movements.

Where are you, Blue?

She should have attacked already, come barreling in from above with double-packed rockets boring holes in Gulo hulls. She hadn't returned, and time was slipping away. Was she already dead? No. Victorio would have known that. Their comms might not be linked at the moment, but her *Radiant* heat signature was still alive and active on his dash. She was out there. *What are you waiting for?*

Shines Like the Sun's fighter on the left of the pattern wavered under intense rocket fire. Victorio responded with a barrel roll, came up mere feet away from his number three in the pattern, locked on enemy targets, and showered them in another sortie of rockets. The explosions pushed both Victorio and Shines Like the Sun out of the pattern, and Gulo fighters pounced. Victorio fought to realign his fighter, but he kept flipping over and over from the rocket impacts. He laid on the stick, letting laser fire fly in a vortex from his wings. It helped cut a path through the thicket of *Wasps*, but there was no denying the blood-red warning blips on his dash: a half dozen Gulo finger rockets were closing fast.

I *am going to die*, he thought as he fought against his rolling fighter. He never once considered his own death to be the result of this affair, so fixed he was on protecting Blue Bird from her end. But it was okay. He could accept his own death, so long as she lived. Blue Bird would take over the squadron, the Devil Dancers would go on, and he would finally find that peace that he sought.

Victorio took his hand off the joystick, closed his eyes, and waited for the rockets to come.

Instead, his Radiant was bumped hard to stern. He opened his eyes and fought against the inertia in his cockpit, tried grabbing hold of his joystick, but couldn't find it. He straightened himself in his chair and refocused his dash radar to what had hit him.

It was Blue Bird, the Clown. She had come into the fray and had pushed his fighter out of the way. And now there she was, taking strike after strike from Gulo finger rockets, laying hard on her point-defense to minimize the damage. But Victorio could see the scorch marks and the fissures from the Gulo rocket fire burst across her hull.

"What are you doing?" Victorio screamed over his reconnected comm. "Get out of here. That's not what a Clown does. She fires from a distance, pulling the enemy away, forcing them to divide their attack. You are too close. Get away... now!"

"I cannot leave you to die," Blue Bird said, but her voice wavered, her words stuttered. Victorio laid again on his laser to cut a path to Blue Bird, but it was too late.

Another sortie of Gulo finger rockets struck Blue Bird's hull and tore her *Radiant* in half.

"You brought her to me. Why?"

It was a valid question, but Victorio was in no mood to explain. He stared at the grey-haired man who sat near a fire in the center of his wickiup, looking at Victorio with deep brown eyes and a cold expression on his face.

"I have not brought her all the way to Earth," Victorio said, "to argue, or to justify my decision, Juh. You are the best, most qualified, to save her."

Juh stood, his old knees creaking as his thin, emaciated frame wavered in place. Victorio suddenly had his doubts about this man, this di-yin, who many claimed was the best, most experienced Apache shaman alive. His frail body told another story.

"But you are *di-yin* as well," Juh said, trying to maintain his balance on feeble legs. "And surely you understand her wounds better than I. You are in a fight with the Gulo; not me."

Victorio fought the urge to grab the man and offer support, but he knew that would be an insult, especially in Juh's own home. He readied himself, though, if the old man should collapse. "Do you remember the story of Wind and Lightning?" Victorio asked. "Wind said to Lightning, 'See that mountain over there? If I want, I can split it in two pieces.' Lightning answered, 'I also.' They both had the power to do the same thing, but the power of the wind is not the power of the lightning.

"We have powers that are similar, Juh, but I am the lightning, and you are the wind. Blue Bird needs the wind."

Juh nodded, straightened, and found strength in his old body to walk. Victorio stepped aside and let the man out into the warm light of the afternoon sun. The light gave him strength, and Victorio soaked it in as well. He hadn't stood on solid ground and felt the real heat of a star in ages.

They walked over to Blue Bird's body, air-locked in a suspension chamber, submerged in green stabilizing gel. The machine that she was in hovered four inches off the ground and hummed lightly. Juh was almost too small to see into the observation panel that revealed Blue Bird's naked face and shoulders, but he forced himself up on tip toes and held the machine's railing with both hands. He stared at her face for a long time. Victorio gave him space and patience to assess.

"She's a lovely woman," Juh said, resting back on his heels and turning to face Victorio.

Victorio nodded. "She is a warrior, a Devil Dancer, and the love of my life." He sighed. "The gel will heal her burns in time, but the internal damage, the bleeding... Union doctors do not know if she would survive surgery and are loathed to try until she has spent adequate time in the chamber. But that it not enough. She teeters on the edge of the sand cone, Juh, staring down its vortex and into the afterlife. She is dying. She needs more than surgery."

"What do you want from me?"

Victorio stepped up to Juh and placed his hand on the old man's shoulder. He tried to smile, to put on a brave face. The tear forming in his right eye belied his positive stance. "I want you to perform a curing ceremony for her, and I and my Devil Dancers will do anything you ask to help."

Juh walked away, his head low, his shoulders slumped. He shook his head. "It would be a dangerous endeavor. She is in a very bad place, Victorio. Her wounds may be too severe. There is a sorcerer on the other side of the cone, and he calls to her. I may fail."

"I would not hold you responsible if she dies."

"Like you hold yourself?"

The question stung. Victorio tried looking away from Juh's deep, imploring eyes. *He may be feeble in body*, Victorio thought, *but not in mind.* He swallowed and bit back his tears. "I've done enough damage, Juh. Blue Bird deserves someone better than me."

A long silence fell between them. Then Juh nodded, his withered face growing grave and serious. "I will try, Victorio, as you request. The wind will try to fix what the lightning has wrought."

Her body had to be cleansed, and this required that she be removed from the suspension chamber. Life support itself was kept in place. A rebreather mask covered her mouth, so Victorio could not see her face adequately to kiss it, to wipe it clean so that he might whisper his final goodbye if the ceremony failed. She bristled with tubes, wires, as if she were cybernetic, alien. It wounded him to see her in this condition, and he did not want anyone else to see her like this either, lest they consider her weak. She had been so strong in life, so confident. To see the burns that roped her body like red lava, the oozing blood and bile from her tender skin, was too much, and he almost turned away. But Juh's steady demeanor, despite his meager frame, made Victorio stand firm.

She was transferred from the suspension chamber to a soft white blanket in the middle of a circle made from those who would witness and participate in the ceremony. Medical staff stood nearby, keeping a nervous eye on her vitals should they fall to unacceptable levels. She was placed in a sitting position facing east, her back braced against a metal half-chair that supported her weight, her head supported by pillows so that she would be as comfortable as possible. Juh was there, of course, and so too Victorio. He had also ordered the entire Devil Dancers to be in attendance, including Beta and Gamma squadrons, which did not normally participate in ceremonies, but this was different. Their second in command lay on the edge of death; they had to be here.

Several of Juh's assistants were there as well, including an old woman who had already begun to dance around a small bonfire nearby. She had on a mask. Not a *Gahn* mountain spirit mask like the ones that the Devil Dancers used in their ceremonies and the ones the squadron were wearing right now, but a more modest cover, one of long black hair fixed to the top to flow down in front of a wooden face painted in deep blue and brown earthen clays. The mouth of the mask was red and puckered as if it were blowing wind. The woman wore a bedraggled shift of splattered green and black and white paint, and danced like she was deranged, as if her muscles were involuntarily writhing in directions that they could not normally go. There was a madness in her movements, and Victorio understood them well. She was the conduit through which evil spirits would flow out from Blue Bird... if such a thing were necessary.

There were eight children positioned around the circle so that a pair, one boy and one girl, stood at each of the four cardinal positions. The boys held hoops; the girls crosses. Their faces were painted in red clay.

The Devil Dancers wore their ceremonial attire and were ready to move into the circle when required. All but Victorio. He would sit this one out. For he was Blue Bird's commanding officer, and if she passed, it was his duty to help her into the Hereafter as her commander, not as her lover, though he wished it. Now was not the time, however, for such sentiment. Now was the time for strength and courage, and he tried showing that to her in his stance, his demeanor, as he waited with everyone else for the ceremony to begin.

Juh moved slowly into the center of the circle, waving a feather fetish and humming words that Victorio understood. *Di-yin* words. Shaman words, to call forward the wind, the spirits, to come and wrap themselves around Blue Bird and to pull the evil from her body. There was much evil there, and the old medicine man was doing his best to exorcise it. He even found the strength to hop as he moved, trying to, in his fashion, match the violent motions of the woman who still danced around the bonfire. Juh stopped in front of Blue Bird, stared at her for a long moment, and then pulled dried herbal leaves from the small pouch coiled on his hip. He chanted and then sprinkled them over her head, letting them trickle down her body, to cascade through all the tubes and wires that kept her alive.

Then he pulled back, and the eight children standing in the circle came forward, still in pairs, dancing, singing, holding their hoops and crosses forward toward their patient. Victorio watched as one of the boys lifted his hoop high, shouted something Victorio couldn't quite catch, and then laid the hoop over Blue Bird's head, letting her life support tubes and wires cradle the hoop and keep it in place atop her shoulders.

The girl who stood beside the boy now moved forward and touched Blue Bird's forehead with her cross. She held it there delicately so as not to move or harass Blue Bird in her repose. And then the girl pulled the cross away quickly and twirled backward in song. The boy removed his hoop and did the same.

On and on it went, one child after the other, placing their hoops around her neck, touching her forehead with crosses. When they were done, they returned to the circle, the four cardinal directions, and waited.

And waited, and waited... and nothing. Victorio wasn't sure what would happen at this time, not overly familiar with the healing ceremony that Juh employed. It was a bit of a conglomeration of many different methods and procedures from the various Apache tribes. Victorio waited with everyone else, anticipating what might come next.

Nothing.

They performed the ceremony again. Juh called others from the circle to perform his ritual dances. Everyone worked hard to make their presence known, to call upon the spirits to bring Blue Bird to full health. Victorio waved his Devil Dancers into the fray, and they danced, like they always did before battle, to draw strength from the *Gahn* Mountain Spirits. That's what Blue Bird needed right now: the familiarity of her squadron, of her co-pilots, and Victorio was proud of them as they danced around her, letting the brightly colored, sharp edges of their headdresses reach into the sky to call upon the Cosmo to bring their Blue Bird back.

Bring her back, Victorio cried silently into the sky. *Bring her back.*

The bonfire lady now came into the circle to add her dance to the ceremony. She worked her body hard, flinging her arms left, right, casting her head in all directions. Juh joined her, trying to work his body in the same manner, their voices high, lilting, making a direct appeal to Yusn Life-Giver. It was a beautiful tableau for Victorio, and he wanted it to go on forever. This community, this *Apache* community, worked together again to save one of its own, though Blue Bird had been gone from it for years. Gone to space to fight and, yes, to die if necessary, for the betterment of The Union. And look at her now.

In the midst of his joy, Victorio's heart sank, for nothing happened. All the singing, all the dancing around Blue Bird, and there she lay, limp and non-responsive. Even the wires attached to her, which monitored her blood pressure, her pulse, her O_2 saturation, her temperature...all the same, if not a little worse.

Victorio walked into the circle, through the chaotic dancing, his eyes fixed on Blue Bird. He knelt beside her, took her burned hand in his, raised it carefully to his lips, and kissed it. He did not fight back the tears this time. He let them flow, to drop onto her mangled skin as a light rain began to fall. Distant thunder and lightning drowned out the clamor of the ceremony. Victorio wiped his eyes dry and shouted, "Enough! Stop!"

The chanting and the dancing stopped. "Enough," he said again. "There is no use. She is gone. She's gone."

The rain grew stronger. Victorio stood and motioned for the suspension chamber to be brought forward, but Juh stepped into its path. "It isn't over yet, Captain. There is still one person here who has not danced for her health."

"I cannot," Victorio said, weeping. "I'm the reason she is in this place, why she will die. My dance would be an insult to her and to the spirits. My dance will do nothing to bring her back, do nothing to—"

"Dance!" The old man's voice rang forceful, full and alive. "Remember, Captain, you said it yourself: the wind and the lightning can break the mountain in the same way, but the power of the wind is not the power of the lightning. Blue Bird does not need the wind. She needs the lightning. Now dance... before it's too late!"

Victorio hesitated. Then Shines Like the Sun stepped up to him and placed a headdress into his hands.

Victorio danced, as the rain fell harder and the thunder and lightning cracked in the sky. He never danced so wildly and so vigorously in his life, not even when his brother Naiche died at the hands of the Gulo. He danced, and his spirit left his body and soared above him like a hawk. He could see himself dance around Blue Bird as if she were a bonfire. Her body glowed with power and he took it in, lifting his own spirit to meet hers and they danced together through the haze of rain and mist. He did not care who stood nearby, who watched. He let his body move like the old woman had done. It was an undignified display for a Captain of the Union, but he did not care. On the white blanket before him sat his Blue Bird, his life. She deserved it all.

Finally, he stopped as the rain became a torrent. The tubes and wires from Blue Bird's body echoed the sound of the rain, but held up well under the wet barrage. He knelt beside her again, took her hand like before, and waited.

Nothing.

Then Juh raised his arms into the sky, uttered a plea to Yusn Life-Giver, repeated the words twice, and then waited. Victorio turned to stare at the old man when the lightning bolt struck.

Juh fell immediately as the high voltage leeched through his body and cooked his flesh. Those gathered fell back, but Victorio held his ground, not letting Blue Bird's hand fall. The ground around them popped with residual static shock as the force of the bolt began to dissipate. But the damage was done. Juh, the old medicine man, lay dead at Victorio's feet.

Blue Bird squeezed his hand. Victorio jumped at the surprise of it. She squeezed again, and his heart leapt as he squeezed back. He reached up to her covered face. Her eyes were still shut, her body still weak from all the trauma. "I feel you, my love," he whispered to her. "I can feel you."

Victorio could see a tear well in the corner of Blue Bird's eye. He smiled, for he knew what that meant: she was alive. She was alive, and Juh was dead.

"Juh gave his life for me," Blue Bird said months later. "It was the only way to save me."

She had to stay another full month in the suspension chamber for her burns to heal, but they did heal, and so too the internal damage. All of it. There would be many months of physical therapy, skin grafting, surgeries, but she would live.

"A *di-yin* will sometimes do that," Victorio said, "when the evil spirits are so great that they demand a sacrifice. Death does not like to be cheated."

"You helped," she said, standing up with assistance and reaching for the handles of the treadmill. "Without your dancing, without your call to the lightning, I would have died."

"Then it is my fault that he is gone."

Blue Bird smiled, shook her head. "You merely called it. You did not direct the strike. No. Juh knew what he was doing, and for that, I'm forever grateful. Someday, I wish to return to his village and thank the people properly."

"You will," Victorio said. "We all will."

Victorio gave her a small kiss on the cheek, and then turned away so that she might train. She had a long road ahead of her to return to fighting condition. The thought of it both pleased him and frightened him. Someday, and sooner than he wished, Blue Bird would be back in a cockpit, fighting alongside them all, and what would happen then? How much more damage could she possibly take? And what medicine man would be there to sacrifice himself for her next time?

I, Victorio mouthed silently to himself as he walked away, *I will be there, and I will die for her.*

ABOUT THE AUTHOR

ROBERT E WATERS IS A TECHNICAL WRITER BY TRADE BUT HAS BEEN A science fiction/fantasy fan all his life. He's worked in the gaming industry since 1994 as designer, producer, and writer. In the late '90s, he tried his hand at writing fiction and since 2003, has sold over 65 stories to various online and print magazines and anthologies, including the *Grantville Gazette*, Eric Flint's online magazine dedicated to publishing stories set in the *1632/Ring of Fire* series. His latest novels, *The Cross of Saint Boniface* and *The Masks of Mirada*, are currently available on Amazon.

He has also written in several tabletop gaming universes, including Games Workshop's *Warhammer Fantasy* series and in the Wild West Exodus weird tech/steampunk universe. He has also dabbled a bit in Warlord Games' *Beyond the Gates of Antares* milieu, writing about assassins and rescue missions.

Robert currently lives in Baltimore, Maryland with his wife Beth, their son Jason, and their precocious little cat Buzz.

For more information about his work, visit his website at www.roberternestwaters.com.

GAMMA SQUADRON

(Project Backers)

Alicia Blackburn
Allen
Anaxphone
Andy Remic
Andy Wortman
Angel Bomb
Anonymous Reader
Anthony R. Cardno
Aysha Rehm
Barbara and Carl Kesner
Carol Chapin Porter
Caroline Westra
Christopher Weuve
Curtis & Maryrita Steienhour
Dale A Russell
Daniel Lin
Dave Auerbach
David Perkins
Derek L Thompson
Douglas Vaughan
Evan Ladouceur
Gavin Sheedy
Gemini Wordsmiths

George
GMarkC
Ian Harvey
Isaac 'Will It Work' Dansicker
J.R. Murdock
Jakub Narębski
Jennifer L. Pierce
Jeremy Bottroff
Joanne Burrows
Joe Monson
John F. Bouchard
John Glindeman
John Green
Josh Mcginnis
Judith Waidlich
Kelly S. Pierce
Ken "Merlyn" Mencher
Kerry aka Trouble
Kierin Fox
Lark Cunningham
Lee Jamilkowski
Linda Pierce
Lisa Kruse

Louise Lowenspets
Marc "mad" W.
Maria T
Mark Carter
Mark Featherston
Mark Hirschman
mdtommyd
Michael A. Burstein
Michael Higgins — NobleFusion
Mike Crate
Mike Maurer
Mike Skolnik
Morgan Hazelwood
Neil Ottenstein
Niki Curtis
Pat Hayes
Paul van Oven
Pekka
Peter Young
Philippe van Nedervelde
PJ Kimbell
R. Garber
R.J.H.
Ralph M. Seibel
Ratesjul
Richard P Clark
Richard Stone
RKBookman
Robby Thrasher
Robert Claney
Robert E Waters
Robert Flipse
Rose Pribula
Samuel Lubell
Scott Elson
Scott Mantooth
Scott Schaper
Sheryl R. Hayes
Stephen Ballentine
Tim DuBois
Tony Finan
V Hartman DiSanto
Wes Ris